CHILDREN OF THE ATOM

by Wilmar H. Shiras

Timothy Paul seemed to be an ordinary child. Too ordinary, thought psychiatrist Dr. Peter Welles. There was something unsettling about how statistically "average" he was.

So Welles decided to befriend Timothy in order to discover the secret he is sure the boy is hiding...and now Welles knows he was right.

Timothy *is* entirely uncommon —the child of a couple who died of radiation exposure following a nuclear plant explosion. Born just before they died, Timothy is more than just an orphan—he is beyond genius...and he is also one of the loneliest people in the world.

United by this secret, Timoth' and Welles enbark on a search find other dispossessed youn(prodigies who hide from a hos world which cannot understa' them...the Children of the At

Bc

children
of the atom

children
of the atom

WILMAR H. SHIRAS

Nelson Doubleday, Inc.
Garden City, New York

To

my husband
RUSSELL

and

my daughter
ALICE

contents

children
of the atom

In HIDING

Peter Welles, psychiatrist, eyed the boy thoughtfully. Why had Timothy Paul's teacher sent him for examination?

"I don't know, myself, that there's really anything wrong with Tim," Miss Page had told Dr. Welles. "He seems perfectly normal. He's rather quiet as a rule, doesn't volunteer answers in class or anything of that sort. He gets along well enough with other boys and seems reasonably popular, although he has no special friends. His grades are satisfactory—he gets B faithfully in all his work. But when you've been teaching as long as I have, Peter, you get a feeling about certain ones. There is a tension about him—a look in his eyes sometimes—and he is very absent-minded."

"What would your guess be?" Welles had asked. Sometimes these hunches were very valuable. Miss Page had taught school for thirty-odd years; she had been Peter's teacher in the past, and he thought highly of her opinion.

"I ought not to say," she answered. "There's nothing to go on—yet. But he might be starting something, and if it could be headed off—"

"Physicians are often called before the symptoms are sufficiently marked for the doctor to be able to see them," said Welles. "A patient, or the mother of a child, or any practiced observer, can often see that something is going to be wrong. But it's hard for the doctor in such cases. Tell me what you think I should look for."

"You won't pay too much attention to me? It's just what occurred to me, Peter; I know I'm not a trained psychiatrist. But it could be delusions of grandeur. Or it could be a withdrawing from the society of others. I always have to speak to him twice to get his attention in class—and he has no real chums."

Welles had agreed to see what he could find, and promised not to be too much influenced by what Miss Page herself called "an old woman's notions."

Timothy, when he presented himself for examination, seemed like an ordinary boy. He was perhaps a little small for his age, he had big dark eyes and close-cropped dark curls, thin sensitive fingers and—yes, a decided air of tension. But many boys were nervous on their first visit to the psychiatrist. Peter often wished that he were able to concentrate on one or two schools, and spend a day a week or so getting acquainted with all the youngsters.

In response to Welles' preliminary questioning, Tim replied in a clear, low voice, politely and without wasting words. He was thirteen years old, and lived with his grandparents. His mother and father had died when he was a baby, and he did not remember them. He said that he was happy at home, that he liked school "pretty well," that he liked to play with other boys. He named several boys when asked who his friends were.

"What lessons do you like at school?"

Tim hesitated, then said: "English, and arithmetic . . . and history . . . and geography," he finished thoughtfully. Then he looked up, and there was something odd in the glance.

"What do you like to do for fun?"

"Read, and play games."

"What games?"

"Ball games . . . and marbles . . . and things like that. I like to play with other boys," he added, after a barely perceptible pause, "anything they play."

"Do they play at your house?"

"No; we play on the school grounds. My grandmother doesn't like noise."

Was that the reason? When a quiet boy offers explanations, they may not be the right ones.

"What do you like to read?"

But about his reading Timothy was vague. He liked, he said, to read "boys' books," but could not name any.

Welles gave the boy the usual intelligence tests. Tim seemed willing, but his replies were slow in coming. *Perhaps*, Welles thought, *I'm imagining this, but he is too careful—too cautious.* Without taking time to figure exactly, Welles knew what Tim's I.Q. would be—about 120.

"What do you do outside of school?" asked the psychiatrist.

"I play with the other boys. After supper, I study my lessons."

"What did you do yesterday?"

"We played ball on the school playground."

Welles waited awhile to see whether Tim would say anything of his own accord. The seconds stretched into minutes.

"Is that all?" said the boy finally. "May I go now?"

"No; there's one more test I'd like to give you today. A game, really. How's your imagination?"

"I don't know."

"Cracks on the ceiling—like those over there—do they look like anything to you? Faces, animals, or anything?"

Tim looked.

"Sometimes. And clouds, too. Bob saw a cloud last week that was like a hippo." Again the last sentence sounded like something tacked on at the last moment, a careful addition made for a reason.

Welles got out the Rorschach cards. But at the sight of them, his patient's tension increased, his wariness became unmistakably evident. The first time they went through the cards, the boy could scarcely be persuaded to say anything but, "I don't know."

"You can do better than this," said Welles. "We're going through them again. If you don't see anything in these pictures, I have to mark you a failure," he explained. "That won't do. You did all right on the other things. And maybe next time we'll do a game you'll like better."

"I don't feel like playing this game now. Can't we do it again next time?"

"May as well get it done now. It's not only a game, you know, Tim; it's a test. Try harder, and be a good sport."

So Tim, this time, told what he saw in the ink blots. They went through the cards slowly, and the test showed Tim's fear, and that there was something he was hiding; it showed his caution, a lack of trust, and an unnaturally high emotional self-control.

Miss Page had been right; the boy needed help.

"Now," said Welles cheerfully, "that's all over. We'll just run through them again quickly and I'll tell you what other people have seen in them."

A flash of genuine interest appeared on the boy's face for a moment.

Welles went through the cards slowly, seeing that Tim was attentive to every word. When he first said, "And some see what you saw here," the boy's relief was evident. Tim began to relax, and even to volunteer some remarks. When they had finished he ventured to ask a question.

"Dr. Welles, could you tell me the name of this test?"

"It's sometimes called the Rorschach test, after the man who worked it out."

"Would you mind spelling that?"

Welles spelled it, and added: "Sometimes it's called the ink-blot test."

Tim gave a start of surprise, and then relaxed again with a visible effort.

"What's the matter? You jumped."

"Nothing."

"Oh, come on! Let's have it," and Welles waited.

"Only that I thought about the ink-pool in the Kipling stories," said Tim, after a minute's reflection. "This is different."

"Yes, very different," laughed Welles. "I've never tried that. Would you like to?"

"Oh, no, sir," cried Tim earnestly.

"You're a little jumpy today," said Welles. "We've time for some more talk, if you are not too tired."

"No, I'm not very tired," said the boy warily.

Welles went to a drawer and chose a hypodermic needle. It wasn't usual, but perhaps— "I'll just give you a little shot to relax your nerves, shall I? Then we'd get on better."

When he turned around, the stark terror on the child's face stopped Welles in his tracks.

"Oh, no! Don't! Please, please, don't!"

Welles replaced the needle and shut the drawer before he said a word.

"I won't," he said quietly. "I didn't know you didn't like shots. I won't give you any, Tim."

The boy, fighting for self-control, gulped and said nothing.

"It's all right," said Welles, lighting a cigarette and pretending to watch the smoke rise. Anything rather than appear to be watching the badly shaken small boy shivering in the chair opposite him.

"Sorry. You didn't tell me about the things you don't like, the things you're afraid of."

The words hung in the silence.

"Yes," said Timothy slowly, "I'm afraid of shots. I hate needles. It's just one of those things." He tried to smile.

"We'll do without them, then. You've passed all the tests, Tim, and I'd like to walk home with you and tell your grandmother about it. Is that all right with you?"

"Yes, sir."

"We'll stop for something to eat," Welles went on, opening the door for his patient. "Ice cream, or a hot dog."

They went out together.

Timothy Paul's grandparents, Mr. and Mrs. Herbert Davis, lived in a large old-fashioned house that spelled money and position. The grounds were large, fenced, and bordered with shrubbery. Inside the house there was little that was new, everything was well-kept. Timothy led the psychiatrist to Mr. Davis's library, and then went in search of his grandmother.

When Welles saw Mrs. Davis, he thought he had some of the explanation. Some grandmothers are easy-going, jolly, comparatively young. This grandmother was, as it soon became apparent, quite different.

"Yes, Timothy is a pretty good boy," she said, smiling on her grandson. "We have always been strict with him, Dr. Welles, but I believe it pays. Even when he was a mere baby, we tried to teach him right ways. For example, when he was barely three I read him some little stories. And a few days later he was trying to tell us, if you will believe it, that he could read! Perhaps he was too young to know the nature of a lie, but I felt it my duty to make him understand. When he insisted, I spanked him. The child had a remarkable memory, and perhaps he thought that was all there was to reading. Well! I don't mean to brag of my brutality," said Mrs. Davis, with a charming smile. "I assure you, Dr. Welles, it was a painful experience for me. We've had very little occasion for punishments. Timothy is a good boy."

Welles murmured that he was sure of it.

"Timothy, you may deliver your papers now," said Mrs. Davis. "I am sure Dr. Welles will excuse you." And she settled herself for a good long talk about her grandson.

Timothy, it seemed, was the apple of her eye. He was a quiet boy, an obedient boy, and a bright boy.

"We have our rules, of course. I have never allowed Timothy to forget that children should be seen and not heard, as the good old-fashioned saying is. When he first learned to turn somersaults, when he was three or four years old, he kept coming to me and saying, 'Grandmother, see me!' I simply had to be firm with him. 'Timothy,' I said, 'let us have no more of this! It is simply showing off. If it amuses you to turn somersaults, well and good. But it doesn't amuse me to watch you endlessly doing it. Play if you like, but do not demand admiration.'"

"Did you never play with him?"

"Certainly I played with him. And it was a pleasure to me also. We—Mr. Davis and I—taught him a great many games, and many kinds of handcraft. We read stories to him and taught him rhymes and songs. I took a special course in kindergarten craft, to amuse the child—and I must admit that it amused me also!" added Tim's grandmother, smiling reminiscently. "We made houses of toothpicks, with balls of clay at the corners. His grandfather took him for walks and drives. We no longer have a car, since my husband's sight has begun to fail him slightly, so now the garage is Timothy's workshop. We had windows cut in it, and a door, and nailed the large doors shut."

It soon became clear that Tim's life was not all strictures by any means. He had a workshop of his own, and upstairs beside his bedroom was his own library and study.

"He keeps his books and treasures there," said his grandmother, "his own little radio, and his schoolbooks, and his typewriter. When he was only seven years old, he asked us for a typewriter. But he is a careful child, Dr. Welles, not at all destructive, and I had read that in many schools they make use of typewriters in teaching young children to read and write and to spell. The words look the same as in printed books, you see; and less muscular effort is involved. So his grandfather got him a very nice noiseless typewriter, and he loved it dearly. I often hear it purring away as I pass through the hall. Timothy keeps his own rooms in good order, and his shop also. It is his own wish. You know how boys are—they do not wish others to meddle with their belongings. 'Very well, Timothy,' I told him, 'if a glance shows me that you can do it yourself properly, nobody will go into your rooms; but they must be kept neat.' And he has done so for several years. A very neat boy, Timothy."

"Timothy didn't mention his paper route," remarked Welles. "He said only that he plays with other boys after school."

"Oh, but he does," said Mrs. Davis. "He plays until five o'clock, and then he delivers his papers. If he is late, his grandfather walks down and calls him. The school is not very far from here, and Mr. Davis frequently walks down and watches the boys at their play. The paper route is Timothy's way of earning money to feed his cats. Do you care for cats, Dr. Welles?"

"Yes, I like cats very much," said the psychiatrist. "Many boys like dogs better."

"Timothy had a dog when he was a baby—a collie." Her eyes grew moist. "We all loved Ruff dearly. But I am no longer young, and the care and training of a dog is difficult. Timothy is at school or at the Boy Scout camp or something of the sort a great part of the time, and I thought it best that he should not have another dog. But you wanted to know about our cats, Dr. Welles. I raise Siamese cats."

"Interesting pets," said Welles cordially. "My aunt raised them at one time."

"Timothy is very fond of them. But three years ago he asked me if he could have a pair of black Persians. At first I thought not; but we like to please the child, and he promised to build their cages himself. He had taken a course in carpentry at vacation school. So he was allowed to have a pair of beautiful black Persians. But the very first litter turned out to be short-haired, and Timothy confessed that he had mated his queen to my Siamese tom, to see what would happen. Worse yet, he had mated his tom to one of my Siamese queens. I really was tempted to punish him. But, after all, I could see that he was curious as to the outcome of such crossbreeding. Of course I said the kittens must be destroyed. The second litter was exactly like the first—all black, with short hair. But you know what children are. Timothy begged me to let them live, and they were his first kittens. Three in one litter, two in the other. He might keep them, I said, if he would take full care of them and be responsible for all the expense. He mowed lawns and ran errands and made little footstools and bookcases to sell, and did all sorts of things, and probably used his allowance, too. But he kept the kittens and has a whole row of cages in the yard beside his workshop."

"And their offspring?" inquired Welles, who could not see what all this had to do with the main question, but was willing to listen to anything that might lead to information.

"Some of the kittens appear to be pure Persian, and others pure

Siamese. These he insisted on keeping, although, as I have explained to him, it would be dishonest to sell them, since they are not pure-bred. A good many of the kittens are black short-haired and these we destroy. But enough of cats, Dr. Welles. And I am afraid I am talking too much about my grandson."

"I can understand that you are very proud of him," said Welles.

"I must confess that we are. And he is a bright boy. When he and his grandfather talk together, and with me also, he asks very intelligent questions. We do not encourage him to voice his opinions—I detest the smart-aleck type of small boy—and yet I believe they would be quite good opinions for a child of his age."

"Has his health always been good?" asked Welles.

"On the whole, very good. I have taught him the value of exercise, play, wholesome food and suitable rest. He has had a few of the usual childish ailments, not seriously. And he never has colds. But, of course, he takes his cold shots twice a year when we do."

"Does he mind the shots?" asked Welles, as casually as he could.

"Not at all. I always say that he, though so young, sets an example I find hard to follow. I still flinch, and really rather dread the ordeal."

Welles looked toward the door at a sudden, slight sound.

Timothy stood there, and he had heard. Again, fear was stamped on his face and terror looked out of his eyes.

"Timothy," said his grandmother, "don't stare."

"Sorry, sir," the boy managed to say.

"Are your papers all delivered? I did not realize we had been talking for an hour, Dr. Welles. Would you like to see Timothy's cats?" Mrs. Davis inquired graciously. "Timothy, take Dr. Welles to see your pets. We have had quite a talk about them."

Welles got Tim out of the room as fast as he could. The boy led the way around the house and into the side yard where the former garage stood.

There the man stopped.

"Tim," he said, "you don't have to show me the cats if you don't want to."

"Oh, that's all right."

"Is that part of what you are hiding? If it is, I don't want to see it until you are ready to show me."

Tim looked up at him then.

"Thanks," he said. "I don't mind about the cats. Not if you like cats really."

"I really do. But, Tim, this I would like to know: You're not afraid of the needle. Could you tell me why you were afraid . . . why you said you were afraid . . . of my shot? The one I promised not to give you after all?"

Their eyes met.

"You won't tell?" asked Tim.

"I won't tell."

"Because it was pentothal. Wasn't it?"

Welles gave himself a slight pinch. Yes, he was awake. Yes, this was a little boy asking him about pentothal. A boy who— Yes, certainly, a boy who knew about it.

"Yes, it was," said Welles. "A very small dose. You know what it is?"

"Yes, sir. I . . . I read about it somewhere. In the papers."

"Never mind that. You have a secret—something you want to hide. That's what you are afraid about, isn't it?"

The boy nodded dumbly.

"If it's anything wrong, or anything that might be wrong, perhaps I could help you. You'll want to know me better, first. You'll want to be sure you can trust me. But I'll be glad to help, any time you say the word, Tim. Or I might stumble on to things the way I did just now. One thing though—I never tell secrets."

"Never?"

"Never. Doctors and priests don't betray secrets. Doctors seldom, priests never. I guess I am more like a priest, because of the kind of doctoring I do."

He looked down at the boy's bowed head.

"Helping fellows who are scared sick," said the psychiatrist very gently. "Helping fellows in trouble, getting things straight again, fixing things up, unsnarling tangles. When I can, that's what I do. And I don't tell anything to anybody. It's just between that one fellow and me."

But, he added to himself, *I'll have to find out. I'll have to find out what ails this child. Miss Page is right. He needs me.*

They went to see the cats.

There were the Siamese in their cages, and the Persians in their cages, and there, in several small cages, the short-haired black cats and their hybrid offspring. "We take them into the house, or let them into this big cage, for exercise," explained Tim. "I take mine into my shop sometimes. These are all mine. Grandmother keeps hers on the sun porch."

"You'd never know these were not all pure-bred," observed Welles. "Which did you say were the full Persians? Any of their kittens here?"

"No; I sold them."

"I'd like to buy one. But these look just the same—it wouldn't make any difference to me. I want a pet, and wouldn't use it for breeding stock. Would you sell me one of these?"

Timothy shook his head.

"I'm sorry. I never sell any but the pure-breds."

It was then that Welles began to see what problem he faced. Very dimly he saw it, with joy, relief, hope and wild enthusiasm.

"Why not?" urged Welles. "I can wait for a pure-bred, if you'd rather, but why not one of these? They look just the same. Perhaps they'd be more interesting."

Tim looked at Welles for a long, long minute.

"I'll show you," he said. "Promise to wait here? No, I'll let you come into the workroom. Wait a minute, please."

The boy drew a key from under his blouse, where it had hung suspended from a chain, and unlocked the door of his shop. He went inside, closed the door, and Welles could hear his moving about for a few moments. Then he came to the door and beckoned.

"Don't tell grandmother," said Tim. "I haven't told her yet. If it lives, I'll tell her next week."

In the corner of the shop under a table there was a box, and in the box there was a Siamese cat. When she saw a stranger she tried to hide her kittens; but Tim lifted her gently, and then Welles saw. Two of the kittens looked like little white rats with stringy tails and smudgy paws, ears and noses. But the third—yes, it was going to be a different sight. It was going to be a beautiful cat if it lived. It had long, silky white hair like the finest Persian, and the Siamese markings were showing up plainly.

Welles caught his breath.

"Congratulations, old man! Haven't you told anyone yet?"

"She's not ready to show. She's not a month old."

"But you're going to show her?"

"Oh, yes, grandmother will be thrilled. She'll love her. Maybe there'll be more."

"You knew this would happen. You made it happen. You planned it all from the start," accused Welles.

"Yes," admitted the boy.

"How did you know?"

The boy turned away.

"I read it somewhere," said Tim.

The cat jumped back into the box and began to nurse her babies. Welles felt as if he could endure no more. Without a glance at anything else in the room—and everything else was hidden under tarpaulins and newspapers—he went to the door.

"Thanks for showing me, Tim," he said. "And when you have any to sell, remember me. I'll wait. I want one like that."

The boy followed him out and locked the door carefully.

"But, Tim," said the psychiatrist, "that's not what you were afraid I'd find out. I wouldn't need a drug to get you to tell me this, would I?"

Tim replied carefully, "I didn't want to tell this until I was ready. Grandmother really ought to know first. But you made me tell you."

"Tim," said Peter Welles earnestly, "I'll see you again. Whatever you are afraid of, don't be afraid of me. I often guess secrets. I'm on the way to guessing yours already. But nobody else need ever know."

He walked rapidly home, whistling to himself from time to time. Perhaps he, Peter Welles, was the luckiest man in the world.

He had scarcely begun to talk to Timothy on the boy's next appearance at the office, when the phone in the hall rang. On his return, when he opened the door he saw a book in Tim's hands. The boy made a move as if to hide it, and thought better of it.

Welles took the book and looked at it.

"Want to know more about Rorschach, eh?" he asked.

"I saw it on the shelf. I—"

"Oh, that's all right," said Welles, who had purposely left the book near the chair Tim would occupy. "But what's the matter with the library?"

"They've got some books about it, but they're on the closed shelves. I couldn't get them." Tim spoke without thinking first, and then caught his breath.

But Welles replied calmly: "I'll get one out for you. I'll have it next time you come. Take this one along today when you go. Tim, I mean it—you can trust me."

"I can't tell you anything," said the boy. "You've found out some things. I wish . . . oh, I don't know what I wish! But I'd rather be let alone. I don't need help. Maybe I never will. If I do, can't I come to you then?"

Welles pulled out his chair and sat down slowly.

"Perhaps that would be the best way, Tim. But why wait for the ax to fall? I might be able to help you ward it off—what you're afraid of. You can kid people along about the cats; tell them you were fooling around to see what would happen. But you can't fool all of the people all of the time, they tell me. Maybe with me to back you up, the blowup would be easier. Easier on your grandparents, too."

"I haven't done anything wrong!"

"I'm beginning to be sure of that. But things you try to keep hidden may come to light. The kitten—you could hide it, but you don't want to. You've got to risk something to show it."

"I'll tell them I read it somewhere."

"That wasn't true, then. I thought not. You figured it out."

There was silence.

Then Timothy Paul said: "Yes, I figured it out. But that's my secret."

"It's safe with me."

But the boy did not trust him yet. Welles soon learned that he had been tested. Tim took the book home, and returned it, took the library books which Welles got for him, and in due course returned them also. But he talked little and was still wary. Welles could talk all he liked, but he got little or nothing out of Tim. Tim had told all he was going to tell. He would talk about nothing except what any boy would talk about.

After two months of this, during which Welles saw Tim officially once a week and unofficially several times—showing up at the school playground to watch games, or meeting Tim on the paper route and treating him to a soda after it was finished—Welles had learned very little more. He tried again. He had probed no more during the two months, respected the boy's silence, trying to give him time to get to know and trust him.

But one day he asked: "What are you going to do when you grow up, Tim? Breed cats?"

Tim laughed a denial.

"I don't know what, yet. Sometimes I think one thing, sometimes another."

This was a typical boy answer. Welles disregarded it.

"What would you like to do best of all?" he asked.

Tim leaned forward eagerly. "What you do!" he cried.

"You've been reading up on it, I suppose," said Welles, as casually as he could. "Then you know, perhaps, that before anyone can do what I do, he must go through it himself, like a patient. He must also study medicine and be a full-fledged doctor, of course. You can't do that yet. But you can have the works now, like a patient."

"Why? For the experience?"

"Yes. And for the cure. You'll have to face that fear and lick it. You'll have to straighten out a lot of other things, or at least face them."

"My fear will be gone when I'm grown up," said Timothy. "I think it will. I hope it will."

"Can you be sure?"

"No," admitted the boy. "I don't know exactly why I'm afraid. I just know I *must* hide things. Is that bad, too?"

"Dangerous, perhaps."

Timothy thought a while in silence. Welles smoked three cigarettes and yearned to pace the floor, but dared not move.

"What would it be like?" asked Tim finally.

"You'd tell me about yourself. What you remember. Your childhood—the way your grandmother runs on when she talks about you."

"She sends me out of the room. I'm not supposed to think I'm bright," said Tim, with one of his rare grins.

"And you're not supposed to know how well she reared you?"

"She did fine," said Tim. "She taught me all the wisest things I ever knew."

"Such as what?"

"Such as shutting up. Not telling all you know. Not showing off."

"I see what you mean," said Welles. "Have you heard the story of St. Thomas Aquinas?"

"No."

"When he was a student in Paris, he never spoke out in class, and the others thought him stupid. One of them kindly offered to help him, and went over all the work very patiently to make him understand it. And then one day they came to a place where the other student got all mixed up and had to admit he didn't understand. Then Thomas suggested a solution and it was the right one. He knew more than any of the others all the time; but they called him the Dumb Ox."

Tim nodded gravely.

"And when he grew up?" asked the boy.

"He was the greatest thinker of all time," said Welles. "A thirteenth-century super-brain. He did more original work than any other ten great men; and he died young."

After that, it was easier.

"How do I begin?" asked Timothy.

"You'd better begin at the beginning. Tell me all you can remember about your early childhood, before you went to school."

Tim gave this his consideration.

"I'll have to go forward and backward a lot," he said. "I couldn't put it all in order."

"That's all right. Just tell me today all you can remember about that time of your life. By next week you'll have remembered more. As we go on to later periods of your life, you may remember things that belonged to an earlier time; tell them then. We'll make some sort of order out of it."

Welles listened to the boy's revelations with growing excitement. He found it difficult to keep outwardly calm.

"When did you begin to read?" Welles asked.

"I don't know when it was. My grandmother read me some stories, and somehow I got the idea about the words. But when I tried to tell her I could read, she spanked me. She kept saying I couldn't, and I kept saying I could, until she spanked me. For a while I had a dreadful time, because I didn't know any word she hadn't read to me —I guess I sat beside her and watched, or else I remembered and then went over it by myself right after. I must have learned as soon as I got the idea that each group of letters on the page was a word."

"The word-unit method," Welles commented. "Most self-taught readers learned like that."

"Yes. I have read about it since. And Macaulay could read when he was three, but only upside-down, because of standing opposite when his father read the Bible to the family."

"There are many cases of children who learned to read as you did, and surprised their parents. Well? How did you get on?"

"One day I noticed that two words looked almost alike and sounded almost alike. They were 'can' and 'man.' I remember staring at them and then it was like something beautiful boiling up in me. I began to look carefully at the words, but in a crazy excitement. I was a long while at it, because when I put down the book and tried to stand up I was stiff all over. But I had the idea, and after that it wasn't hard to figure out almost any words. The really hard words are the common ones that you get all the time in easy books. Other words are pronounced the way they are spelled."

"And nobody knew you could read?"

"No. Grandmother told me not to say I could, so I didn't. She read to me often, and that helped. We had a great many books. Of course, I liked those with pictures. Once or twice they caught me with a book that had no pictures, and then they'd take it away and say, 'I'll find a book for a little boy.'"

"Do you remember what books you liked then?"

"Books about animals, I remember. And geographies. It was funny about animals—"

Once you got Timothy started, thought Welles, it wasn't hard to get him to go on talking.

"One day I was at the Zoo," said Tim, "and by the cages alone. Grandmother was resting on a bench and she let me walk along by myself. People were talking about the animals and I began to tell them all I knew. It must have been funny in a way, because I had read a lot of words I couldn't pronounce correctly, words I had never heard spoken. They listened and asked me questions and I thought I was just like grandfather, teaching them the way he sometimes taught me. And then they called another man to come, and said, 'Listen to this kid; he's a scream!' and I saw they were all laughing at me."

Timothy's face was redder than usual, but he tried to smile as he added, "I can see now how it must have sounded funny. And unexpected, too; that's a big point in humor. But my little feelings were so dreadfully hurt that I ran back to my grandmother crying, and she couldn't find out why. But it served me right for disobeying her. She always told me not to tell people things; she said a child had nothing to teach its elders."

"Not in that way, perhaps—at that age."

"But, honestly, some grown people don't know very much," said Tim. "When we went on the train last year, a woman came up and sat beside me and started to tell me things a little boy should know about California. I told her I'd lived here all my life, but I guess she didn't even know we are taught things in school, and she tried to tell me things, and almost everything was wrong."

"Such as what?" asked Welles, who had also suffered from tourists.

"Well . . . she said so many things . . . but I thought this was the funniest: She said all the Missions were so old and interesting, and I said yes, and she said, 'You know, they were all built long before Columbus discovered America,' and I thought she meant it for a joke, so I laughed. She looked very serious and said, 'Yes, those people all came up here from Mexico.' I suppose she thought they were Aztec temples."

Welles, shaking with laughter, could not but agree that many adults were sadly lacking in the rudiments of knowledge.

"After that Zoo experience, and a few others like it, I began to get wise to myself," continued Tim. "People who knew things didn't want to hear me repeating them, and people who didn't know, wouldn't be taught by a four-year-old baby. I guess I was four when I began to write."

"How?"

"Oh, I just thought if I couldn't say anything to anybody at any time, I'd burst. So I began to put it down—in printing, like in books. Then I found out about writing, and we had some old-fashioned schoolbooks that taught how to write. I'm left-handed. When I went to school, I had to use my right hand. But by then I had learned how to pretend that I didn't know things. I watched the others and did as they did. My grandmother told me to do that."

"I wonder why she said that," marveled Welles.

"She knew I wasn't used to other children, she said, and it was the first time she had left me to anyone else's care. So she told me to do what the others did and what my teachers said," explained Tim simply, "and I followed her advice literally. I pretended I didn't know anything, until the others began to know it, too. Lucky I was so shy. But there were things to learn, all right. Do you know, when I first went to school, I was disappointed because the teacher dressed like other women. The only pictures of teachers I had noticed were those in an old Mother Goose book, and I thought that all teachers wore hoop skirts. But as soon as I saw her, after the little shock of surprise, I knew it was silly, and I never told."

The psychiatrist and the boy laughed together.

"We played games. I had to learn to play with children, and not be surprised when they slapped or pushed me. I just couldn't figure out why they'd do that, or what good it did them. But if it was to surprise me, I'd say 'Boo' and surprise them some time later; and if they were mad because I had taken a ball or something they wanted, I'd play with them."

"Anybody ever try to beat you up?"

"Oh, yes. But I had a book about boxing—with pictures. You can't learn much from pictures, but I got some practice too, and that helped. I didn't want to win, anyway. That's what I like about games of strength or skill—I'm fairly matched, and I don't have to be always watching in case I might show off or try to boss somebody around."

"You must have tried bossing sometimes."

"In books, they all cluster around the boy who can teach new games and think up new things to play. But I found out that doesn't work. They just want to do the same thing all the time—like hide and seek. It's no fun if the first one to be caught is 'it' next time. The rest just walk in any old way and don't try to hide or even to run, because it doesn't matter whether they are caught. But you can't get the boys to see that and play right, so the last one caught is 'it.' "

Timothy looked at his watch.

"Time to go," he said. "I've enjoyed talking to you, Dr. Welles. I hope I haven't bored you too much."

Welles recognized the echo and smiled appreciatively at the small boy.

"You didn't tell me about the writing. Did you start to keep a diary?"

"No. It was a newspaper. One page a day, no more and no less. I still keep it," confided Tim. "But I get more on the page now. I type it."

"And you write with either hand now?"

"My left hand is my own secret writing. For school and things like that I use my right hand."

When Timothy had left, Welles congratulated himself. But for the next month he got no more. Tim would not reveal a single significant fact. He talked about ball-playing, he described his grandmother's astonished delight over the beautiful kitten, he told of its growth and the tricks it played. He gravely related such enthralling facts as that he liked to ride on trains, that his favorite wild animal was the lion, and that he greatly desired to see snow falling. But not a word of what Welles wanted to hear. The psychiatrist, knowing that he was again being tested, waited patiently.

Then one afternoon when Welles, fortunately unoccupied with a patient, was smoking a pipe on his front porch, Timothy Paul strode into the yard.

"Yesterday Miss Page asked me if I was seeing you and I said yes.

She said she hoped my grandparents didn't find it too expensive, because you had told her I was all right and didn't need to have her worrying about me. And then I said to grandma, was it expensive for you to talk to me, and she said, 'Oh, no, dear; the school pays for that. It was your teacher's idea that you have a few talks with Dr. Welles.' "

"I'm glad you came to me, Tim, and I'm sure you didn't give me away to either of them. Nobody's paying me. The school pays for my services if a child is in a bad way and his parents are poor. It's a new service, since 1956. Many maladjusted children can be helped—much more cheaply to the state than the cost of having them go crazy or become criminals or something. You understand all that. But—sit down, Tim!—I can't charge the state for you, and I can't charge your grandparents. You're adjusted marvelously well in every way, as far as I can see; and when I see the rest, I'll be even more sure of it."

"Well—gosh! I wouldn't have come—" Tim was stammering in confusion. "You ought to be paid. I take up so much of your time. Maybe I'd better not come any more."

"I think you'd better. Don't you?"

"Why are you doing it for nothing, Dr. Welles?"

"I think you know why."

The boy sat down in the glider and pushed himself meditatively back and forth. The glider squeaked.

"You're interested. You're curious," he said.

"That's not all, Tim."

Squeak-squeak. Squeak-squeak.

"I know," said Timothy. "I believe it. Look, is it all right if I call you Peter? Since we're friends."

At their next meeting, Timothy went into details about his newspaper. He had kept all the copies, from the first smudged, awkwardly printed pencil issues to the very latest neatly typed ones. But he would not show Welles any of them.

"I just put down every day the things I most wanted to say, the news or information or opinion I had to swallow unsaid. So it's a wild medley. The earlier copies are awfully funny. Sometimes I guess what they were all about, what made me write them. Sometimes I remember. I put down the books I read too, and mark them like school grades, on two points—how I liked the book, and whether it was good. And whether I had read it before, too."

"How many books do you read? What's your reading speed?"

It proved that Timothy's reading speed on new books of adult level varied from eight hundred to nine hundred fifty words a minute. The average murder mystery—he loved them—took him less than half an hour. A year's homework in history, Tim performed easily by reading his textbook through three or four times during the year. He apologized for that, but explained that he had to know what was in the book so as not to reveal in examinations too much that he had learned from other sources. Evenings, when his grandparents believed him to be doing homework, he spent reading other books, or writing his newspaper, "or something." As Welles had already guessed, Tim had read everything in his grandfather's library, everything in the public library that was not on the closed shelves, and everything he could order from the state library.

"What do the librarians say?"

"They think the books are for my grandfather. I tell them that, if they ask what a little boy wants with such a big book. Peter, telling so many lies is what gets me down. I have to do it, don't I?"

"As far as I can see, you do," agreed Welles. "But here's material for a while in my library. There'll have to be a closed shelf here, too, though, Tim."

"Could you tell me why? I know about the library books. Some of them might scare people, and some are—"

"Some of my books might scare you too, Tim. I'll tell you a little about abnormal psychology if you like, one of these days, and then I think you'll see that until you're actually training to deal with such cases, you'd be better off not knowing too much about them."

"I don't want to be morbid," agreed Tim. "All right. I'll read only what you give me. And from now on I'll tell you things. There was more than the newspaper, you know."

"I thought as much. Do you want to go on with your tale?"

"It started when I first wrote a letter to a newspaper—of course, under a pen name. They printed it. For a while I had a high old time of it—a letter almost every day, using all sorts of pen names. Then I branched out to magazines, letters to the editor again. And stories—I tried stories."

He looked a little doubtfully at Welles, who said only: "How old were you when you sold the first story?"

"Eight," said Timothy. "And when the check came, with my name on it, 'T. Paul,' I didn't know what in the world to do."

"That's a thought. What did you do?"

"There was a sign in the window of the bank. I always read signs, and that one came back to my mind: 'Banking By Mail.' You can see I was pretty desperate. So I got the name of a bank across the Bay and I wrote them—on my typewriter—and said I wanted to start an account, and here was a check to start it with. Oh, I was scared stiff, and had to keep saying to myself that, after all, nobody could do much to me. It was my own money. But you don't know what it's like to be only a small boy! They sent the check back to me and I died ten deaths when I saw it. But the letter explained. I hadn't endorsed it. They sent me a blank to fill out about myself. I didn't know how many lies I dared to tell. But it was my money and I had to get it. If I could get it into the bank, then some day I could get it out. I gave my business as 'author' and gave my age as twenty-four. I thought that was awfully old."

"I'd like to see the story. Do you have a copy of the magazine around?"

"Yes," said Tim. "But nobody noticed it—I mean, 'T. Paul' could be anybody. And when I saw magazines for writers on the newsstands, and bought them I got on to the way to use a pen name on the story and my own name and address up in the corner. Before that I used a pen name and sometimes never got the things back or heard about them. Sometimes I did, though."

"What then?"

"Oh, then I'd endorse the check payable to me and sign the pen name, and then sign my own name under it. Was I scared to do that! But it was my money."

"Only stories?"

"Articles, too. And things. That's enough of that for today. Only— I just wanted to say—a while ago, T. Paul told the bank he wanted to switch some of the money over to a checking account. To buy books by mail, and such. So I could pay you, Dr. Welles—" with sudden formality.

"No, Tim," said Peter Welles firmly. "The pleasure is all mine. What I want is to see the story that was published when you were eight. And some of the other things that made T. Paul rich enough to keep a consulting psychiatrist on the payroll. And, for the love of Pete, will you tell me how all this goes on without your grandparents' knowing about it?"

"Grandmother thinks I send in box tops and fill out coupons," said Tim. "She doesn't bring in the mail. She says her little boy gets such a big bang out of that little chore. Anyway that's what she said when I was eight. I played mailman. And there were box tops—I showed them to her, until she said, about the third time, that really she wasn't greatly interested in such matters. By now she has the habit of waiting for me to bring in the mail."

Peter Welles thought that was quite a day of revelation. He spent a quiet evening at home, holding his head and groaning, trying to take it all in.

And that I.Q.—120, nonsense! The boy had been holding out on him. Tim's reading had obviously included enough about I.Q. tests, enough puzzles and oddments in magazines and such, to enable him to stall successfully. What could he do if he would co-operate?

Welles made up his mind to find out.

He didn't find out. Timothy Paul went swiftly through the whole range of Superior Adult tests without a failure of any sort. There were no tests yet devised that could measure his intelligence. While he was still writing his age with one figure, Timothy Paul had faced alone, and solved alone, problems that would have baffled the average adult. He had adjusted to the hardest task of all—that of appearing to be a fairly normal, B-average small boy.

And it must be that there was more to find out about him. What did he write? And what did he do besides read and write, learn carpentry and breed cats and magnificently fool his whole world?

When Peter Welles had read some of Tim's writings, he was surprised to find that the stories the boy had written were vividly human, the product of close observation of human nature. The articles, on the other hand, were closely reasoned and showed thorough study and research. Apparently Tim read every word of several newspapers and a score or more of periodicals.

"Oh, sure," said Tim, when questioned. "I read everything. I go back once in a while and review old ones, too."

"If you can write like this," demanded Welles, indicating a magazine in which a staid and scholarly article had appeared, "and this"— this was a man-to-man political article giving the arguments for and against a change in the whole Congressional system—"then why do you always talk to me in the language of an ordinary schoolboy?"

"Because I'm only a little boy," replied Timothy. "What would happen if I went around talking like that?"

"You might risk it with me. You've showed me these things."

"I'd never dare to risk talking like that. I might forget and do it again before others. Besides, I can't pronounce half the words."

"What!"

"I never look up a pronunciation," explained Timothy. "In case I do slip and use a word beyond the average, I can anyway hope I didn't say it right."

Welles shouted with laughter, but was sober again as he realized the implications back of that thoughtfulness.

"You're just like an explorer living among savages," said the psychiatrist. "You have studied the savages carefully and tried to imitate them so they won't know there are differences."

"Something like that," acknowledged Tim.

"That's why your stories are so human," said Welles. "That one about the awful little girl—"

They both chuckled.

"Yes, that was my first story," said Tim. "I was almost eight, and there was a boy in my class who had a brother, and the boy next door was the other one, the one who was picked on."

"How much of the story was true?"

"The first part. I used to see, when I went over there, how that girl picked on Bill's brother's friend Steve. She wanted to play with Steve all the time herself and whenever he had boys over, she'd do something awful. And Steve's folks were just like I said—they wouldn't let Steve do anything to a girl. When she threw all the watermelon rinds over the fence into his yard, he just had to pick them all up and say nothing back; and she'd laugh at him over the fence. She got him blamed for things he never did, and when he had work to do in the yard she'd hang out of her window and scream at him and make fun. I thought first, what made her act like that, and then I made up a way for him to get even with her, and wrote it out the way it might have happened."

"Didn't you pass the idea on to Steve and let him try it?"

"Gosh, no! I was only a little boy. Kids seven don't give ideas to kids ten. That's the first thing I had to learn—to be always the one that kept quiet, especially if there was any older boy or girl around, even only a year or two older. I had to learn to look blank and let my mouth hang open and say, 'I don't get it,' to almost everything."

"And Miss Page thought it was odd that you had no close friends of your own age," said Welles. "You must be the loneliest boy that ever walked this earth, Tim. You've lived in hiding like a criminal. But tell me, what are you afraid of?"

"I'm afraid of being found out, of course. The only way I can live in this world is in disguise—until I'm grown up, at any rate. At first, it was just my grandparents scolding me and telling me not to show off, and the way people laughed if I tried to talk to them. Then I saw how people hate anyone who is better or brighter or luckier. Some people sort of trade off; if you're bad at one thing you're good at another, but they'll forgive you for being good at some things, because you're not good at others and they can balance that off. They can beat you at something. You have to strike a balance. A child has no chance at all. No grownup can stand it to have a child know anything he doesn't. Oh, a little thing, if it amuses them. But not much of anything. There's an old story about a man who found himself in a country where everyone else was blind. I'm like that—but they shan't put out my eyes. I'll never let them know I can see anything."

"Do you see things that no grown person can see?"

Tim waved his hand towards the magazines.

"Only like that, I meant. I hear people talking, in street cars and stores, and while they work, and around. I read about the way they act—in the news. I'm like them, just like them, only I seem about a hundred years older—more matured."

"Do you mean that none of them have much sense?"

"I don't mean that exactly. I mean that so few of them have any, or show it if they do have. They don't even seem to want to. They're good people in their way, but what could they make of me? Even when I was seven, I could understand their motives, but they couldn't understand their own motives. And they're so lazy—they don't seem to want to know or to understand. When I first went to the library for books, the books I learned from were seldom touched by any of the grown people. But they were meant for ordinary grown people. But the grown people didn't want to know things—they only wanted to fool around. I feel about most people the way my grandmother feels about babies and puppies. Only she doesn't have to pretend to be a puppy all the time," Tim added, with a little bitterness.

"You have a friend now, in me."

"Yes, Peter," said Tim, brightening up. "And I have pen friends, too. People like what I write, because they can't see I'm only a little boy. When I grow up—"

Tim did not finish that sentence. Welles understood, now, some of the fears that Tim had not dared to put into words at all. When he grew up, would he be as far beyond all the other grownups as he had, all his life, been above his contemporaries? The adult friends whom he now met on fairly equal terms—would they then, too, seem like babies or puppies?

Peter did not dare to voice the thought, either. Still less did he venture to hint at another thought. Tim, so far, had no great interest in girls; they existed for him as part of the human race, but there would come a time when Tim would be a grown man and would wish to marry. And where among the puppies could he find a mate?

"When you're grown up, we'll still be friends," said Peter. "And who are the others?"

It turned out that Tim had pen friends all over the world. He played chess by correspondence—a game he never dared to play in person, except when he forced himself to move the pieces about idly and let his opponent win at least half the time. He had, also, many friends who had read something he had written, and had written to him about it, thus starting a correspondence-friendship. After the first two or three of these, he had started some on his own account, always with people who lived at a great distance. To most of these he gave a name which, although not false, looked it. That was Paul T. Lawrence. Lawrence was his middle name; and with a comma after the Paul, it was actually his own name. He had a post office box under that name, for which T. Paul of the large bank account was his reference.

"Pen friends abroad? Do you know languages?"

Yes, Tim did. He had studied by correspondence, also; many universities gave extension courses in that manner, and lent the student records to play so that he could learn the correct pronunciation. Tim had taken several such courses, and learned other languages from books. He kept all these languages in practice by means of the letters to other lands and the replies which came to him.

"I'd buy a dictionary, and then I'd write to the mayors of some towns, or to a foreign newspaper, and ask them to advertise for some pen friends to help me learn the language. We'd exchange souvenirs and things."

Nor was Welles in the least surprised to find that Timothy had also taken other courses by correspondence. He had completed, within three years, more than half the subjects offered by four separate universities, and several other courses, the most recent being Architecture. The boy, not yet fourteen, had completed a full course in that subject and, had he been able to disguise himself as a full-grown man, could have gone out at once and built almost anything you'd like to name, for he also knew much of the trades involved.

"It always said how long an average student took, and I'd take that long," said Tim, "so, of course, I had to be working several schools at the same time."

"And carpentry at the playground summer school?"

"Oh, yes. But there I couldn't do too much, because people could see me. But I learned how, and it made a good cover-up, so I could make cages for the cats, and all that sort of thing. And many boys are good with their hands. I like to work with my hands. I built my own radio too—it gets all the foreign stations, and that helps me with my languages."

"How did you figure it about the cats?" asked Welles.

"Oh, there had to be recessives, that's all. The Siamese coloring was a recessive, and it had to be mated with another recessive. Black was one possibility, and white was another, but I started with black because I liked it better. I might try white too, but I have so much else on my mind—"

He broke off suddenly and would say no more.

Their next meeting was by prearrangement at Tim's workshop. Welles met the boy after school and they walked to Tim's home together; there the boy unlocked his door and snapped on the lights.

Welles looked around with interest. There was a bench, a tool chest. Cabinets, padlocked. A radio, clearly not store-purchased. A file cabinet, locked. Something on a table, covered with a cloth. A box in the corner—no, two boxes in two corners. In each of them was a mother cat with kittens. Both mothers were black Persians.

"This one must be all black Persian," Tim explained. "Her third litter and never a Siamese marking. But this one carries both recessives in her. Last time she had a Siamese short-haired kitten. This morning—I had to go to school. Let's see."

They bent over the box where the new-born kittens lay. One kitten was like the mother. The other two were Siamese-Persian; a male and a female.

"You've done it again, Tim!" shouted Welles. "Congratulations!"

They shook hands in jubilation.

"I'll write it in the record," said the boy blissfully.

In a nickel book marked "Compositions" Tim's left hand added the entries. He had used the correct symbols—F_1, F_2, F_3; Ss, Bl.

"The dominants in capitals," he explained, "B for black, and S for short hair; the recessives in small letters—s for Siamese, l for long hair. Wonderful to write ll over ss again, Peter! Twice more. And the other kitten is carrying the Siamese markings as a recessive."

He closed the book in triumph.

"Now," and he marched to the covered thing on the table, "my latest big secret."

Tim lifted the cloth carefully and displayed a beautifully built doll house. No, a model house—Welles corrected himself swiftly. A beautiful model, and—yes, built to scale.

"The roof comes off. See, it has a big storage room and a room for a play room or a maid or something. Then I lift off the attic—"

"Good heavens!" cried Peter Welles. "Any little girl would give her soul for this!"

"I used fancy wrapping papers for the wallpapers. I wove the rugs on a little hand loom," gloated Timothy. "The furniture's just like real, isn't it? Some I bought; that plastic. Some I made of construction paper and things. The curtains were the hardest; but I couldn't ask grandmother to sew them—"

"Why not?" the amazed doctor managed to ask.

"She might recognize this afterwards," said Tim, and he lifted off the upstairs floor.

"Recognize it? You haven't showed it to her? Then when would she see it?"

"She might not," admitted Tim. "But I have to take some risks."

"That's a very livable floor plan you've used," said Welles, bending closer to examine the house in detail.

"Yes, I thought so. It's awful how many house plans leave no clear wall space for books or pictures. Some of them have doors placed so you have to detour around the dining room table every time you go from the living room to the kitchen, or so that a whole corner of a room is good for nothing, with doors at all angles. Now, I designed this house to—"

"You designed it, Tim!"

"Why, sure. Oh, I see—you thought I built it from blueprints I'd bought. My first model home, I did, but the architecture courses gave me so many ideas that I wanted to see how they would look. Now, the cellar and game room—"

Welles came to himself an hour later, and gasped when he looked at his watch.

"It's too late. My patient has gone home again by this time. I may as well stay—how about the paper route?"

"I gave that up. Grandmother offered to feed the cats as soon as I gave her the kitten. And I wanted the time for this. Here are the pictures of the house."

The color prints were very good.

"I'm sending them and an article to the magazines," said Tim. "This time I'm T. L. Paul. Sometimes I used to pretend all the different people I am were talking together—but now I talk to you instead, Peter."

"Will it bother the cats if I smoke? Thanks. Nothing I'm likely to set on fire, I hope? Put the house together and let me sit here and look at it. I want to look in through the windows. Put its little lights on. There."

The young architect beamed, and snapped on the little lights.

"Nobody can see in here. I got Venetian blinds; and when I work in here, I even shut them sometimes."

"If I'm to know all about you, I'll have to go through the alphabet from A to Z," said Peter Welles. "This is Architecture. What else in the A's?"

"Astronomy. I showed you those articles. My calculations proved correct. Astrophysics—I got A in the course, but haven't done anything original so far. Art, no; I can't paint or draw very well, except mechanical drawing. I've done all the Merit Badge work in scouting, all through the alphabet."

"Darned if I can see you as a Boy Scout," protested Welles.

"I'm a very good Scout. I have almost as many badges as any other boy my age in the troop. And at camp I do as well as most city boys."

"Do you do a good turn every day?".

"Yes," said Timothy. "Started that when I first read about Scouting—I was a Scout at heart before I was old enough to be a Cub. You know, Peter, when you're very young you take all that seriously, about the good deed every day, and the good habits and ideals and all that. And then you get older and it begins to seem funny and childish and posed and artificial, and you smile in a superior way and make jokes. But there is a third step, too, when you take it all seriously again. People who make fun of the Scout Law are doing the boys a lot of harm; but those who believe in things like that don't know how to say so, without sounding priggish and platitudinous. I'm going to do an article on it before long."

"Is the Scout Law your religion—if I may put it that way?"

"No," said Timothy. "But 'a Scout is Reverent.' Once I tried to study the churches and find out what was the truth. I wrote letters to pastors of all denominations—all those in the phone book and the newspaper—when I was on a vacation in the East, I got the names, and then wrote after I got back. I couldn't write to people here in the city. I said I wanted to know which church was true, and expected them to write to me and tell me about theirs, and argue with me, you know. I could read library books, and all they had to do was recommend some, I told them, and then correspond with me a little about them."

"Did they?"

"Some of them answered," said Tim, "but nearly all of them told me to go to somebody near me. Several said they were very busy men. Some gave me the names of a few books, but none of them told me to write again, and . . . and I was only a little boy. Nine years old, so I couldn't talk to anybody. When I thought it over, I knew that I couldn't very well join any church so young, unless it was my grandparents' church. I keep on going there—it is a good church and it teaches a great deal of truth, I am sure. I'm reading all I can find, so when I'm old enough I'll know what I must do. How old would you say I should be, Peter?"

"College age," replied Welles. "You are going to college? By then, any of the pastors would talk to you—except those that are too busy!"

"It's a moral problem, really. Have I the right to wait? But I have to wait. It's like telling lies—I have to tell some lies, but I hate to. If I have a moral obligation to join the true church as soon as I find it, well, what then? I can't until I'm eighteen or twenty?"

"If you can't, you can't. I should think that settles it. You are legally a minor, under the control of your grandparents, and while you might claim the right to go where your conscience leads you, it would be impossible to justify and explain your choice without giving yourself away entirely—just as you are obliged to go to school until you are at least eighteen, even though you know more than most Ph.D.'s. It's all part of the game, and He who made you must understand that."

"I'll never tell you any lies," said Tim. "I was getting so desperately lonely—my pen pals didn't know anything about me really. I told them only what was right for them to know. Little kids are satisfied to be with other people but when you get a little older you have to make friends, really."

"Yes, that's a part of growing up. You have to reach out to others and share thoughts with them. You've kept to yourself too long as it is."

"It wasn't that I wanted to. But without a real friend, it was only pretense, and I never could let my playmates know anything about me. I studied them and wrote stories about them and it was all of them, but it was only a tiny part of me."

"I'm proud to be your friend, Tim. Every man needs a friend. I'm proud that you trust me."

Tim patted the cat a moment in silence and then looked up with a grin.

"How would you like to hear my favorite joke?" he asked.

"Very much," said the psychiatrist, bracing himself for almost any major shock.

"It's records. I recorded this from a radio program."

Welles listened. He knew little of music, but the symphony which he heard pleased him. The announcer praised it highly in little speeches before and after each movement. Timothy giggled.

"Like it?"

"Very much. I don't see the joke."

"I wrote it."

"Tim, you're beyond me! But I still don't get the joke."

"The joke is that I did it by mathematics. I calculated what ought to sound like joy, grief, hope, triumph, and all the rest, and—it was just after I had studied harmony; you know how mathematical that is."

Speechless, Welles nodded.

"I worked out the rhythms from different metabolisms—the way you function when under the influences of these emotions; the way your metabolic rate varies, your heartbeats and respiration and things. I sent it to the director of that orchestra, and he didn't get the idea that it was a joke—of course I didn't explain—he produced the music. I get nice royalties from it, too."

"You'll be the death of me yet," said Welles in deep sincerity. "Don't tell me anything more today; I couldn't take it. I'm going home. Maybe by tomorrow I'll see the joke and come back to laugh. Tim, did you ever fail at anything?"

"There are two cabinets full of articles and stories that didn't sell. Some of them I feel bad about. There was the chess story. You know, in 'Through the Looking Glass,' it wasn't a very good game, and you couldn't see the relation of the moves to the story very well."

"I never could see it at all."

"I thought it would be fun to take a championship game and write a fantasy about it, as if it were a war between two little old countries, with knights and foot-soldiers, and fortified walls in charge of captains, and the bishops couldn't fight like warriors, and, of course, the queens were women—people don't kill them, not in hand-to-hand fighting and . . . well, you see? I wanted to make up the attacks and captures, and keep the people alive, a fairy-tale war you see, and make the strategy of the game and the strategy of the war coincide, and have everything fit. It took me ever so long to work it out and write it. To understand the game as a chess game and then to translate it into human actions and motives, and put speeches to it to fit different kinds of people. I'll show it to you. I loved it. But nobody would print it. Chess players don't like fantasy, and nobody else likes chess. You have to have a very special kind of mind to like both. But it was a disappointment. I hoped it would be published, because the few people who like that sort of thing would like it *very* much."

"I'm sure I'll like it."

"Well, if you do like that sort of thing, it's what you've been waiting all your life in vain for. Nobody else has done it." Tim stopped, and blushed as red as a beet. "I see what grandmother means. Once you get started bragging, there's no end to it. I'm sorry, Peter."

"Give me the story. I don't mind, Tim—brag all you like to me; I understand. You might blow up if you never express any of your legitimate pride and pleasure in such achievements. What I don't understand is how you have kept it all under for so long."

"I had to," said Tim.

The story was all its young author had claimed. Welles chuckled as he read it, that evening. He read it again, and checked all the moves and the strategy of them. It was really a fine piece of work. Then he thought of the symphony, and this time he was able to laugh. He sat up until after midnight, thinking about the boy. Then he took a sleeping pill and went to bed.

The next day he went to see Tim's grandmother. Mrs. Davis received him graciously.

"Your grandson is a very interesting boy," said Peter Welles carefully. "I'm asking a favor of you. I am making a study of various boys and girls in this district, their abilities and backgrounds and environment and character traits and things like that. No names will ever be mentioned, of course, but a statistical report will be kept, for ten years or longer, and some case histories might later be published. Could Timothy be included?"

"Timothy is such a good, normal little boy, I fail to see what would be the purpose of including him in such a survey."

"That is just the point. We are not interested in maladjusted persons in this study. We eliminate all psychotic boys and girls. We are interested in boys and girls who succeed in facing their youthful problems and making satisfactory adjustments to life. If we could study a selected group of such children, and follow their progress for the next ten years at least—and then publish a summary of the findings, with no names used—"

"In that case, I see no objections," said Mrs. Davis.

"If you'd tell me, then, something about Timothy's parents—their history?"

Mrs. Davis settled herself for a good long talk.

"Timothy's mother, my only daughter, Emily," she began, "was a lovely girl. So talented. She played the violin charmingly. Timothy is like her, in the face, but has his father's dark hair and eyes. Edwin had very fine eyes."

"Edwin was Timothy's father?"

"Yes. The young people met while Emily was at college in the East. Edwin was studying atomics there."

"Your daughter was studying music?"

"No; Emily was taking the regular liberal arts course. I can tell you little about Edwin's work, but after their marriage he returned to it and . . . you understand, it is painful for me to recall this, but their deaths were such a blow to me. They were so young."

Welles held his pencil ready to write.

"Timothy has never been told. After all, he must grow up in this world, and how dreadfully the world has changed in the past thirty years, Dr. Welles! But you would not remember the days before 1945. You have heard, no doubt, of the terrible explosion in the atomic plant in 1958 when they were trying to make a new type of bomb? At the time, none of the workers seemed to be injured. They believed the protection was adequate. But two years later they were all dead or dying."

Mrs. Davis shook her head, sadly. Welles held his breath, bent his head, scribbled.

"Tim was born just fourteen months after the explosion, fourteen months to the day. Everyone still thought that no harm had been done. But the radiation had some effect which was very slow—I do not understand such things—Edwin died, and then Emily came home to us with the boy. In a few months she, too, was gone.

"Oh, but we do not sorrow as those who have no hope. It is hard to have lost her, Dr. Welles, but Mr. Davis and I have reached the time of life when we can look forward to seeing her again. Our hope is to live until Timothy is old enough to fend for himself. We were so anxious about him; but you see he is perfectly normal in every way."

"Yes."

"The specialists made all sorts of tests. But nothing is wrong with Timothy."

The psychiatrist stayed a little longer, took a few more notes, and made his escape as soon as he could. Going straight to the school, he had a few words with Miss Page and then took Tim to his office, where he told him what he had learned.

"You mean—I'm a mutation?"

"A mutant. Yes, very likely you are. I don't know. But I had to tell you at once."

"Must be a dominant, too," said Tim, "coming out this way in the first generation. You mean—there may be more? I'm not the only one?" he added in great excitement. "Oh, Peter, even if I grow up past you I won't have to be lonely?"

There. He had said it.

"It could be, Tim. There's nothing else in your family that could account for you."

"But I have never found anyone at all like me. I would have known. Another boy or girl my age—like me—I would have known."

"You came West with your mother. Where did the others go, if they existed? The parents must have scattered everywhere, back to their homes all over the country, all over the world. We can trace them, though. And, Tim, haven't you thought it's just a little bit strange that with all your pen names and various contacts, people don't insist more on meeting you? People don't ask about you? Everything gets done by mail? It's almost as if the editors are used to people who hide. It's almost as if people are used to architects and astronomers and composers whom nobody ever sees, who are only names in care of other names at post office boxes. There's a chance—just a chance, mind you—that there are others. If there are we'll find them."

"I'll work out a code they will understand," said Tim, his face screwed up in concentration. "In articles—I'll do it—several magazines and in letters I can enclose copies—some of my pen friends may be the ones—"

"I'll hunt up the records—they must be on file somewhere—psychologists and psychiatrists know all kinds of tricks—we can make some excuse to trace them all—the birth records—"

Both of them were talking at once, but all the while Peter Welles was thinking sadly, perhaps he had lost Tim now. If they did find those others, those to whom Tim rightfully belonged, where would poor Peter be? Outside, among the puppies—

Timothy Paul looked up and saw Peter Welles' eyes on him. He smiled.

"You were my first friend, Peter, and you shall be forever," said Tim. "No matter what, no matter who."

"But we must look for the others," said Peter.

"I'll never forget who helped me," said Tim.

An ordinary boy of thirteen may say such a thing sincerely, and a week later have forgotten all about it. But Peter Welles was content. Tim would never forget, Tim would be his friend always. Even when Timothy Paul and those like him should unite in a maturity undreamed of, to control the world if they chose, Peter Welles would be Tim's friend—not a puppy, but a beloved friend—as a loyal dog, loved by a good master, is never cast out.

OPENING DOORS

Timothy Paul, age fourteen-next Wednesday, and Dr. Peter Welles, psychologist-psychiatrist, were on their way to the post office.

Tim was bursting with excitement, but he said never a word. Welles, watching him silently, knew why. One word from either of them and the floods of talk which would be loosed would never do in public. For they were going to get the first replies to the advertisement which they had placed in newspapers and magazines covering the nation.

The advertisement had been drafted by Tim himself, and he was very proud of it. He was in a fever of impatience to find the other children who were like him—if they existed, as there was reason to hope. Welles had intended to use other means, and within a week expected his first report from the detective agency which was tracing the children of all the parents who had died after the atomic explosion of 1958.

"Orphans, b c 59, i q three star plus," read the advertisement.

"We'll get all sorts of crazy replies," Tim had said, "but I want it to be plain enough so they can't miss it."

"We can weed them out," Welles had answered. "We can sell the writers neckties by mail, or something of the sort. We can explain it all by saying that I, as a psychologist, wanted to see what answers a cryptic nonsense ad would get."

"The b stands for born, and the c for circa," Tim had explained, pointing. "And the 59 is the year; they must all have been born in 1959 or very close to it. The rest is plain enough; they'll all be orphans, and it makes a catchy first word."

"Yes," Welles had replied patiently.

"I didn't mean to explain," apologized Tim, abashed. "Excuse me, Peter. It's only that I'm so used to having people never figure anything out by themselves."

"This seems almost too plain," said the psychologist. "But we'll see."

Well, at the worst, they'd get replies about bright children, and it would not do any harm for Tim to get in touch with bright children, even if they were only in the IQ 150-200 class.

Peter Welles unlocked the post-office box, and without a word began to divide the seven letters it contained, one for Tim and one for himself, one for Tim and one for himself, so that the odd one fell to the boy. Peter marched quickly out of the post office, and when Tim—who went slowly, examining the outsides of the envelopes—reached the street, he found that the doctor had flagged a taxi.

"Speed is the need of the moment," remarked Welles.

Tim smiled with his lips closed. The psychologist saw that the boy did not dare part his lips, lest indiscreet speech burst out. It was always hard to remember that this child, whose intelligence surpassed that of superior adults, was still emotionally only about thirteen years old.

"Hold everything, pal," said Welles encouragingly. "It won't be long now."

When they reached the doctor's office, which was also his home, Tim leaped from the cab and tore inside. By the time Peter got there, the first letter had been opened and read.

"This one thinks we're looking for child stars for the radio or the movies," said the boy. "But she doesn't know why orphans, she says, unless there is something wrong with our proposition."

"What shall we answer?" asked Peter, ripping open an envelope.

"Tell her we don't want the child's parents to get any of the child's salary," said Tim. "That'll settle her, all right. What's your first grab?"

"Thinks it must be some sex stuff, because it's cryptic," said Welles, tossing the letter into the fireplace.

Tim paid no attention; he was deep in the second letter which had fallen to him.

"This looks possible!" cried the boy. "It's obscure . . . but—"

"This one," interrupted Welles, "asks whether we are offering orphans for adoption or whether we want to adopt one. That's no good. But we must answer." He ripped open another, and cried, "Hello! This is in code!"

They read it together and laid it aside for the moment, with the other letter which had seemed possible but obscure.

"This one collects strange ads, so he says," Tim reported after a glance over his third letter. "Might be a possibility, but I don't think so. We can follow it up cautiously. And the last of all . . . hey! this is interesting, at any rate!"

He read the letter aloud:

"Dear Sir,

Your advertisement seems to deserve a wider audience, so I am broadcasting it over my short-wave set on the hour every hour this week. May I say that I take a personal interest in this matter? I would appreciate hearing from you further.

Jay Worthington."

"I think he's one," cried Tim. "That is, if there really are any more like me."

"Could be. We must figure out a reply to him; but it must be less plain than the ad, Tim. In fact, we'd better make some sort of reply to all the letters, just to be on the safe side."

"All but the one you threw into the fire," said Tim. "Let's see the code letter again."

They bent over it.

"Door-head tooth-head hand hook-tooth house-head-fish fish ox-serpent-fist serpent—"

Tim began to giggle. In many ways he was a very normal small boy.

"—mouth-head-fish-sign-tooth door fish-prop ox-sign-water hand-back of the head goad-camel goad-fish-goad-hand."

"Anything else?"

"Not a word except the name and address on the envelope. Marie Heath—a girl!"

"There would be girls too, no doubt," said Tim, with elaborate carelessness which might have fooled the casual observer. "But why did she use this paper? It's folded like a greeting card. Open it all the way out flat, Peter."

Welles opened the paper to its fullest extent.

"Here's a bit of a scribble in pencil. A doodle. No, let me have a good look . . . Tim, it's Hebrew!"

"I don't know Hebrew. Do you? Then I'll stop in the main library before I go home, and transliterate it. Now for the obscure one."

Timothy read it aloud slowly:

"*Dear Box Number:*
It leaps to the eye that this is my cue. But perhaps you are as much in the dark as I am and it is probably better so.
B. Burke."

"Sounds promising," said Welles.

Tim muttered a moment and then exclaimed, "Better in the dark!" and fled from the room. By the time Peter Welles had got to his feet there was a shout from Tim, summoning Welles to his own bedroom, and there was Tim beckoning from the clothes closet. They shut themselves in the closet and in the dark they could make out words dimly luminous between the lines of typing:

"If there was a mental Boomfood in my bottle when I was a baby it might explain a great deal. Were others fed the same food? I must take this risk, I must find out. Beth Burke."

"Another girl," exclaimed Tim in triumph. "Look, we've found two already and I can't wait to see about this code. If we turn the Hebrew word into English letters it may help us; otherwise we'll have to ask somebody who knows the language."

"Run along, then, and give me a buzz when you have anything to report."

"Not over the phone," said Tim cautiously. "I'll get in touch, though."

"Don't you spring any codes on me, young fellow. If this keeps up, we'll have plenty of puzzles on our hands. Scamper! You need a good run."

"And how!" agreed Tim. He dashed off.

He was ringing Welles' doorbell frantically a little later.

"I've got it! When I opened the encyclopedia to transliterate the Hebrew letters, it gave the meaning of each character. Look—door is daleth, that's d, and head is resh, that's r—"

He had written it on a separate piece of paper.

"Dr sr y ws brn n—and the next must be figures. The letters have a numerical value too—1-9-50-9. It makes a good code, for there are no vowels. This means, 'Dear sir, I was born in 1959.' And then it goes on, prnts d ns—I don't know what that means—atm y q lg lnly. That's all."

"Parents dead, and I don't get the ns either; maybe the writer got a little mixed. The number values would be 50-60. But atm is atom, of course, and the next is, IQ large. What's lnly?"

"Lonely," said Tim confidently.

"Seems to me these are almost too easy," worried Welles. "But I suppose they wouldn't give much away to anyone who doesn't know about the Wonder Children." He caught his breath, but it was too late. Tim merely grinned.

"So that's what you call us?"

"Not you, Tim. The rest of them . . . well, I had to call them something."

"Yes? I call them 'mine,' I think. I say to myself, 'Can we find any more of mine?' But that's silly, too. Now we can fit names to some of them; but we ought to think up a proper name for the group, and use it, Peter. That is, if we ever get a group, really."

"Timothy, it's almost your supper time," said Welles, as the clock struck six. "Run!"

"May I write answers to them?"

"Yes, but don't send them until I see them," conceded the doctor.

Writing answers was the most delightful game that Tim had ever played. Boys and girls of thirteen and fourteen have very little privacy about their incoming mail; all letters must be carefully coded and "tailored to fit" the letter they were answering, besides. Tim worked in references to Shaw's "Back to Methuselah" and Counts' "Country of the Blind."

The first list from the detective agency came two days later, and Welles dismissed a patient hurriedly and went with long strides to the school where Timothy spent his days. Miss Page raised an eyebrow when Welles beckoned to Timothy from the doorway, but nodded permission for the boy to go.

Welles hustled the boy into the middle of the empty corridor where they could not be overheard, and spoke softly.

"I have the list—nineteen names on it, this first batch. One of them, a girl, is in an insane asylum. She's probably perfectly sane. I must go to her at once."

"She must have given herself away and nobody believed her." Tim was shocked and grieved. "You can get her out, can't you, Peter?"

"I don't know. She may be insane. And I have no right to interfere. But I'll do what I can."

"Can I do anything? Or did you just want me to know you are going away?"

"You can pray hard, Tim. And here's the list I got. Make out a letter we can send to all of them, if you want to. But hold it until I come back."

Tim glanced at the list and grinned.

"Here's one of my pen pals, Gerard Chase. I thought some of my pen pals might belong. I'll write to him, all right. Look, can I send all my pen pals a copy of the ad, and just say I saw it and isn't it odd?"

"Sure. Go right ahead on that. And get the mail, too, if you like. Here's the key to the box."

Timothy pocketed the key and went back to his eighth-grade class.

Poor kid, thought Welles as he hastened to the airport. Somehow he must meet all those other kids, before too long. But not this trip.

The asylum was a small private hospital, three hours away by plane. It had pleasant grounds, flowers, trees. Dr. Mark Foxwell was in charge. Could Dr. Foxwell see Dr. Welles? Certainly, sir; this way, please.

"Elsie Lambeth is a patient here, yes," said Foxwell. He was a big man, heavier than Peter by fifty pounds at least; perhaps fifteen years older. He looked as dependable as a rock, thought Peter. And kind; he looked kind and patient. Good!

"The fact is," said Welles, "I have been asked by a friend of—well, one might say, a friend of Elsie's parents—I'll explain it all later, Dr. Foxwell. Shall we say that I have a friendly interest in the little girl, although I did not know of her existence until this morning. My credentials—"

Foxwell glanced over Welles' professional credentials and nodded.

"Heard of you," he murmured. "What do you want to know? Or do you want to see the child?"

"If possible, I want to hear all about her," said Peter. "And I want to see her, later, if I may. In exchange, I can tell you of a very interesting case, doctor—a boy about the same age. I have reason to think the cases may be related."

"Fine!" said the big doctor heartily. "Elsie's case is puzzling, and that's a fact. Nothing I'd like better than some light on her case. The whole town knows all about it; you might as well be told frankly all I know. Her uncle is her guardian; the child's parents died when she was a baby. She was brought to us when she was not quite six years old—completely unmanageable, that was the complaint."

"Dangerous?"

"Not particularly; but violent. Tantrums, alternating with fits of depression and sullen spells. Abusive language—said everyone was stupid. Wouldn't play with other children at all. In fact, that was where the real trouble started. She wouldn't go to school. Before she reached the age of five, the chief problem was that she was always running away. But always to the same place. Where would you guess a child of three would always run to?"

"The library, in this case," said Peter.

"Humph! You must know something I don't." Dr. Foxwell, genuinely startled, rubbed his chin thoughtfully. "You never heard of Elsie until today? Who told you that?"

"Nobody," said Peter. "I told you I knew a case that might be similar."

"Well—the library. Yes. She'd take a book at random, open it anywhere, hold it upside-down as like as not, and look at it by the hour. Turning pages faster than any adult can read, but more slowly than an idle child would flutter the pages. The librarians would call her aunt, and down would come auntie in a rush. But that was no go. Elsie all but tore the place apart."

"Did she damage the books?"

"No, never. Smash a chair to pieces—push a table over—scream and rage and kick—but never damage a book. No, I take that back; she did once. Tore a book to shreds. She said it told lies. Child of three!"

"Did it?"

"I don't know. Before my time. But the librarian was used to children, and she told Elsie if she ever did such a thing again she couldn't come to the library at all. And then she suggested that, since the child was perfectly quiet while she was looking at books, that she be allowed to stay there if she liked. After that, when she showed up, somebody would phone her aunt, and on his way home from work her uncle would look in every night and see if she was there, and take her home to supper."

"Would she go quietly then?"

"Usually. Sometimes not."

"Depending on what she was reading, I suppose," said Welles. "And what happened when she was five?"

"She wouldn't go to kindergarten. Something like the old joke about the little boy who told his mother, 'All right, if you want me to grow up to be a bead-stringer, I'll go.' But Elsie wouldn't go. She might start off to school, but she seldom ended up there. She'd land at the library, or at the Junior College. The students used to smuggle her in, and she'd sit in back where the instructor could not see her. The students thought that was funny, to have her sit there and appear to take everything in. Trouble was, after the first week or so, she wouldn't be quiet. She'd shout out, 'Oh, you don't know what you're talking about,' or other little compliments of the same sort. She'd call the students stupid and silly when they tried to recite. One professor stopped his lecture to say that she'd better come up and teach the class if she knew so much, and Elsie said, 'I could do it as well as you, but would I get paid for it?' "

Welles chuckled. "Didn't he offer to pay her?"

"He didn't, but a few days later another instructor did. And Elsie said, 'It's no use; these stupid people don't want to learn anything anyway.' "

"Sweet child," murmured Welles. "Let me ask a question now. Did Elsie actually know anything herself? Did she ever prove that she did?"

"Not a thing we could ever prove. Sometimes she'd say, 'It's all in the book; can't you read?' or 'You've heard that often enough; any fool should know it by now.' But the child actually could read by that time, I'm sure. I didn't come on the scene until later. Well, the long and short of it is that Elsie became a public nuisance. Even the librarians got out of patience sometimes. Elsie was usually quiet at the library, but one day when people were getting out books she walked up and said, 'What do you want that junk for?' and on another day, when a man chanced to say to a librarian that only four people had ever read the Encyclopedia Britannica through, Elsie popped up at his elbow and said, 'I'm the fifth and sixth, then. I've read it through twice.' "

Foxwell stopped to light a cigarette.

"You can laugh," he commented rather acidly, "but this isn't a joke. The child is here in this asylum because people didn't think it funny very long. Her aunt and uncle had no control over her, and finally they brought her here. She had been here a year or so when I came and took charge of this hospital."

"Didn't she run away?"

"They kept the child locked up. Had to. But when I came I took another line. Elsie, I said, you want to go to the library? Well, if you'll be a good girl, you don't have to be locked up. No running away, no tantrums, no naughty talk, and I'll let you go to the library and get books out every week. Then you can read them here, in your room or out in the nice big yard. Just so you stay on the grounds, Elsie, I said, and be a good girl. It worked pretty well. We had to lock her up a couple of times, until she saw I meant it."

"What does she do besides read?"

"She writes," said Foxwell. "A scribble nobody can make out. Looks like some kind of shorthand. She keeps it locked in a drawer in her room and wears the key on a ribbon around her neck. I allow it, but once in a while she has to let somebody glance through it— make sure nothing out of the way is there, you know—matches or other contraband. She knows if she doesn't behave she can't keep it locked. Once in a while she goes through it and burns up a lot of stuff. That is, of course, somebody else burns it; she stands by and sees that it is done. She has a radio; likes it low, so we have no trouble about that."

"What's the diagnosis?"

"Who can say? We call it something for the books."

"What is her IQ?"

"We'll never know. She won't answer. Superior intelligence, no doubt, but not co-operative. She and I get along fine now, though. I know what she won't do and what she will do, and we get along fine. She won't talk, she won't answer questions, she won't take tests or play games. But she cleans up her room and makes her bed and all that, she has learned several kinds of handwork, sews nicely—makes some of her own clothes—she helps with the gardening, and she knows how to talk politely now. 'Elsie,' I said, 'no saucy speeches here; you've got to be nice to people, if you want us to be nice to you. Never mind what you think, you keep still if you can't talk like a lady.' And she makes polite small talk when her aunt and uncle come to see her, just as nice as anyone could wish. I told her she must answer when she is spoken to, be nice, and not be naughty and stubborn. There are no other children here, but Elsie doesn't mind that; she hates children. She doesn't mix much with the other patients, yet she seems to take a sort of interest in them. I started to tell her a little about the other cases, so she wouldn't be frightened at their odd ways, and she would listen as solemnly as a judge. It can't be coincidence, either, the little ways she helps with them. We have one wide-eyed old gal who always wants to run the power mower. Drives the gardener nuts, but Elsie will drop everything and get over there and do something to distract the old gal. The gardener swears that once when Elsie lured the old gal off, the child turned and winked at him."

"You think she is crazy?"

"She isn't normal. She doesn't behave normally. What do you mean, crazy?"

"Could she behave in a sane manner if she wished to?"

"Most likely she could. Where does that get you? Elsie doesn't wish to. She says she likes it here."

Foxwell went to the window and pointed.

"There she is, over there under the tree. Reading, as usual. Want to go over and speak to her? I don't promise she will make an answer, not one worth hearing."

"Small talk, such as she has been taught, eh?" mused Welles. "Does it ever sound like a caricature?"

"It usually does," admitted Foxwell. "I thought she was trying hard to please us. Maybe you're right—there was something a bit sarcastic about it, always. Or as if she is having a game with us. Humph! Want to hear about that case of yours! Well, come on."

The two men walked out into the grounds and advanced towards Elsie. She was absorbed in her book, and did not heed their approach.

"Good afternoon, Elsie," said Dr. Foxwell.

The child looked up, rose to her feet, and answered: "Good afternoon, doctor," in a sweet childish voice. She was a wiry little girl with black curls; she was dressed like any other child of her age.

"Dr. Welles, may I present Elsie Lambeth?"

"How do you do, Elsie?"

"How do you do?" The girl kept her finger in her book to mark the place. She was perfectly polite, completely disinterested.

Peter raised his eyebrows at Foxwell, who nodded, understanding the request.

"I have come here to see you, Elsie," said Peter. "I know a boy whose case is something like yours. So I came here to see if you are ready to leave this place. Dr. Foxwell says that you won't answer his questions or take the tests he wants to give you. Perhaps when you have heard my story you will think differently about things."

Elsie stared at him. She lowered her eyes after a moment, and the color rushed to her face.

"It's all right, Elsie," he went on. "I am going to tell Dr. Foxwell my story, and then we can send for you and tell you about it."

"You're going pretty fast," said Foxwell, nudging Welles. "She may not be ready to leave us. She may not want to live outside."

"There are problems about living outside, aren't there, Elsie? But perhaps we can solve them. The boy I am going to tell you about has solved them. But then he is a very bright boy."

The look Elsie shot at Dr. Welles made him smile as he nodded back at her.

"He had the breaks. But now things are going to break right for some other girls and boys. You'll listen to my story, won't you, Elsie?"

"I want to hear it first," said Foxwell, a little roughly. "Got to be sure it's worth telling her. Maybe she won't be much interested."

Welles winked at the child and turned to go.

The doctors walked off together in high satisfaction.

"Got her interested," remarked Foxwell. "But it's nothing to the way you've got me interested, Welles! Hints, hints! You must be very sure of yourself."

"We must not be overheard. Tim's case is secret."

"My office is completely soundproofed."

"I'm sure you've already taken the hints?"

"Wouldn't be surprised if I have. You think Elsie is too bright and didn't have a fair chance to get adjusted. By the time I came on the scene, she had been here a year, and I couldn't do much with her."

"Do you think she is sane?"

"I couldn't prove it. Now, what's your case, Dr. Welles?"

They went into Foxwell's office and locked the door; and then Peter Welles told the story of Timothy Paul.

Foxwell listened, agape.

"You think Elsie is shamming?"

"Hiding. She hasn't chosen the best way to do it, and by now it would tax a better brain than hers to find a way out. Her wilfulness and her quick temper got her into trouble before she was old enough to devise a wiser way to manage her life; and now what can she do?"

"What have you to offer, Dr. Welles?"

"If she can prove herself sane, she can be taken out of here and into a different environment. You have taught her self-control and good manners; she could easily make a new start where her record is not known. That would be my suggestion. But she is under your care."

Foxwell waved an expansive arm.

"She is under your care now if you can do anything for her. You think your Timothy could help her adjust?"

"Possibly," said Welles. "It would be worth trying. He wants to be a psychiatrist himself. And it would do him a world of good to meet some of the other children."

"I'd like to meet your Tim."

"Certainly you must meet him. And if we could take Elsie there and let them meet . . . but perhaps he should meet some of the others first."

Dr. Foxwell said slowly: "It might be best if he meets Elsie first of all."

Welles nodded. "I see. Yes, you are right."

"If she is sane, it will still take time for her to adjust," said Foxwell. "You must help me with it."

"I had hoped you would say that. And I hope you will be able to help me with the other children if I find them. It is too big a job for one man to handle; and not many would be qualified to do it. It must be kept top secret for a while."

There was a tap at the door; a nurse reminded Dr. Foxwell that dinner time was at hand. The men ate quickly and absentmindedly, saying little. After dinner, Elsie was sent for.

The child was in her own room, nervously pacing about.

"Dr. Foxwell wants to see you now," said the nurse. "His friend is with him."

Elsie nodded obediently.

"I do hope you'll be good, Elsie," said the nurse pleadingly. "You've been such a good child lately. If you'd only talk to the doctor and answer his questions—"

"They are waiting," said Elsie sharply. "Why don't we go at once?"

"Well," cried the nurse, a little indignantly. "At least you're willing to go. Come on."

The nurse went with Elsie to the office and then was dismissed.

"Sit down, my dear, and let Dr. Welles tell you about the boy whose case is like yours," said Foxwell.

"No case is like mine," said Elsie.

"I think Tim is a little more intelligent than you are," said Welles thoughtfully. "He had all the breaks, and he made the most of them. Now things are breaking right for you."

"You said that before," said the child.

"I may say it again before I am through. But now for the story," and without further preamble, Peter plunged into the story of Timothy Paul.

Elsie listened with concentrated attention.

"Now, I know you are the child of parents who were also exposed to the same radiation," he concluded, "and who died of its effects not long after your birth. I think, and Dr. Foxwell thinks, that you are also sane and of greatly superior intelligence. If you are sane, you can leave this asylum and, under our direction, lead the kind of life such a brilliant girl should lead. But, if you are sane, you must prove it."

"Of course I am sane," said the child calmly. "I could have proved it any time these past five years."

"Why didn't you?"

"I didn't see what good it would do. I would have had to go back to school with a lot of stupid babies, and act like a little girl, and live with my stupid aunt and uncle. I can't be myself here, but I have more freedom than I would have outside. I was always unhappy until I came here."

"I am glad to see that you will answer my questions," said Peter, smiling at the child until she smiled back. "Weren't your aunt and uncle good to you?"

"They spoiled me rotten," said Elsie frankly. "Is that good? They didn't teach me to control my temper, or to be polite to people, or anything."

"They tried, didn't they?"

"Not very hard. My aunt always said she couldn't do anything with me. I was an awful brat. But grown people ought to have more control over a baby, even a bright baby. They didn't try to tell me things. I could have understood if they had told me. Dr. Foxwell did it right away. Why didn't they talk sense to me, the way he did? First they laughed and laughed and thought I was funny, and then they got mad with me. Stupids!"

"I don't think you behaved very wisely yourself, Elsie."

"Dr. Foxwell talked to me, and then I read more books, about how to bring up children, and about psychology. Then I knew how foolish I had been to be so naughty. But I couldn't think what to do, except to stay here."

"What is all this writing that you do?" asked Welles curiously.

"Poetry and stories and my diary and things. I am going to publish a lot of things when I get out of here. I meant to get out as soon as I was grown up, of course."

"What do you mean to do now?" asked Dr. Foxwell.

"I mean to get out of here and publish things now," said Elsie in some surprise. "Didn't you both say I could? Timothy Paul does."

"You'll have to behave as well as he does, and be accepted as a sane member of society," said Foxwell.

"Well, if I have pretended to be crazy for all these years," said Elsie tartly, "I can pretend to be normal if I like."

"What do you mean? Pretended to be crazy?"

"As soon as I saw where being uncontrolled got me, of course I knew how I ought to behave. But I had to keep on throwing tantrums and being sulky and not talking, so I could stay here in peace."

"You made the wrong adjustment, my dear," said Peter gently.

"I know that. I've known it for a long time. But I'm still only a little girl, and I couldn't stand living with my aunt and uncle and other children. They are all so stupid!"

"Elsie," said Dr. Foxwell, "I am glad to hear you talking so much; but you must erase that word 'stupid' from your vocabulary. It may be apt and it may not; but let's leave it out."

"Yes, sir," said the child obediently.

"Now about that writing," said Welles. "Can you write so people can read it?"

"Yes; but I had to have a secret writing for my private papers, or everyone would know I am sane. I'll copy everything out for you any time you want me to."

"You are sure the writings are sane?"

Elsie mused a moment.

"Yes, I am sure. Shall I tell you a little about them? A little is all I have time for, tonight, I suppose." She was plainly eager to tell, and the doctors urged her to go on talking.

"There's one drawer full of things I found wrong in books and papers I read, and the things people said; answers to magazine articles and book reviews and things that were wrong. I couldn't correct people out loud any more, so I wrote it all down. That got it off my mind. But no magazines would print it; most of it is out of date by now. Some books say the craziest things. And teachers, too. Some of those teachers at the Junior College—one of them said we couldn't know anything! He said there was no such thing as truth, and if there was, we couldn't know it, or ever know we knew it. Such crazy people, to try to teach! and—"

"Elsie," said Dr. Foxwell, "you must not call people crazy. That is not nice, either. Cut it out."

"A privilege reserved for you," said Elsie, with an impish grin which quite took the doctor's breath away. And then she added briskly: "You see you must not call me crazy either. I can even make jokes."

"You took the words right out of my mind," Welles joked back. "Go on. What else did you write?"

"I can't say the poems off by heart, and any other way would spoil them. But the play is nice. You'll like the play I have just finished. Do you liked Shakespeare, Dr. Welles?"

"Er . . . yes."

"So do I—in some ways. But sometimes he is cr . . . I mean, I don't always like him as well as I do sometimes," said the girl sedately, her eyes twinkling. "I thought he missed a good chance to write about Cataline—"

"Cataline?" said Dr. Foxwell weakly.

"Yes, and Cicero, you know. So I thought I'd write a play like 'Julius Caesar,' about the conspiracy of Cataline, and put some of Cicero's grand speeches into blank verse, and—I thought it would be an amusing hoax if I could pretend it was really by Shakespeare, undiscovered until now, but a hoax would be dishonest, so I decided against trying it. It is my first play," she added modestly, "but I like it. It was such fun. I'm so glad that you can read it, both of you. The really hard part has been keeping everything a secret. If I can be free like Tim—my aunt and uncle were snoopy. His grandparents must be wonderful. They trust him, don't they? Would you trust me?"

"That shouldn't be necessary," said Welles. "You can confide in us, you know. Now, it's getting late, and we must send you to bed. If Dr. Foxwell gives you the tests tomorrow, will you take them properly?"

"Yes, doctor."

"And answer everything we ask you?"

"Yes, doctor."

"And then what shall we do with you?"

The little girl chewed her thumbnail and screwed up her forehead.

"You could tell everybody that Dr. Welles came to town with a new treatment," she said triumphantly. "He could talk to me and pretty soon you could both say the new treatment had worked. There are always new kinds of psychotherapy being tried."

"Elsie, do you practice saying these big words when you are alone?" groaned Dr. Foxwell.

"Of course. I had to learn how to talk, didn't I?" was the cool response. "Well—could I go and live near Tim somewhere? Would his grandmother help me? But no, you said she doesn't care for children, except her grandson. And I couldn't live with you, of course, Dr. Welles, because I'm a girl."

"She thinks of everything," marveled Foxwell.

"Of course I do," Elsie flashed back. "I may be crazy but I am not stupid. I . . . oh, doctor, please excuse me, I forgot!"

"Excused," laughed the big doctor. "Welles? Have you a solution to these difficulties?"

"There must be some woman with whom she could board," said Peter, "and I have one in mind. But there is no need to tell anyone about Elsie. She must copy Tim, and present a normal face to the world. We can explain that she has not been well, had a nervous breakdown or something, that she is spoiled and needs training, and that she must be allowed to amuse herself in any proper way like other girls. When Dr. Foxwell releases you, Elsie, we think you should be away from here, and go somewhere away from all your past."

"That was one reason why I didn't see any point in being cured," said Elsie. "This whole town would think everything I did was cra . . . was odd, no matter what I did."

"Will her guardians agree to let her leave town?"

"Her uncle will gladly pay her board and care anywhere. They are eager to do their best for the child, although they do not understand her—and I can't blame them, now I see that I didn't understand her very well myself."

"I must have been a very difficult child," said the girl.

"Yes, I think you were," said Dr. Foxwell.

"Bring on your tests," said Elsie, waving her hands. "But if I'm not sane, then I want to stay here. I don't want to pretend I'm sane if I'm not. How many other boys and girls are there? Can we all live together?"

"That's my dream," admitted Welles, "but it may not be possible. You are all children, and nothing can be done without the consent of your guardians. I'll see your uncle and aunt the first thing after the tests are finished tomorrow."

"They'll agree," said Elsie. Her eyes suddenly filled with tears. "They're dreadfully stu . . . slow, poor things. But they do mean well. And they'll be so happy to think I'm going to be all right. It's been hard on them, too."

She ran out of the room, banging the door behind her.

The rest was easy. The next morning Dr. Foxwell gave Elsie the tests, and, as Timothy Paul had done, so also did Elsie. She went through the top of the IQ and C.M. tests, and on the Rorschach tests she gave normal, obviously unrehearsed answers which often made her examiners smile. Her uncle and aunt, when they were told as much as was good for them to know, were unfeignedly glad to know that Elsie could be "cured" and gave ready consent that she should move to be near Dr. Welles and under his care, as Dr. Foxwell recommended, and to board with any woman Dr. Welles suggested, to complete her adjustment to normal life.

Peter took the afternoon plane back, and reached his home city just in time to catch Tim leaving school.

"It's all right," he said. "It's all right. Come to my office after supper."

The boys were shouting to Tim to come and play ball.

"Yes, I'm coming," Tim shouted back. "May I go now, sir? Thank you, doctor," and he bounded away.

Welles watched him admiringly. The years of rigid self-control had wrought wonders. Nobody would ever have guessed that Peter had said anything of significance, anything to interest a boy whose schoolmates wanted him for a game.

The psychologist went into the school building and sat on Miss Page's desk. That brisk lady batted her eyes mischievously at him and asked concerning his health.

"I'm fine. And you, Miss Page?"

"Oh, fine, but getting no younger. Thirty-odd years of teaching age a gal before her time."

"I wondered . . . that is, have you any special plans for the summer?"

"No," said the teacher, stacking papers efficiently. "Nothing special. Can I do anything for you?"

"That depends. You see, there's a little girl . . . do you like bright children, Pagey?"

"That's hard to say. One meets so few of them."

"I'm serious for once. Many adults resent a bright child, and I need to find a woman who likes them."

"I have had one or two in my time," admitted Miss Page, "and I know what you mean. But I like them. There was one in particular—" her voice trailed off into silence.

"So you have found out that Timothy is brighter than most people think?" said Welles, gratified.

"I always thought he was. He wasn't the boy I had in mind. That one grew up to be a psychologist—but I'm beginning to think he isn't so bright after all."

Scarlet, Peter found himself laughing.

"Pagey, my love, my head is so full of a number of things that it has no room for me in it at all! Now, listen! Could you take this girl, a new patient of mine from out of the city, as a boarder for the summer? A girl of thirteen."

"A bright girl? Yes, I can, and gladly. How bright?"

"Too bright," said Welles. "A bit of a problem."

"You'll take care of the problem, no doubt. School is out in four weeks. When is she to come? Does she go to school?"

"She has not gone to school. Er . . . privately taught. She is not used to other children. That is one thing wrong with her."

"Bring her along, Peter. If she comes early, she can spend some time in my class if you like. It might do her good to visit school a short time before vacation."

"It would, I think. But you'd rather wait until school is out, wouldn't you?"

"If the child needs your care, Peter, why not begin?"

"Pagey, you're a gem!"

When Timothy came to the psychologist's house that evening, he had three letters in his hand.

"I figured that ns out," he said, beginning to talk almost before the door was opened to him. "The letters shouldn't be together. The two should be separated. The n stands for *in* and the s is the date—60. Parents died in 1960, that's what it means."

Peter Welles, who had forgotten all about the code letter, stared in amazement for a few seconds. Then he got what the boy was talking about, and in the next second realized what desperate excitement must lie beneath this prepared talk of other things. He shut the door behind Tim and spoke quickly.

"The girl is all right," he said. "Everything is all right. We'll have to help her a little; but she is coming here to live with Miss Page for the summer. I've been telephoning to her doctor just now. Next Sunday he is going to bring her up here. Now, do you want to hear all the details?"

The boy hesitated.

"Would it be all right? I don't want to pry. Does she know about me?"

"Yes, she knows nearly all that I know about you—as much as I had time to tell. So does her doctor. I had to tell them, you see."

"Then tell me all about her."

An hour later, they remembered the three letters.

"This one is promising. A boy says he feels like Gulliver—he's always much bigger or much smaller than the people he is with, but he says he leaves it to us to guess which is mental and which is physical. That's Robin Welch. And this girl says she was aptly named Alice—her last name is Chase—that she is out of communication with everything, even her own feet, and what was in that bottle labeled 'Drink Me' that she does not even recall having drunk. I think she belongs, too. The third is no good; it advertised a boarding school with special attention to orphans. Well, Peter, I have to start home; you know grandma's rules. When . . . when can I see Elsie?"

"Sunday evening at seven. We'll have to take her to Miss Page's first, and let her unpack and get located a bit. Dr. Foxwell and I will have her here for supper, I think, and you can come over right after supper."

They filled up the intervening days as best they could, with their separate daily routines, and with the writing of letters. Welles had explained to Tim that he intended to spend his vacation, in August, getting to see as many of the boys and girls as he could, but that for the present he could only pave the way by writing letters. Tim prepared a card index of possible names, and kept a file of information gathered.

Sunday evening! Timothy, scrubbed until he shone, presented himself with the punctuality of one who had been waiting outside for the exact moment, and he was introduced formally to Dr. Foxwell and to a shy, eager Elsie.

"Elsie has brought some of her writings to show you," said Dr. Foxwell, "and she hopes you can help her decide which to offer for publication."

"Take them into my study, you two kids," suggested Peter. "Have a drink, Foxwell?"

"Thanks, I will. Good idea, Welles," he added, as the children disappeared, "but I'm dying to hear what goes on."

"There would be nothing to hear if we sat and stared at them. Give them ten minutes. How is she doing lately?"

"Fine! Just fine! She spent every minute of her spare time working over this stuff she is showing him now. Amazing stuff, Pete! By the way—I've had an offer for the hospital. I've been thinking, maybe I could sell out and come up here. Join in the work, you know." The big doctor was talking very rapidly, and he accepted his drink without looking up. "Don't want to poach. But there's Elsie—"

"That's all agreed," said Welles. "Any time you can manage it. Elsie is your patient. But I think the two children ought to be kept together, and others with them if it can be managed. But how can we arrange things? Can we get the other children here? And how can we live, if we take too much time over the children?"

They discussed the matter briefly, but without coming to any conclusion. Their minds were not on the subject; and as soon as the ten minutes had elapsed, Peter got a pitcher of fruit juice and a plate of cookies from the kitchen, and led the way quietly to the study. The men paused by the open door and listened to the chatter of the children.

"This is great," Timothy was saying. "These poems—but they're almost too good, Elsie! 'The slow sweet curve of light'—that's grand! But I don't know if it would sell."

"I know poetry doesn't sell. I wanted you to see it, that's all. I'm typing out everything."

"That whole poem about infinity and creation, honestly, it's grand. This other stuff is good, and I think this novel will sell, too. There was a novel, *The Snake Pit*, and it made a big hit when it first came out, away back thirty years or so ago, or something like that. Yours, from the synopsis and first pages, is . . . oh, hello, Peter! and Dr. Foxwell."

"We thought you might like a little refreshment," said Welles, advancing with the tray.

"Sure—thanks," said Tim, pushing papers out of the way politely. "Say, do you know what Elsie has done? She has read all the books about the sciences she could, and then turned them into poetry!"

"Is that good?" asked Foxwell, selecting a cookie.

"Is that good! Say, it's great! She tells you what things *mean*, you know! Not just the mechanism and the equations and all that, but what it's all about. She makes you see it. And she has three novels done, she says, and some are sure to sell. She showed me the synopses of them tonight, and a sample chapter. We'll have to think up a whole raft of pen names, Elsie."

"How many do you have, Timothy?"

"Oh, I don't know—I keep a card index of them. Couple of dozen, I guess. Have some punch?" Tim filled the glasses.

"You haven't typed out all the novels, have you?" asked Dr. Foxwell.

"No, not yet," said Elsie. "The rest of this here is articles and short stories and a lot of poems. I wanted to get the short stuff typed up first. May I have a cookie?"

When it was time to take Elsie home, Dr. Foxwell lingered in the hall a moment.

"Keep notes," he begged Welles in a whisper. "I've got to take the night plane back and miss all of this. But keep notes, son!"

"We'll never know the whole of it," Welles answered. "But what we have heard tonight . . . this past hour—"

"I'll run up next Sunday . . . no, Saturday," promised Foxwell.

Monday, Elsie sat quietly in class. Tim scarcely spoke to her all day, and she replied in monosyllables when he did. He went home without a glance her way; but he was at Miss Page's house ten minutes later.

Miss Page admitted him and left the children alone together.

"Listen," said Tim, "you've got to make friends with the other girls."

"I don't like them. They're silly."

"They can do a lot of things better than you can. Play games and things. Now, listen—you've got to, that's all, Elsie. You know what the doctors told you."

"I want to be with you, that's all," said Elsie frankly. "The others have no sense. And you didn't even walk home with me."

"Gosh, no! Do you want all the kids to say you're my girl?"

Elsie stared at him in horror.

"Of course not! That's stupid!"

"Well, you have to make friends. Miss Page made it easy. She told the kids last week, that a new girl was coming—"

"They don't like me. Nobody spoke to me, except 'Hello.'"

"Miss Page told them you were shy, that's why. She said you

hadn't been to school, and that you weren't used to being with other girls and boys, because you had been sick, see? They think you used to have heart trouble or something, and you're just getting over it. They smiled at you, I saw them. They're trying to be polite, and not rush you too much the first day. Now, listen! you've got to practice playing with them, and getting along nice—or I won't help you get things published."

"You don't have to," said Elsie, turning her face away. "There are other boys and girls like us. They may be nice to me."

"Isn't anybody going to be nice unless you are nice, too. You might as well begin," said Tim ruthlessly. "You think fine, and you write fine, but what else can you do?"

"I never had a fair chance," Elsie flashed at him.

"You're having it now," said the boy grimly.

They glared at one another for a minute defiantly, and then both began to laugh.

"All right," said Elsie. "I know I'm maladjusted, and I have to get right. You had a head start on me, but I can catch up with you. Just give me a little time."

"We'll practice basketball for a while," said Timothy. "Come over to my place. I have a basket there to practice, myself. And then I'll show you my cats, if you like."

Peter Welles, who had reserved the last hour before supper for Elsie, was obliged to seek her out. He found the children at Timothy's, bent over the cat cages, admiring some kittens. But what were they saying?

"Are we dominants or recessives?" Elsie was asking earnestly. "Both my parents got the radiations, and both of yours."

"Yes, and so it can be recessive. We'll have to find out," Tim replied. "But we can find out if any others had only one parent exposed to it. If it's a recessive, you and I and some of the others will carry it double, but—"

"But if we marry outside the group, what then? No, we've got to know. And that is another reason for getting the whole group together."

"Statistics," gloated Tim, his eyes alight. "Bales and bales of statistics, graphs, charts, tests—too bad we can't experiment. Hello, here's Peter. I was showing Elsie the kittens. Look, I mated a silver Persian tom to one of these Siamese, and see what I got! Silver tabby!"

"They're the most beautiful of all," crooned Elsie. "I like short-haired cats best, anyway."

"You can have a couple of these," offered Tim.

"But Miss Page might not want me to have cats," the little girl objected.

"She won't mind. Peter can tell her you need pets," replied Timothy with assurance. "What did you tell her, Peter?"

"I told her that Elsie was very bright, very much maladjusted, and that she needed to live near me so I could treat her," replied Welles. "And I'd rather you two went easy when Miss Page can overhear you, but we may have to take her into our confidence before very long, if we take any steps toward having more of you children here. I still can't see how we are going to manage that."

"We'll think of a way," said Tim.

"Meanwhile, Elsie was due at my place half an hour ago."

The two children flushed.

"Oh, I'm sorry," she cried. "I didn't know it was so late. We've been playing ball, and then—"

Timothy also was trying to apologize, but Welles waved his hand and said he would forgive them this once. They finished off Elsie's scheduled hour in Tim's workshop, and he gave her some of his published writings to take away and read. The kittens, he said, would be ready to leave their mother in about a week, and Elsie could get Miss Page's consent meanwhile.

Peter did not see Tim for several days, but he knew the two children were together much of the time, discussing manuscripts, playing games, chattering constantly, and becoming well acquainted. On Friday he sought Tim out, and began to ask questions.

"Well, Timothy? Do you like her?"

"Oh, yes! I hope all the others are as good," said Tim happily. "It's wonderful to be able to talk to another person my own age and have them get everything I say, snap! just like that! no matter what I talk about. I can say anything I want to, just the way I can to you. She doesn't know exactly the same things I do, of course, but she understands everything."

"I wonder which of you is the more intelligent," hinted Peter Welles.

Timothy thought it over.

"I have been wondering that, too," he said, "and trying to judge, but it is hard to judge, being one of the two myself. I'd say we aren't exactly alike, so we can't be measured like that. She looks at things in a different way, you know. She wants to know what things mean, and I want to know what to do about things. We both have a lot to teach each other. Her memory and mine work differently, too. Of course we both read so much that we can't remember everything, or even a very big part of what we read; we remember the way we understood things, what they mean to us. She remembers sciences as if they were poems or pictures, and thinks about the significance of these things; but I remember the way things work, and think about inventions and social service and things like that, things she doesn't care about. I think of what practical use things are, and the theory of them. And yet in some ways she is much more practical than I am. She thinks about the philosophy of things and how they fit into the whole concept of everything. You can't measure any two people with the same yardstick, can you, Peter?"

"I guess not," laughed the psychologist. "Have you found out about her, some things I have been wondering? Can you tell me, perhaps, where she got that odd shorthand of hers?"

"She told me," Tim answered. "When she was little she saw that people did not print when they wrote; the letters were different from printed ones. But no two handwritings were alike, and she heard her uncle say he couldn't read somebody else's handwriting; so when she was real little she thought everybody made up an arbitrary penmanship of his own. So she did, too. And then she found it so useful that she kept it up."

"Could it be broken as a simple substitution code, then?"

"I don't know; I haven't seen enough of it. Perhaps it could; at any rate, she never let people examine it carefully, you know, while she was in the hospital. She had some special signs for common words and frequent-letter-combinations, but mostly she spells things correctly; it is not a phonetic alphabet."

"And why did she hold books upside down so often? Was that part of her pose?"

"I didn't ask her that, but probably she could read as easily one way as another. I can; can't you? I usually don't, because it looks odd; she may have done it on purpose to look odd. But everybody does it more or less."

"And why would she always tell people they were wrong, but never tell them what was right?" asked the doctor. "She refused to instruct them. Why was that?"

Tim laughed. "She didn't say; but I think I know. She wanted to be right all the time. She despised others because they were stupid, but she couldn't stand the thought that she might make a mistake. I guess she read stories about demigods and magic princesses and stuff like that, when she was real little. Maybe she even got some idea that if she did make a mistake she wouldn't be so wonderful any more; sort of break the spell, or spoil the magic, or something like that. Anyway, I'm pretty sure that is what was wrong—she couldn't spoil this idea she had of herself as somebody who knew a million times as much as everybody else. Then as she grew older, and read more, and found out things, she must have found out how silly that was, and also she learned that other people she met—Dr. Foxwell for one—were much smarter than she had thought other people could be. So she wouldn't tell on herself. She's all right with me—she doesn't mind telling me that there are things she does not know, or can't do, or can't remember."

"I think she is all right, Tim. She must have been completely sane for some years, if not always. Perhaps she was a little queer for a while there, but I don't think it ever could have been called insane. Still, if you notice anything that I ought to know—we'll call Elsie your first patient, Tim—call me into consultation."

Timothy grinned. "I wouldn't keep anything from you, Peter. You're the doctor. She's making friends with the other girls at school. When is Dr. Foxwell coming back up here, Peter?"

"Tomorrow, I think."

"My grandmother wants to see both of you, while he is here," said Tim. "Can you come over tomorrow night?"

"Why, yes, I guess so. What's up?"

"Oh, she wants to talk to both of you," said Tim carelessly. "Grandfather is out of town this week end, or he would be there, too."

"We'll be over," said Peter.

The June days were long, and the doctors found Elsie skipping in at the gate as they neared Timothy's house. Her face fell when she saw them.

"Tim said I could get my kittens tonight," she said, "and Miss Page said I could come. Did you want me?"

"Not right now. We came to see Mrs. Davis," said Dr. Welles.

"I'll run ahead and ring the bell for you," said Elsie, suiting the action to the word.

"Big place," remarked Foxwell, looking about the grounds.

"Yes; Tim's grandparents are very well off, and he has a private workroom out back here, which used to be the garage. I'll take you out to see the workshop if there is time after we see Mrs. Davis," said Welles. "She probably wants to know who Elsie is, since the two kids have been spending so much time together. She lets Tim do about as he likes in some ways, but she is very strict about the company he keeps."

"How did he ever get away with so much? You say she has no idea he is anything out of the ordinary."

"She takes pains to see that he is a good boy and that he gets into no mischief. His writing and model-building and all that, she takes for ordinary schoolwork and boyish play, I suppose; she has never seen any of it. He convinced her that his cat-breeding experiments were the result of random curiosity. One can scarcely blame her for not suspecting anything like the truth."

Tim had opened the door, and was waiting for the doctors. They hastened their steps, and were taken into the house and presented to Mrs. Davis.

"And now you and your little friend may go outside and play," said that lady to her grandson, when she had received her guests. "Do sit down, Dr. Foxwell, and Dr. Welles. I have a little plan—a proposal which I dare to think may interest you. And since your time is valuable, and I know that you have little of it to spare on this visit, Dr. Foxwell, I intend to come to the point at once. My husband is not in the city at present, but he is aware of the proposal I am to make, and approves of it. Timothy, my grandson, has told me that you two men wish to start an experimental school for children who are a little above the average in intelligence. There are a few schools in this country, I understand, which take children whose intelligence quotient—I believe that is the correct term?—is above 150. I do not know what figure you had in mind, my dear Dr. Welles; perhaps something less extreme; but children above the average, Timothy tells me. I understand also that your plans and methods are as yet untried, something rather new in education. But we have every confidence in you, Dr. Welles, and since Timothy has hinted that he might, because of your interest in him, perhaps be considered as a pupil in such a school under your management—" Mrs. Davis paused, and raised her eyebrows.

The astounded doctors exchanged glances.

"Yes," said Peter feebly, "Timothy would certainly be . . . er . . . considered."

"And he tells me that you know a great architect, Paul T. Lawrence," continued the good lady, after referring to a slip of paper on which the name was apparently written. "Do you think he could be persuaded to design the buildings?"

"Er . . . yes, I think he could."

"For many years, we have had it in mind, my husband and I, to build a memorial to my daughter and to her husband. But nothing suitable has suggested itself until now. Timothy's references to this plan of yours have interested us deeply, and we have actually . . . ah . . . pumped him; I believe that is the expression. Well, Dr. Welles, if you and Dr. Foxwell are agreeable, we propose to let you have the use of a large tract of land which my husband owns, just beyond the edge of town, and we propose to erect suitable buildings for the school, whatever you may require. Estimates, of course, and such business details, we must settle later. And how many pupils did you have in mind?"

"Not very many," said Peter, trying to keep his voice steady. "Perhaps not more than ten, to start with; perhaps as many as forty or fifty. I really must explain that it is all a dream of mine. I have made no effort to contact possible pupils for such a school. I—"

Mrs. Davis bowed graciously.

"I understand all that, Dr. Welles. We thought perhaps you would care to inquire as to possible students this summer, the building could be started in the fall, and the school opened the following fall, when Timothy would be ready to enter High School. I do not expect you to tell me immediately whether you will accept this offer of ours; I realize that you have made no definite plans, and that there must be an enormous amount of figuring to be done. Let me say, briefly, what it is I propose. The use of the land; proper buildings; but, for we must be businesslike, all to remain in my husband's name, leased to you at a dollar a year for a period of, perhaps, five years, with privilege of renewal at the same figure. Your salaries, and those of a suitable number of assistants, to be guaranteed for the same length of time; and expenses also guaranteed. You will perhaps wish to put some of your own capital into the venture, and in that case we can work out some arrangement of sharing the expenses and the profits; but to my mind this is not a moneymaking venture, but an experiment in education."

The doctors hastened to agree with Mrs. Davis.

"It is true, Mrs. Davis, that if any such school is opened, there may be no profit at all, but heavy losses," Dr. Foxwell said earnestly.

"I am aware of that," said the lady serenely, "but the land will remain, and the buildings; and when we have lost all we can afford to lose, we shall simply close the school. Meanwhile, Timothy and the other children will have had the benefit of your guidance. You are to be in full charge, Dr. Welles, subject to whatever state laws exist; I contract not to interfere with your management of the school in any way, provided of course that the state authorities have no objections to raise. You understand, Dr. Foxwell, that I address myself largely to Dr. Welles, and put him in charge, because he is Timothy's friend and we know him well; but I wanted you to be present when the offer was made, and to share in it, since Timothy told me the idea is partly yours and that his new little friend, Elsie, would be one of the pupils. She is really a very bright little thing, isn't she? And such nice manners. And now, shall I tell my husband on his return that you are giving the matter your most serious consideration?"

Somehow the men stammered their thanks, and promised to spend the summer in trying to carry out her plans. Then Mrs. Davis dismissed them, saying that she knew it must be nearly little Elsie's bedtime—a statement which carried a definite hint that it was certainly nearing her grandson's bedtime.

"The children will be out with the cats," said Peter Welles. "We can find our way."

As soon as they were out of the house, the older man turned to Peter and demanded, "Does she mean it?"

"Certainly she does. The point is, do *we* mean it?"

"But how did she know?" marveled Foxwell. "She knows more than we do ourselves about our dream for the group! And yet she still hasn't the faintest idea what it is all about!"

"Don't let Tim hear you talking like this. It's as plain as ABC to him, and he expected us to get it in a flash. That's why he didn't even trouble to warn us."

"Oh! It's his doing? But he is only a child. And Mrs. Davis seemed to think it would surprise him."

"He knows how to manage her, all right."

"But, confound it all! Are we to be managed, too, by a kid like—"

"By a kid like Tim, Foxwell, it's an honor. Don't worry; everything will be done right."

"I'll be darned if I'll be shoved around by a kid that size," protested the big doctor. "Why, we don't even know what he's doing!"

"It'll be your own fault if you don't. *Shh!* Here they are."

The children ran up to the men, and Elsie asked eagerly:

"Doctor, what do you think caused us? I read that people never use more than a very small part of their brains. Do you think the radiation stepped up our brains so we could use more of them? Tim doesn't think that's it."

"Well, it's an idea," said Tim slowly. "I don't know much about it. Maybe we can rig up some tests to tell us more about it. Or it could be something about our glands, for all I know."

"I haven't the least idea," said Peter, "and I'd rather leave it for later. Tim, did you know what your grandmother wanted to tell us?"

Tim's eyes danced.

"I wouldn't be surprised. But she probably thinks I would. Well? Will you do it?"

"I sure will," said Welles, "and Foxwell probably will, when he calms down enough to believe it."

"It'll cost a fortune," objected Foxwell. "Your grandmother doesn't realize . . . why the architect's fee alone will be—Who is the fellow she spoke of, anyway?"

"Me," said Tim. "She doesn't know that. I'm not famous, but she thinks so. Anyway, I can do the buildings, and one of you men can represent me and oversee the workmen and the contractor. Now listen—I've got to go in soon. But I'll be drawing up the plans. Units of ten, I think, so we can build one or two, and more later on as we need them; it's better than starting with one huge building that would never be just the right size. A private workshop for each student, with a sink and a hood and some tables and chairs and shelves and cabinets—and the windows high, so nobody can peep in from outside—and glass in the doors like a regular school—the walls ought to be soundproofed, and—"

"Just a minute! How about classrooms?"

"We'll only have one grade. Sort of ungraded, rather. A high school, let's see—we'll have an auditorium, so we can put on plays and things, and we can have lectures and big classes there, and perhaps some small classes could meet in one of the workrooms, or outside, or somewhere."

"All you need is a log with a student on one end and a teacher on the other," muttered Foxwell.

"Well, sure. What we must have is lab facilities and quiet places to study and think, and a place where we can be together. Television equipment—we can listen in on lectures at the big universities all over the world. And a dormitory for the girls and women on this side—" Tim was sketching rapidly on a pad.

"Women!" shouted Dr. Foxwell.

"Miss Page, and whoever else we get," said Tim. "And the boys and men on this side . . . I suppose you'll both live there?"

"Us?" gasped the big doctor.

"Well, Peter, then, if you aren't coming."

"I am coming!" roared Foxwell. "Everybody said I could! Try and keep me out! But you go too fast for me, my boy."

"Gymnasium," Tim was scribbling rapidly, "and a swimming pool, maybe. We might build that ourselves."

"What are you going to use for money?" demanded Dr. Foxwell.

"Aren't you going to buy in?" asked Tim, surprised. "I am, and I thought you'd all want to, and the other boys and girls surely will, too."

"I can't," wailed Elsie, her face suddenly crumpled in grief.

"Of course you can!" cried Tim. "Wait until you start selling, that's all. You—"

"Timothy, there are laws regulating schools," said Peter Welles.

"Oh, you can get away with anything around here if you call it an experimental school," said Tim carelessly. "Give it out as a high IQ school, and it won't matter what we do. All they ask is whether you can pass Subject A and have gym every semester. And enough bathrooms for everybody. I made it a high IQ school because then we won't have to hide so much, either. It gives us a lot more freedom. But we must be careful not to make a show of it."

"Suppose others try to get in? People who aren't of the group?"

"If they test high enough, we might let them in, if we have room. They'll give us a norm to copy in public, higher than we ever had before, so that will be a big help. And it will do them good. You know a person with an IQ of 152 is as far from the average as a person with an IQ of 48. And most schools don't do a thing for the kids above 120."

"Please tell me exactly what you plan to do," said Peter Welles, "and all about it. Skip the buildings."

"I don't know that I can," said Timothy. "I haven't verbalized it yet. It's all new in my mind, you see. I only began to think of it this week, because of Elsie. We've got to set them all free, you understand. We've got to set them all free right away. I thought I was in hiding and in bondage, but when I heard about Elsie then I knew we have to do something about the others right away. This school is the best way, because we won't have to hide so much—we can pretend to be about 150 instead of 100—and we can all be together, and you two doctors can look after us and straighten out anybody that needs it. If any of the others aren't free or aren't adjusted, it's a million times worse for them than it was for me, don't you see? And a school seems so natural. If we don't advertise it, I don't think we have to let in anyone who asks, and in any case we can have tests and say we have our quota full or that applicants don't quite make it. And don't worry about the money—it'll come in fast enough. I am sure that several of them have money already, like me, and once we are free we can all earn ever so much more. And don't you see, we've got to learn how to work together and help each other, all of us children? We can't wait much longer, or we'll all be set in habits of solitude and secrecy, so we'll never be right. We can be together, and be free and independent, and have friends, and be helped, and help each other, and all work toward the same things, and—"

Tim had been talking so fast that he ran out of breath at last and had to stop and gasp.

"Toward what things?"

Tim waved his arms.

"Towards whatever we have to do. For everybody."

"The things God meant us to do," agreed Elsie, who had been standing rapt, her hands clasped, taking it all in.

"Some of them may not believe in God," said Welles. "Many people don't."

Elsie turned on him swiftly and snapped: "I don't know how to talk about people like that if I can't say either 'stupid' or 'crazy.'"

"Well, don't bite me; I'm a Thomist," replied Welles mildly.

"What's that?"

"I'll lend you the Summa tomorrow and you can read it through before lunch," replied Welles.

A bell rang violently in the workshop.

"My alarm clock," said Tim. "I've got to go in. I'll do the plans, and we'll get together pretty soon on all this."

"What do I have to do?" Peter Welles inquired. "It sounds to me as if you plan to do it all yourselves."

"Oh, no, Peter!" Tim cried in alarm. "It all depends on you. You've got to front for us, and find the others, and be the teachers too probably."

"Teachers!" roared Dr. Foxwell.

"That's just it. We need Peter and you especially to teach us how to be what we ought to be, to keep us on the right track, to help us work together right; you can see what Elsie needed! Others too must need help dreadfully. And we are only children after all. Nothing takes the place of experience. You can weld all these individuals into one group where each can help all and yet nobody's individuality will be sacrificed—"

"Timothy! Timothy!" came the call from the house.

"Yes, grandma!" Tim shouted back. "I'm coming!"

"Good night, Tim," said Welles, pushing the others toward the gate.

"My kittens!" Elsie remembered, and Tim hastily selected two and thrust them into her arms.

The men took her to Miss Page's door in a silence broken only by the child's crooning endearments to the struggling, crying kittens.

"Good night," said Mark Foxwell to the child.

She looked up at him.

"Tim forgot to mention it," she said, "but the school will have to have a dining hall and a kitchen. We can use the dining hall for a classroom, sometimes. And we'll need a cook."

"Yes."

"My aunt is a wonderful cook," said Elsie. "My uncle can sell his grocery store and buy one up here. He can give us a rate on all the things we'll need to buy. And my aunt can do the cooking."

"Do you mean you want them to come up here and live near you?" asked Foxwell.

Elsie wriggled.

"I think they'd like to," she said. "And . . . I feel different now, about them. One can feel sorry for a hen trying to bring up a duckling—ugly or not!"

She ran into the house with her kittens.

The doctors went on to Welles' home without a word, except that Dr. Foxwell shook his head and muttered to himself occasionally.

"Well?" said Mark Foxwell, when his pipe was alight. "You've chosen, yourself, to go into this thing, if it can be done?"

"There is no choice," said Welles. "I have found my life work. These kids, barely into their teens, need all kinds of help and they need it the worst way. Somehow or other, within the next few years, they have to come out of hiding and get into the adult world. I'm going to do what I can to see that they have the chance to do it right. And Tim has given us the opportunity—laid the chance of a lifetime in our laps."

Foxwell shook his head slowly.

"That's true. Most kids with IQ's of over 160 have to adjust on a lower level in order to live in this world at all. It always seemed to me a great waste. And these—what will they be like when they grow up?"

"That's more or less up to us, now," said Peter Welles. "They need each other, they need us. Tim's right—Elsie shows us."

"You mean the others may be warped in all kinds of ways!" cried the big doctor.

"They may be. Some of them must be. The bright child has all too often grown up to be a queer, maladjusted, unhappy adult. Or else he has thrown away half of his intelligence in order to adjust and be happy and get along as a social being. These children are bright beyond anything the world has ever known—if Tim is at all a fair sample, and Elsie is full as well endowed. Think of such intelligence combined with a lust for power, a selfish greed, or an overwhelming sense of superiority so that all other people, of average intelligence or a little more, would seem as worthless as . . . as Yahoos."

"Elsie—" began Dr. Foxwell in horror.

"Elsie is all right. She adores you, she obeys you and she follows the advice that you and I and Tim give her. She only needed to be set free. But the others—"

"It's an awful responsibility," said Foxwell. "And did you hear those kids talking about heredity, last week?"

"Yes," said Peter.

"They'll be so far above us when they are adult," moaned Dr. Foxwell, "I swear I'm afraid to think of it."

"Timothy Paul has the answer, I think. A school, where they can work together under our direction, and have as much freedom as they can stand, combined with the psychotherapy that you and I can give them where it is needed. They are much like normal children in many ways, I think—looking to adults for help, emotionally still children. But Tim has solved his own problems fairly well up to now, and I think he can help us with the school. I don't doubt that he has all his plans made, as to how the school is to be run, but he looks to us for the adult supervision and for the psychological guidance that the young people must have."

Foxwell rubbed his chin and shook his head, puffed at his pipe, found it had gone out, and relighted it.

"I'm beginning to believe all this at last," he said.

"It does take time to grasp the possibilities."

"Lectures by television," mused Mark Foxwell. "A private laboratory for each child. The students contribute to the upkeep of the place—invest their own money in it, money they earned in competition with the whole adult world, and . . . Pete, tell me, do you honestly think you can find enough of these kids to make a school?"

"You have met two of them. Timothy and I are in correspondence with at least half a dozen more, and Mrs. Davis gives us the school and guarantees all expenses."

"Where's your phone?"

"In the hall."

The big doctor lumbered out of the room. He returned in a few minutes and held a match to his pipe again.

Welles waited.

"I phoned the fellow that wants my hospital," Foxwell said. "It's sold. I can leave it in a month or so. Come on now Pete and let's do some practical planning! The kid is miles ahead of us already. Most likely he always will be, but I'd like to pretend we're the bosses for a few months yet."

NEW FOUNDATIONS

"And that's the full story to date of Timothy Paul and Elsie Lambeth, the Wonder Children," concluded Welles.

Miss Page caught her breath.

"I should have guessed it," she said, "or something like it. But who could have guessed anything like that? Tim seemed like such an ordinary little boy. And even since Elsie came I hadn't dreamed of anything of such proportions. They didn't seem like super-wonderful intellects, although anyone could see they were quite bright."

"They were hiding from you," Welles smiled, "under orders. But now that we propose to start a school for these children, and need teachers and matrons, you are the first one Dr. Foxwell and I want. Will you join us?"

"Indeed I will! When is the school to open?"

"We must get the scholars first. I plan to spend August touring the country to see the children and arrange with their guardians. Meanwhile we have been able to write to some of the children and make preliminary arrangements. When I go to the Psychiatrists' Convention next week, I intend to see Jay Worthington. I'm leaving here a day early for that purpose."

He unlocked a drawer—they were talking in his office—and leafed through some papers until he came to those he wanted.

"Here's the correspondence. Jay wrote us that he had seen our advertisement and thought it deserved wider attention, adding that he took a personal interest in the matter. A few days later, his name turned up on the list. The detective agency has by now found nearly all the children for us, checking everyone who was exposed to the radiations, and eliminating those who are known to have died child-less."

There was a tap on the door, and two impatient children popped their heads in.

"What does she say?" demanded Elsie.

"She says yes," laughed Peter.

"Can't you talk him into getting started sooner, Miss Page?" begged Tim. "That's a thing I don't understand about grown people. You have so much less time than we do, and yet you don't seem to think time matters at all."

"Older people have learned to make haste slowly," Dr. Welles replied. "The idea of the school is scarcely a month old. Believe me, Tim, we are as impatient as you are, but things must be planned and done in order."

Elsie moved restlessly.

"If you see the children next month," she complained, "I don't see why you can't start the month after. We don't need all those buildings Tim planned."

Tim was prompt to agree.

"We're already fourteen years old," said he, "and in a few years we'll be grown up and scattered. Let's just have some prefabricated houses put up quickly, and get started this September, can't we?"

Peter Welles shook his head.

"At a week to interview each child and make arrangements with the guardians, it will take months."

"Why a week?" cried both children.

"Because," said Peter somberly, "there may be more difficulties than you can imagine."

"Jay Worthington?"

The boy nodded. "You must be Dr. Welles," he said in a rapid treble voice. "Come right in, doctor." He was vibrating with excitement. A tall, lanky boy, awkward and what Tim's grandmother would have called "high-strung," Jay was clearly bursting to talk. He led the way into the living room, chattering at double speed all the while.

"My aunt's out," he said, "and my uncle has gone for a walk. I tried to get rid of them, but we'll have to watch out. There is so much to say, I don't know where to begin. But that's for you to say, isn't it, Dr. Welles? There must be something very special back of all this, and a reason for your visit, and for your asking about my parents. The Curtises aren't really related to me, you know; they adopted me when I was ten months old. This is the best chair, and here's an ash tray if you want one."

"Our letters have been brief because yours were," said Dr. Welles, accepting the chair, "and it is better policy. But now by all means let us get to the point, without fencing. You must have a pretty good idea of what this is all about."

Jay bobbed his head vigorously. "I'd rather you said it, though," he replied.

"You answered our ad and said that you had a personal interest in children born in 1959 who were of very high intelligence."

"That's putting it bluntly," said Jay, catching his breath. "I didn't mean to be so plain . . . if I meant . . . I—"

"We're talking straight now. That is what the ad meant, and you knew it. Your name was also on the list given me by a detective agency which has been busy tracing the children born of parents who died as yours did. You know how they died?"

"Yes, the atomic plant explosion."

"Right. Putting these two things together, we knew where we stood. So Tim wrote to you that we were starting a school for children of high I.Q. and that you would be interviewed."

"That was a body blow," said Jay. "I couldn't see how you knew my age. And then I realized that you hadn't actually said you did know, and perhaps I had misread you. I realized that you might mean you thought I knew some bright children. So I wrote back and said I didn't know any such intelligent children, and then Tim replied that since I was born in the same year he was, I must know some of the things he was interested in. Then I was pretty sure something was up, but I replied with a line saying that perhaps Dr. Hollingworth's books were what he was interested in having, and he answered on a postcard that they were too elementary. And while I was still wondering what to say next the air mail letter came that you would be here a week after my fourteenth birthday with greetings and a message. You seem to know more about me than I can account for, but I still don't know how much you know."

"I'll be perfectly frank. The atomic explosion gave slow death to hundreds of men and women. But before they died, some of the couples exposed to the radiations had children, and some, perhaps all, of these children are mutants of extraordinary high intelligence. We want to gather them all together, where they can have the benefit of one another's company and develop as they should."

"That is just about as I figured it," said Jay with a sigh of relief. "Tim is one of them, of course? And Elsie?"

"I have much to tell you about them. But let me find out about you first. I know that your uncle is John Curtis the historian. Who are you?"

"Why . . . I'm his adopted son, Jay Worthington. The Curtises had me keep my own name because—"

"That isn't what I meant," said Dr. Welles. "I meant your pen name, or the name you take out patents in, or whatever you do. You don't use your own name for things like that, do you?"

Their eyes met and there was a moment of tense silence.

"You do know, then," said Jay. "I'm James Vernon Worth."

This was too great a shock for Peter Welles to take unblinking. He even gulped. When he could speak again he asked, "Does your uncle know that?"

"Of course not. That's the whole point. If people knew, they would say it was all his work, or that he helped me so much it might as well be. And if he had known what I was doing at first he would have tried to help me. I didn't want that. Of course I have to help him; but that's different."

"You help *him?*"

"Yes," said the boy. "He is blind."

The phone rang while Peter was still trying to take in the implications of what he had heard. Jay, with a muttered word of apology, dashed out of the room.

James Vernon Worth—this boy? Those three magnificent biographies written by this child? But if he was the adopted son of John Curtis, and helped Curtis with his work—

Jay was back, breathless but talking almost before he had opened the door.

"We haven't much more time," he said. "My uncle will probably be back in a few minutes. He doesn't take long walks."

"Well, here's the situation," said Peter, and he talked rapidly for ten minutes, while Jay listened intently and bobbed his head in eager agreement.

"It sounds wonderful," said Jay at last, drawing a deep breath. "I wish I could be with you. But I can't."

"We'll find some way to arrange it."

But Jay shook his head.

"You see, it's different with me," he explained. "I'm getting along all right. People think it is quite natural for me to know things, for since my uncle's blindness five years ago I have read to him every day, and even before that. And I have always been with people who talked about things all around me. My aunt is a very brilliant woman in her own right. The amateur radio station is really hers. She got it so Uncle could talk to people all over the world when he couldn't read any more. Everybody knows they asked for a bright baby to adopt, and the rest is credited to my environment and upbringing. This is a university town, and people are used to bright boys and they like them. So I don't have to hide very much. Of course nobody knows I write books. But I get along very well. And of course I have to stay with my uncle and aunt. They have nobody but me. And really I'm happy here. There are the dogs to train, for the blind, you know. I didn't train my uncle's dog, Grigio, of course, but we bought Guarda soon after and we train her pups to be guide dogs, and give them to people who need them. My aunt and I train them, and Uncle helps."

A car pulled up in front of the house and a brisk woman, fortyish, jumped out.

"My aunt," explained Jay in all haste. "Quick, please! Come out and look at the pups. We have two for sale now for pet stock. They don't all measure up to be guide dogs."

Peter allowed himself to be led out the back door and to the kennels.

"I see what you mean, Jay," he said, "but we can't leave it at that."

"We must," said Jay. "But we can correspond, and you'll let me know what goes on, won't you?"

Peter scribbled on a card. "Here's my hotel. I'll phone you soon, and we can meet a time or two before I have to leave, can't we?"

"Oh yes—please do."

As the boy knelt down to scratch a pup's head through the wire of the enclosure, Peter's quick eye saw signs of tears.

"We'll arrange it, Jay," he promised.

"No," said Jay, gulping. "I wouldn't go. I wouldn't go if I could. I'm going to stay with my uncle, always."

A few minutes later, after a perfunctory inspection of the pups, Peter Welles went away, feeling greatly depressed.

A telegram signed by Mark Foxwell awaited Peter at his hotel.

"Agency reports another prospect same city. Stella Oates, 432 Vine Avenue."

Peter stared at the telegram for a full minute. And how, he wondered, am I to approach this girl, knowing nothing about her, or her background, or her present home or guardians, am I to walk in without any warning and whisk her off to the other side of the continent? What can I say to her family? How can I get a chance to talk with her alone? Should I phone or write first and pave the way?

But Peter knew that he could not wait. He must see her that very night. The psychiatrist looked at his watch; it was nearly six o'clock. Well, dinner first, and perhaps he could think of something.

At half past seven, ringing the doorbell at 432 Vine Avenue, Peter had still not decided what to say.

Uproar broke out behind the closed door before the bell had ceased ringing. The doctor's trained mind sorted out the sounds and identified them. The crashes and shrieks on the left sounded like two or three children charging through the same doorway at once, bumping one another and complaining about the bumps. The rapid series of thumps was someone in heavy shoes rushing down the stairs. The slower heavy tread and rumbling voice probably indicated a man trying to restore order, and the quick pattering steps were, very possibly, the lady of the house on her way to the door.

A woman in a gay apron opened the door. A hand behind it pulled the door open more widely, disclosing several dark-haired children in their early teens. In a doorway on the right stood a tall man with a newspaper in his hand. And behind him, in the room he had just left, sat a plump, blond young girl with a book in her lap. So detached was she from the noisy quartet staring and giggling and nudging one another as they hastily retreated, helped by the woman's good-natured pushes—with such a cool disdain did the blond girl view the scene in the crowded hallway—that Peter spoke instinctively to her.

"Stella," he said.

The girl rose quietly and came slowly toward him with a smile.

"You must excuse this rabble," the woman was saying. "They were expecting some friends—"

"That's quite all right," said Peter, and suddenly a worse uproar than ever broke out all around him. In the street behind him a rattling car appeared, honking loudly. To the shouts and screams of the young people in the car were added shrieks and yells from the waving quartet in the hall. Dr. Welles moved out of the doorway with all haste; the four shouting adolescents pushed through it and were gone.

"I'm glad Stella wasn't going with them since you want to see her," said the woman. "I'll get back to my dishes, then," and she was gone, too.

Peter turned to the tall man in the doorway.

"Are you Mr. Oates?"

"Yes. Come on in."

"My name is Welles. Dr. Peter Welles."

The men shook hands. Peter began to laugh.

"This reminds me," he said, "of the Queen's advice to Alice: 'Curtsy while you're thinking what to say.'"

"'Begin at the beginning,'" quoted the little girl, "'and go on until you come to the end. Then stop.'"

Mr. Oates looked from one to the other with a blank stare.

"You want to talk to me, too?" he asked. "Is it something about her health?"

"No, Mr. Oates. You are Stella's guardian?"

"Yes. Her uncle. She's my brother's child. Have a chair."

They sat down, Stella's expectant eyes fixed on Peter.

The shabby old house and the swarm of half-grown children decided Peter. The only possible approach was the free-scholarship one.

"It has been suggested," he said, "that Stella might be eligible for one of the free scholarships that we have to offer."

The man's face hardened.

"First let me tell you who I am," said Peter, smiling disarmingly. "I am a medical man, attending the convention of physicians here this week. At home, I am the psychologist for the city schools of Oakland, California; but I am resigning the position to take charge of a school to be opened there by a wealthy couple, Mr. and Mrs. Herbert Davis, as a memorial to their daughter and her husband. It is their wish that the school educate and care for other children who were orphaned at the same time and in the same way as their grandson."

"In the same way?" repeated Mr. Oates. "You mean the radiation deaths?"

"Yes," said Dr. Welles. "You will find my name in tonight's paper in the list of those attending the convention of psychiatrists here. Let me show you some identification. I can give you the names of local men who can vouch for me."

The tall man looked over the papers which Peter offered him, and nodded.

"The school is to take young people through high school and college," Dr. Welles went on, "and is to open within a few months. The young people must pass certain tests first, and if they do so satisfactorily they may apply for a scholarship which will pay part or all of the student's expenses. I don't know whether you would care to have Stella go so far away from home, but if you would consider allowing her to take the tests, and she passes them—"

"Are you trying to sell us something or give us something?" asked Stella's uncle.

"If she passes the tests, whether you pay anything at all is up to you," said Peter. "Those who can pay and are willing to do so, pay as much as they wish. You have, I believe, several children of your own to educate?"

"The four you met in the hall are mine."

"Then in your case it could probably be arranged that all of Stella's expenses could be paid by the school. The aim of Mr. and Mrs. Davis is to educate these other children as a memorial to the parents of their grandson. You can easily satisfy yourself that Stella will be in good hands."

Mr. Oates looked again at the papers he held.

"What did you say your part is in all this?"

"I manage the school," replied Peter, "and Dr. Mark Foxwell is associated with me in the work. Miss Emily Page is to be Dean of Girls. One of our prospective students, Elsie Lambeth, is staying with Miss Page until the school opens."

"Well, sir," said Mr. Oates, "if all this is as you say, and can be proved to be all right, I don't mind telling you that we might think it over and decide to do it. That is, if Stella likes the idea."

Both men turned to look at the child, who had been listening without a word.

"I think I would, Uncle Ralph," said Stella.

"Suppose you go along then and make coffee and cut some cake for us," suggested her uncle. "Give me a little while to talk business with Dr. Welles here." He walked to the other end of the room, and Stella came to the doctor's side and said in low, urgent tones: "You were *sent* to me, weren't you?"

"You might put it that way," replied the psychiatrist. What did she mean?

Her uncle was returning with cigarettes and matches, and Stella left the room.

"I wanted her to go so I could speak right out," he said.

Dr. Welles accepted a cigarette.

"The fact is, Stella isn't happy here," said her uncle, "and there isn't much I can do about it. But I tell you fairly, we have no money for expensive schooling."

"No money is needed, Mr. Oates."

"She and her cousins don't get on. They tease her a lot and I can't wonder they do. Stella's notional. Sort of affected. She puts on that superior air of hers, and the other kids don't like it. They torment her and make her miserable. I moved to this house on purpose so she could have a little room of her own, and I told mine to keep out of it and let her things alone. Bits of poetry she used to try to write, they'd read out loud and laugh over. She's a bright little thing, Stella is, but sometimes sullen. I've often thought if she could go away to school it would be the making of her."

"She is different from her cousins, then."

"Yes, she's a hop out of kin, all right. And she takes a sort of pride in being different, too. I went so far as to have a talk with her teacher about her last May. She told me Stella isn't much like any other kids and she might grow up to be a genius. I favor her all I can, but she's beyond me to understand. She has me get the most outlandish books out of the library for her to look at, nothing a normal child would take any interest in."

"What sort of books?"

"Oh, old languages, with different alphabets, and ancient history, and things about Asia and Africa. No harm in it that I could see, but I don't know where she ever even heard of such things. She does well in school—much better than the rest of them. That shows them up, of course, and they don't like it a little bit. Mine have good heads enough but they're always carrying on and gadding about in a noisy crowd and they don't take any interest in their books. My wife's as good as she can be to Stella, and yet it's hard all around. Mine act up and make a racket on purpose when they know Stella wants to be quiet, and she shows plain she don't like it. She always has her nose in a book. She likes deep stuff, too. She says the others are just like savages. Of course kids will call names, and mine say she just tries to show off. They say she only pretends to read those history books."

"What do you think?"

"I can't make head or tail of the books myself, and I doubt if Stella can, but it seems to interest her. Now, you see how I'm placed. If I send her away to school at my own expense, mine would feel sort of slighted, you see? They don't grudge their cousin her fair share, and never did, but that would be a good big slice more than her share. I don't have too much to do with. So if there is any way it could be managed so as not to take away from my own children, Dr. Welles, let me tell you it would be a godsend."

"Mr. Oates, I am glad you have told me all this, and I can see your problem," said Peter Welles.

"You said you were the school psychologist where you live," said Ralph Oates, "and I thought likely you'd understand the girl better than we do."

"If you trust her to us, I promise that you'll never regret it."

"I'll want to be sure, you know. Look up your references and all that."

"I'll give you a list of local men who know me," said Peter, scribbling rapidly on the back of a used envelope. "Call these. And others in the West," he scribbled more. "The school will not be open for some months," said Peter, who had just had a brilliant idea, "but you can send or bring Stella to us any time. Miss Page would be glad to take her. Miss Page has been teaching in the public schools of Oakland for thirty years or more; she was one of my teachers when I was a boy. Stella might as well live with her and go to public school as Elsie does, and I will do what I can for her. You think, don't you, that she needs some special attention?"

"Yes, I do. I don't know much about such things, but she doesn't seem to adjust well at school, or at home where she has lived all her life. I think mine will be better off with her gone, and she'll be better off away from them. They're too different to get along, and it gets worse all the time."

When Stella came in with the coffee and cake for which she had been sent, it was already settled that Dr. Welles would spend the day after next giving her the required tests.

Maybe all I'll get is the problem children, thought Peter ruefully as he went back to the hotel. What sort of problem is Stella? We can't do without Jay; but he's right, he can't leave. Is there any way out of that? And what is all this about Stella? As for the convention meetings, which he had come to attend, it looked as if he wouldn't get to many of them. Peter took a sleeping pill and went to bed early.

Mrs. Oates opened the door to Dr. Welles at nine o'clock on the appointed morning.

"I sent the others off on an all-day picnic," she said as she ushered him in. "My husband was up until midnight night before last, telephoning and sending telegrams. He says to tell you he has been investigating you, and you seem to be all right."

I forgot to ask them not to tell anyone about the children, moaned Peter inwardly. Well, I suppose it was sure to get out sooner or later, but—

"We don't want you to make any mistake," Mrs. Oates continued. "We love Stella like she was our own. I took her when she was a little baby the same age as my Polly and I meant to raise them like twins. But Stella was a different kind of child. Still, that's no matter. We've no more wish to be rid of her than any of the others, except if it's for her own good. Ralph says you told him to satisfy himself about you, and he's doing it."

Yes, but why didn't I think to ask him not to tell why he wanted to know? Peter groaned behind a smiling face. Oh, why didn't I say it was a high intelligence school, and say nothing about the parentage of the children? But how then could I have known anything about Stella? Obviously nobody thinks she is very intelligent. She, like Tim, keeps her intelligence concealed. Peter suffered a wave of horror as he realized that he had, as yet, no proof that all of these children were gifted. Then he told himself that Tim, Elsie and Jay surely were, and—what was the woman saying?

". . . But I told him maybe you didn't want your affairs talked about, the school and all, or the children's affairs, their parents or anything, so he never said a word about it."

"Thank you, Mrs. Oates," said Peter in heartfelt relief. "It is true that we do not wish a premature revelation of our plans. Only those most concerned should know about it. We hope to give as little publicity as possible to the school and its pupils. It is not good for children to live in the spotlight." I'm babbling, he told himself, and stopped.

"Well, I told Ralph it's for you to say what you want told, not us. He has a friend in the police department and a friend on a newspaper here. They got in touch with the Oakland chief of police and the superintendent of schools, and asked about you and that other doctor and the teacher you mentioned, and about the Davis people, too. They got night letters and phone calls all day yesterday, your description and your photograph even; I believe they said somebody might be posing as you here and asked if you were here. I hope you don't mind all this, Dr. Welles, but we had to be sure."

"Certainly you had to be sure. I hope now I can use you as a reference when I contact guardians of other children."

"Ralph said to tell you," continued Mrs. Oates, "that if you'd rather take her when you go, and board her with Miss Page, that would save her taking the trip alone so far. We can pay her fare and the board bill, and her board at the school too, if she can have her tuition and books free like you said. It seems awful sudden to me, but Ralph said you spoke as if you might like it that way. She can come straight home to us if she doesn't like it there. I wouldn't have it any other way."

"Certainly. And she shall write to you faithfully. But how does Stella feel about all this?"

"The child is wild to go. She keeps saying you're sent to her, whatever she means by that. Of course, she may change her mind again for all I know. She shan't be sent away from here unless she likes. Now, I'll call her; or was there anything else you want to say to me?"

"Only to ask that you allow her to be alone with me for the tests. They are partly psychological, and—"

"I understand that. A child's always distracted if people stand around and watch. What are the tests for? To show she's up to her grade in school?"

"Yes, and to find out where her chief interests and abilities lie, and how well balanced she is, and things of that sort."

"She's up to her grade all right, and in some ways beyond; but she doesn't take a real interest in her studies. She's quick, though, and she has a wonderful memory. There now, she's coming. Come in, Stella. Now you be a good girl, and do what Dr. Welles says, and I'll be in the laundry room if you want me, or the back yard."

As soon as her aunt had gone, Stella sat down opposite Dr. Welles and asked, "You *were* sent to me, weren't you?"

"Well, I'm here," said Peter. "I think that is enough for now."

Oddly enough, this seemed to satisfy Stella, even to please her.

But when the first pages of the Army Alpha test were set before her, Stella waved it away.

"Puzzles and games like that bore me," she said.

"Have you ever taken a test like this at school?"

"They gave us one once. I couldn't be bothered with it just then."

"The hard parts do take effort," said Dr. Welles.

Stella stared at him.

"What hard parts?" she asked.

"What did you do with the test at school?" asked the psychiatrist. "Push it away like this?"

"Oh, no. You can't do things like that at school. I put down answers to some of it. But really I was writing a poem, so I couldn't take time to bother with puzzles just then. I have to write poems when I'm in the mood."

Peter took a deep breath and counted ten.

"Are you writing a poem now?"

"No," said the child, her eyes wide.

"If you want to be in my school you must pass my tests," he said.

"But . . . I thought you *knew*," and the girl looked alarmed.

"I do know," said Peter. "I know a great deal more about you than you think I do. But we must have some proof."

"Then it isn't because I'm an orphan and somebody wants to be kind to orphans like me. I thought I was right about that," said Stella. "It's something else you want to prove about me. How my parents died is only an excuse."

This speech, confused though it sounded, brought hope to the doctor again. For the first time in this extraordinary interview, Peter felt able to talk frankly to her.

"You have, I believe, a very superior intelligence," he told her. "That is what I want to prove, using several standardized tests."

"Oh well, if this must come first," said Stella. She picked up the pencil, and Dr. Welles looked at his watch.

"Fifty minutes is par," he said. "You can do it in much less."

And Stella did.

"Shall we take another test, or talk a little first?" said Peter when she had finished.

"I'd rather talk. What are the other tests?"

"One of the Stanford-Binet superior adult tests, a Rorschach, and the Bellevue-Wechsler test, and a personality-quotient test."

"I hope they'll be more interesting. Now will you tell me what you came to me for?"

"I think you know enough right now," said the doctor. "Let me find out more about you, Stella. Tell me about yourself. How old are you? Fourteen?"

"I'll be fourteen in October."

"You have lived with your uncle and aunt all your life. Is your health good?"

"Yes."

"Do you sleep well?"

"Yes."

"Do you dream very much?"

Stella hesitated, and said she did not dream; but this was an obvious fib.

"Are your uncle and aunt good to you?" asked the doctor.

"They mean to be."

"Your cousins?"

"I guess so."

Peter asked a number of ordinary questions until Stella was answering freely and then he tried a surprise question.

"What is your pen name?"

"I thought you might know that," she said.

"I know you write. Poetry, isn't it?"

"I'm Estelle Starrs."

Much suddenly became clear to Peter. Among poets, Estelle Starrs was most frequently compared with Emily Dickinson; among novelists, with Marie Corelli. Her first novel had not had a very wide sale, and the second was newly published. Peter had not read them, but he had heard his brother practitioners discussing them with considerable professional interest. *The Star Child* had provoked much argument, and *Incarnation in Egypt*, one authority had remarked, must have been written by a slightly wacky wife of some expert Egyptologist. Naturally nobody had dreamed that the author was a girl of thirteen.

"Who knows you write these things?"

"Nobody. Not even the publisher knows who I am."

"How do you collect your money?" asked Peter.

"They keep it for me," replied Stella placidly. "I couldn't spend it, could I? When I am grown up I can get it. I wrote them I would ask for it when I wanted it."

Peter Welles opened his suitcase again and laid some papers before her. But again the child hesitated.

"I can't take this," she said.

"It's a personality-quotient test," he said. "I want to find out what sort of girl you are, your tastes and all that. You can't possibly fail. There are no wrong answers."

"I know the answers I ought to give," she said. "Anybody can see what is wanted. I can't take it and be honest. You'll find out what I am like soon enough."

There was something to that, Peter conceded.

"Just ask me questions yourself, instead of this made-up test," she suggested. "You can tell without asking, can't you?"

"I can tell you some things about yourself," he agreed. "Let's see how well I can do. Pretend I'm a fortune teller at the beach. You believe that nobody understands you, that it is your destiny to live alone forever, and that you will not be appreciated at your true worth until after you have been long dead."

"I feared that might be true," said the child gravely, "but now that you have come to me, won't everything be different?"

"If you come with me, things will be better for you," Peter replied with equal gravity, "but it may take time."

He put away the test she had rejected, and took out the Rorschach cards. Stella enjoyed this test and chattered freely during it.

"I notice," said Dr. Welles, "that your answers show, as your books do, an interest in Egypt and India and the Orient generally. Isn't this an unusual interest for a girl of your age?"

"Perhaps."

"How did you come to take a special interest in things like this?" he asked.

The child replied stiffly, "It is not permitted me to tell."

The psychiatrist tried another tack.

"How can you tell me about your books, when you can't tell even the publisher?"

"I knew you would believe me," said Stella.

"Wouldn't your family believe you?"

"Possibly. But they would not understand," said the child, with marked distaste.

"How do you get along with your family?"

"I live here as a stranger," said Stella.

"You mean they don't understand you?"

"Of course not. And I have no sympathy with them. We are too different."

Mrs. Oates knocked at the door and called them to lunch. The little girl ate well and normally, and washed the dishes while the psychiatrist talked with her aunt. Then the questioning and testing of Stella was resumed. By the time he was ready to leave, Dr. Welles was satisfied as to Stella's intelligence, and he phoned the airport for a reservation for her on his plane four days later. She was certainly one of the Wonder Children, and she needed his help.

After supper, at his hotel, Peter wrote up his notes. Birth, normal. Infancy, normal. General health, good. Not a "nervous child." (Jay's record would probably be the opposite in that respect.) No serious illnesses. No delusion of persecution, but strong feeling on both sides that Stella did not fit in with the rest of the family. Stella admitted to having had childish fancies, years before, that she might not be related to them at all, but said she now knew better than to think she could be a changeling, a fairy princess, or royalty in disguise. She was sure that she really was the child of Ralph Oates' brother, and thought perhaps her own father and, especially, her own mother, might have understood her better. "Though not entirely," she had added.

"Why do you think they would?"

"My uncle understands me better than the others in this family," explained Stella. "So his brother, my own father, probably would have understood me better yet. My aunt isn't really related to me at all, by blood, and her children take after her. I suppose I must take after my own mother."

"Why wouldn't your own mother understand you entirely?"

"I just don't think she would," replied Stella firmly. And on this she refused to elaborate.

As regards her emotional state, Stella said that she was happier than she had formerly been, since she had begun to have things published, but that she had never expected to be truly happy in such an uncongenial environment.

"My uncle tries to be sympathetic, and sides with me all he can," she said, "but I don't think he really tries to understand me much."

Stella admitted to "seeing things" in the hypnagogic state, but said they "usually don't mean anything. It's like dreaming, only I'm not quite asleep." She showed no sign of any hallucinations, illusions or delusions, and admitted to no more obsessions, phobias and compulsions than are normal in an imaginative, lonely youngster. Her frankness in discussing these matters spoke well for her. She had excellent powers of observation, and could reason nimbly when she chose to do so, but her reading had been very limited because, as she explained, children under sixteen were not allowed in the adult section of the library at all. Stella was, therefore, limited to the books she could borrow from friends or ask her uncle to get for her. She was overjoyed to hear that in Oakland she could choose books freely from the adult sections.

When she was asked what she would pack to take with her—Dr.

Welles' idea being to check on the practical side of her nature—
Stella promptly named the necessary articles, described her clothing
in terms of summer and winter weight, asked about the climate to
which she would be moving, and then suggested that Peter look over
her dresses to see which would be suitable to take.

"Your aunt will know that," he replied.

"Please," begged Stella. There was a new look in her eyes, and anxious lines in her face. For the first time she seemed nervous. Obediently, the doctor rose and followed her.

Upstairs in her room, with the door shut, Stella turned to him,
and said in a fierce whisper, "You won't tell?"

"No," he assured her, mystified.

"She'll see if I pack them. Please, will you take them—now?"

"Oh! Manuscripts?" he guessed.

"Yes, and notes. If you move that chest of drawers quickly—
there's a loose board underneath it, if I pull out a nail. There." She
knelt, reached in under the floor and produced a bundle wrapped in
newspaper.

"May I look?" Peter opened the wrappings and picked up a thin
sheaf of papers, fastened with a paper clip, top sheaf of a dozen or
more.

"*Mercer's Ethiopic Grammar*, 'with chrestomathy and glossary,'"
he read in an awed undertone. "What is chrestomathy, may I ask?"

"It's from the Greek *chrestos*, useful, and *mathanein*, to learn,"
replied the little girl. "It means extracts from books in a foreign language, with notes, so you can learn."

She reached under the floor boards again and produced a second
bundle and a third.

"That's all," she said. "Notes, and a few manuscript poems. Put
them all in this brief case—it's my school case, but my aunt will
think it's yours. She doesn't notice very much."

Stella indicated the books in the small bookcase by her bed.

"These are story books and poems and things. May I take the
books?"

"Your uncle can ship them to you." He could see some of the titles; Stella's three books were there. Her poems were called *Sheaves
of Stars*.

"*Shh!* Here's my aunt," said Stella, and Peter thrust the three bun-
dles of paper into the brief case, while Stella snatched a dress from
the closet and held it up before him.

"You'll need some fairly warm things for next winter, and for the cool nights even now," he was saying when Mrs. Oates opened the door.

"I'll see to it," said Mrs. Oates. "I was going to make the girls some dresses this summer; I'll send Stella's to her as fast as I can finish them."

Peter Welles, pondering all these things in his hotel room that evening, added a line to his page of notes, and opened the brief case.

"A Conversation-Grammar of the Hindustani Language," he read. "Biblical Hebrew. Introduction to Literary Chinese. Arabic Language and Grammar. An Anglo-Saxon Reader. Modern Persian Reader. A Short Grammar of Attic Greek." There were more, but Peter felt unable to face them. He opened the second package. "E. Naville's The Ancient Egyptian Faith," he read, "Breasted's History of Egypt from the Earliest Times to the Persian Conquest." There were notes about India, Tibet, Babylon, Persia. Peter looked no more. With a slight shudder, he returned all the notes to the brief case and closed it firmly. Stella should carry it all the way across the continent with her own hands. All those pages of notes in a careful, minute handwriting must have cost long hours of hard labor in secret. These were the odd books she "just wanted to glance over" in which "no child could possibly be interested." These were the source materials for her books.

Peter attended the rest of the conferences he had come to attend. He telephoned Stella daily, but did not see her again. A telegram to Miss Page telling her to expect the child was followed by a letter giving the story. Peter met Jay almost daily, and talked to him about all they were doing and planning to do, but he did not tell the two children anything about each other. Jay, throbbing with eagerness to hear all that Dr. Welles would tell him about Tim and Elsie and the school, exacted a promise that Peter and the others would write often to him, but steadfastly refused to think about attending the school. It was, he said, impossible, and there was no use in thinking about it.

In the taxi to the plane, Stella asked a question.

"The other children—are they anything like me?"

"Not very much," replied Peter. "I hope you will like them and get along with them as well as you can. But I don't think they will share your special interests to any great extent."

Stella, who had been looking puzzled, looked even more so.

"What do we have in common?" she asked. Peter signed her to silence, but at the airport he walked with her to a place where they could not be overheard and began the explanation and the warning he realized she must be given.

"We are trying to gather you all together because most of you have had difficulty in adjusting to the world of normal children. Naturally the tastes and interests of each child are personal and different from those of the others. Tim and Elsie and you are as unlike as children can be, except that you all have exceptionally high intelligence. You should be able to adjust to one another if you make the effort, and you can learn from one another and teach one another. It is probable that you all have a wide range of interests; although your special interests are different there must be many things you can share."

Stella looked bewildered, then extremely thoughtful, and then she nodded. What was going on in her mind was more than Peter could guess.

"I'll leave it to you to tell them as much or as little about yourself as you choose," he said. "There is, I know, much that you have not told me."

Thus warned, Stella said little about herself to Elsie or to Tim at first, and even less to Miss Page and to Dr. Foxwell. The children read her published works with some mystification, and she read theirs.

"Tim certainly can do almost everything," she confided to Dr. Welles. "He knows something about almost everything, too."

"But you know more about the Orient and about Africa," he replied.

"It's right what you told me about their having different interests from mine."

"Your interests will widen, no doubt," said Dr. Welles, "and so will theirs. It is good that you have different specialized branches of knowledge to share with one another."

Dr. Foxwell, after his first meeting with Stella, and recalling Peter's letter concerning her, had made a dire prediction that when Stella and Elsie were brought together, the ringing clash between the two personalities would probably resound for several miles. But Elsie was making tremendous efforts to overcome her faults, particularly her tendency to outspoken criticism of everything which differed in the least from her own notions, and she was determined to get along with the other Wonder Children or die in the effort. Stella's habits were rather toward withdrawal than toward violence when she was not "understood," and as for Tim, nothing human was alien to that ardent would-be psychiatrist. To all three children, what really counted was that they had found others of their own age who were of the same mental level, and they were eager to share their interests and to help one another. Their clashes were indeed frequent, and misunderstandings rife, but the bond which bound them together was stronger than their differences.

Dr. Welles was conscious that Stella had something on her mind and that she was trying to think something out. It seemed that until she had done so she was avoiding any definite statements except those of indisputable fact. She often stared at the others as if puzzled, and they seemed puzzled about her.

For the first fortnight, Dr. Welles made no effort to quiz Stella, but left her largely to the society of Elsie and Tim, and observed her as much as he could. Offered her choice of a pet, Stella said that since all the others were breeding cats she would be content with only one of her own, and she chose a coal-black, short-haired, green-eyed tom which she had neutered. She named it Hegai; and Peter Welles had almost as hard a time tracking down that name as he had in identifying the Grigio for which Jay's guardian's guide-dog was named. Stella and Elsie went almost daily to the main library and returned loaded with volumes. Miss Page privately kept a list of the titles.

"There is no point in the reading that I can see," she reported to Dr. Welles. "Stella is going on a sort of reading jag, reading anything she lays her hands on; and Elsie is going through the library reading everything they didn't have in the library of her home town. They each read most of what the other brings home. I should think it would give them both colic."

"And are they getting enough exercise and play?"

"Oh yes, I see to that. And Tim comes over nearly every afternoon, or they go to play with him."

Elsie spent one evening a week with Dr. Welles and one with Dr. Foxwell. Tim no longer had professional consultations with the doctor, and both of the doctors were extremely busy, for Peter had not yet given up his work with his patients, and Dr. Foxwell was occupied with business affairs connected with plans for the school. .

"How do you get along with Stella?" Dr. Welles asked Elsie one evening.

"All right," said Elsie. "Sometimes she makes me mad, though. She did today."

"Tell me about it."

"We read each other's stuff, of course," Elsie said, "and when I showed her a sonnet sequence, she said it was wordy and stylized. *Wordy!*"

"I haven't had time to read any of her poems yet. What are they like?" inquired the psychiatrist.

"She has a new one she calls 'Figures.' Figures of speech, she means. No rhyme, nothing much to them. Just little short things."

"Well, I suppose a person who calls sonnets 'wordy' would have to write very short things," smiled Peter. "Can you repeat one?" Elsie struck a pose and declaimed:

> "'Branches of trees outstretched—
> Your arms.
> I am a timid bird
> Huddled in them.'"

"Is that all?"

"The rest are like that. Or worse. So, of course, I didn't show her my new sequence, the Summa one." The last sentence was sarcastic.

Elsie and Tim had been reading the *Summa Theologica*. Tim, as the psychiatrist knew, was most impressed by its mathematical quality, and kept saying that it ought to be possible to reduce it to equations, if one could but find the right symbols. But Elsie saw it as a work of art, each question-section as concise and disciplined as a sonnet; and she was actually engaged in turning out examples of what she meant—each objection expressed in the octave, the reply and answer to the objection in the sestet. This exquisitely difficult task was her most cherished secret; no one knew of it except Dr. Welles.

"And how is the Summa sequence getting along?"

"Terrible!" Elsie's eyes were bright with enthusiasm. "I have to set every word in place like . . . like God setting the stars in the sky. I'll never get even one of the sonnets to suit me. It's better poetry in the original. But it is fun to try."

What odd definitions these children had for *fun*, mused Peter.

"I remember another of Stella's things," said Elsie, and she repeated it:

> "'I am the dull earth,
> You are lightning,
> Tying me to heaven
> An instant.'"

"She does it well," said Peter, with some severity. "You can't say it is not poetry."

"Yah!" said Elsie, with great simplicity. "She gets a good idea or phrase and she throws it on to paper and that's all there is to it. She doesn't work with it, that's what is wrong. But what can you expect? She believes in inspiration."

Her head held high, Elsie left the consultation room, and the psychiatrist was left with his thoughts.

After a few moments he picked up the telephone and called Miss Page.

"Hello? Peter Welles speaking. I think we'd better give the children a little studying to do this summer . . . No, nothing burdensome . . . An essay to read together and discuss was what I had in mind . . . Yes, you're right, there's a reason for it . . . Poe's 'Philosophy of Composition' will do to start with."

"How he wrote 'The Raven'?" Miss Page's voice came over the wire. "It will be worth the price of admission to hear what they say about it."

"Give them each a copy tomorrow after supper, or as soon as you can get three copies," Peter directed, "and let me know beforehand. You and I have some work to do while they read."

So a few evenings later, Dr. Welles and Miss Page ostensibly busied themselves with plans and calculations at one end of the living room, while the three children, curled in easy chairs or sprawled on the floor, read the essay and exploded into talk. Never was a man more thoroughly disagreed with. And yet it soon became apparent that there was considerable disagreement among the children themselves. "It depends on just what he means," they often remarked, but they doubted whether masterpieces were often written backwards, and even more did they question whether Poe actually wrote as he said he did.

"I think he rationalized it afterwards," Tim insisted, while Elsie was inclined to think the essay an elaborate hoax, and Stella considered it a defense against "those fool people who keep asking how you do it, and wouldn't understand if you told them."

All of the children jeered at Poe's remarks about Beauty, not even Stella being willing to concede that Beauty makes one weep. Tim stoutly maintained that death is not a very melancholy topic to a Christian, and Elsie couldn't see anything beautiful about the loss of a loved one, "especially if you howl about it all your life." To the surprise of the listening elders, all three children thought that Poe greatly exaggerated originality.

"Only people who don't know much and have never read much think you can ever be original," said Elsie.

"Yes, almost everything possible was done or thought thousands of years ago," agreed Stella, "in a literary way, I mean."

"It's a sort of pride, I think," Tim mused. "As if to say, nobody else in all creation has ever had a mind as good as mine; I can think of things never thought before."

"Well, he does admit that it's only the combinations that can be original," Elsie pointed out. "Like his stanza form."

"Yes, but I bet that could be duplicated if you hunted long enough," said Tim. "Let's keep our eyes open for that kind of stanza when we read."

"Poe tries so hard to be gruesome that half the time he's only funny," Elsie said.

"The silly old raven would soon starve to death sitting on that bust," giggled Tim. "I think the poem is much too long, too; and the refrain dates it."

The girls disagreed with him there. There were times, said Elsie, when a refrain belonged in a poem, even though it had been done to death in some periods.

"But the whole essay is all wrong," said Stella heatedly. "It makes it all so mechanical. We couldn't write that way, and I don't believe anybody could."

"Maybe if they didn't write anything very good," said Elsie. " 'The Raven' isn't really good."

"I should think you'd be too busy with the mechanics to accomplish anything," said Stella. "And he doesn't say a bit about imagination."

"I read something else of his once," Tim frowned as he tried to remember it, "how he chose the name Lenore by choosing the most musical consonants and vowels and combining as many of them as he could in one name, or something like that."

The girls shouted.

"Well, if he doesn't know how to write without all that rigmarole," Elsie said violently, "he's not much of a writer."

"He doesn't claim to be inspired," said Stella.

"But he's always talking about intuition," said Elsie, "and he doesn't much like it."

"What is intuition?" asked Tim briskly. "And inspiration that some writers used to believe in—do you?"

"Of course I do," said Stella indignantly. "That's how I know Poe wasn't really a poet. He doesn't even know what inspiration is. He works like a robot."

"Well, I don't know what it is, either," retorted Elsie, "I just work until it comes out right. And I don't work like a robot at all."

"No, of course you don't," Stella said. "But I think you work over things too much," she added kindly. "Why don't you put your things down as they come, unspoiled?"

Elsie gaped at her.

"Just *raw?*"

Tim, who had never written poetry, was intensely interested. The adults, who had been completely forgotten, had long since given up the pretense of work.

"You don't write the way he says, do you?" demanded Stella.

"No, of course not," replied Elsie, "but I don't claim to be inspired. What do you think, Tim?"

"Well, isn't it possible," said Tim, with an excellent though unconscious caricature of Peter Welles' professional manner, "that Poe really did go through all that he says he does, very rapidly indeed, and then went back and analyzed it and described it as if it had been deliberate and purposive? Your thought processes are so rapid, Stella, that you probably don't know you think at all, it seems to come in one burst."

"I know it's inspiration," said Stella firmly. "I write poems that aren't like anything I ever thought. They come to me. I woke up one night last week and wrote a long one and it amazed me. It wasn't at all like anything I had ever thought in all my life, and at first I couldn't even understand it. But it had great meaning for me— although maybe not for anyone else."

"If it had such great meaning for you and for nobody else," said Elsie, "it must have come from something in yourself—your own experience and thoughts—so it couldn't be inspired from outside yourself."

"Like dreams," suggested Tim. "Sometimes you can't figure out where they come from, but . . . Peter can tell us!" he cried confidently, remembering the presence of the grownups. And the children all rushed across the room, shouting questions in chorus.

"Professionally, I know nothing about inspiration," Dr. Welles answered. "My patients do sometimes suffer from hallucinations in which voices speak to them; but you mean something rather different. Miss Page, may we consult your dictionary? Ah. Here we have it. From *inspirare*, to blow upon or into, to breathe into. 'To fuse or suggest ideas or monitions supernaturally; to communicate divine instructions to the mind.' In this sense we speak of the writers of Sacred Scripture as inspired. They wrote under the guidance of God."

"That wouldn't apply to our poetry, surely," said Elsie to Stella, who flushed hotly and made haste to agree.

" 'To infuse ideas or poetic spirit,' " read Peter. "It doesn't say by whom this is done. Who or what inspires your poetry, Stella?"

The child looked stunned.

"I don't know. I never thought about that."

"Well, I don't understand about the Bible," began Tim, but the doctor silenced him.

"Leave that for now. It is irrelevant. Well, Stella?"

As Stella did not answer, Elsie took it upon herself to do so.

"I should think that's the whole point, *who* inspires you," she said. "I wouldn't want to be dictated to by just anybody or anything. It might be a hallucination, or a demon, or my own imagination. I think it's just ideas that come into your head and you don't stop to think where they come from, but they all have a natural explanation."

"Might be largely unconscious or subconscious, as in the case of dreams," suggested Tim. "Then it would be hard to track down sometimes, as dreams often are."

"Yes, and if you get a good idea you don't stop to fret about the psychology of its coming, you just grab it quick before it gets away," Elsie volunteered. "What about intuition, Dr. Welles? Do you know?"

"About that I think I do know and can explain. There are, in what Jung calls the psyche, four basic functions, of which intuition is one."

"The psyche? Does he mean soul?"

"More or less. Jung's term also includes the unconscious. Terminology differs considerably. Poe referred, you notice, to . . . where's the place . . . 'the object Truth, or the satisfaction of the intellect, and the object Passion or the excitement of the heart.' The scholastics say that the soul has intelligence and free will; the intellect seeks to know, to grasp the truth, while the will desires happiness. Love resides in the will."

"I thought love would reside in the emotions," interrupted Elsie.

"Depends on the definition," Tim said promptly.

"It is impossible that the human will be deeply moved by an object, says St. Thomas Aquinas, without passion being aroused in the sense appetite. Spiritual love flows from the will, and the emotions and sense appetites follow along with it. In all these matters we must understand the words as they are meant, and recognize, on the one hand, identity of thought under difference of terminology, and, on the other hand, difference of thought in many cases where the words used are identical. The word love, for example, has many meanings."

Miss Page marveled anew at the children, who were drinking it all in with concentrated interest.

"What Jung calls 'thought' corresponds to what Poe and the scholastics call 'intellect' and others call 'reason,' and this function evaluates by means of cognition from the viewpoint 'true-false.' Is that clear?"

"Yes. Go on," chorused the children.

"What Poe calls 'passion' and the scholastics call 'the will' is what Jung calls 'feeling' which evaluates by means of emotions, he says, from the viewpoint 'agreeable-disagreeable.' We choose, or love, or desire, what seems *good* to us, in other words."

"Morally good?" asked Tim.

"Any kind of good. Good art—good pie—a good time. The will chooses a thing under its aspect of good, invariably—because of the good in it. It may be morally bad to take a pie, but you may take it because it is a good pie. Now these two functions of the psyche are called rational functions, because they deal with values. Sensation and intuition, on the other hand, are called irrational, because they work with mere perceptions. Sensation takes things as they are, without valuing them or thinking about them."

"But people do think about—"

"Yes, but that's using another function, you see. The sensation type of person will look at a picture or a landscape and see the details—name the trees, the colors of the different flowers, and all that; or he notices an event in the same way, but not the significance, the meaning of things. Such a person in an art gallery will count the cherubs flying about a saint's head, and think you are lacking in observation if you cannot tell how many there were. Intuition also perceives, but in a special way, seeing the inner meanings and the potentialities of things, getting impressions rather than definite, photographic details. Where's the dictionary? Oh, yes. 'The act of knowing by direct perception or comprehension without reasoning or deduction; a first or primary truth; insight; apprehension.'"

"But if it concerns truth, why is there no reasoning or deducting?" Tim wanted to know.

"The axioms, and so forth, which are prerequisite to the reasoning process, must come from somewhere," explained Dr. Welles. "Self-evident truths, as we sometimes call them, are too simple to be demonstrated. The axioms of geometry, the first facts such as 'I exist' and 'I think' are known directly. You'd better all have a go at a textbook on Criteriology—Glenn's is on my shelves somewhere. This is the study of the tests and norms by which one may judge what is true and certain in human thinking, reasoning and knowledge. Now, to get back to intuition. As it is often used the word refers to a guess, hunch, or even an impulse which may be false or evil. You may think you know intuitively that you can trust a certain person, and he would steal your last cent. I'm not the intuitive type myself. But a thing may be perceived intuitively and then checked by reason. There are men of the intuitive type, of the thinking type and of the intuitive-thinking type. Similarly a thing may appeal to the senses and then be rejected by the will. The pie which would be taken at the dictation of the senses because it is good to eat, might be rejected by the will, which seeks a higher good, a moral good. We might go into all this at length"—Dr. Welles glanced at the clock— "but I see it is time for Tim to go home, and rather too near bedtime for you girls."

"Imagination," pleaded Elsie. "What's that?"

"Just very briefly," wheedled Tim.

"Oh, imagination is the power by which we recall or project images of things the senses have perceived. St. Thomas says it is the ability to picture material things in their absence. Jung calls it a creative power which brings up an image out of the material of the unconscious. You can not imagine what you have not first seen, but you can combine different images into one. If you wish to imagine a mermaid, you combine a woman's upper part with a fish's tail. Or if you try to imagine a scene on Venus or Mars, you might think of a plant shaped like grass, the size of a tree, colored like the sky, with a flower like a cat's head, having eyes like a bee and feelers like a snail. Do you understand me?"

"You mean we can't imagine anything?" cried Stella.

"It's like Poe's originality—only the combinations can be original?" Elsie exclaimed.

"Of course, a man born blind can't imagine red or blue," said Tim. "Try imagining a new color. Go on, try."

"Well, think it over and read up on it," advised Dr. Welles. "I'll lend you books if you like. Goodnight, all of you, please! Miss Page and I will finish off our work here."

The girls went up to their rooms, and Timothy left the house.

"What in the world will they make of all that?" Miss Page wondered.

"Tim understood, and Elsie got most of it." Dr. Welles replied. "What Stella thinks is the question. I'll let it all soak in for a while, and see what comes of it."

"They are all so different."

"Yes. And Jay is unlike them all. He tells me in his last letter—I forgot to bring it along—that he has learned several languages. It seems that when his aunt first began to read aloud to his uncle, because of Mr. Curtis' failing sight, Jay demanded lessons. His aunt gave him a month's instruction with special emphasis on pronunciation, and after that he could read German aloud and said he wanted to learn another language. Apparently they still think he does not understand what he reads and has merely learned how to pronounce the words to help his uncle, as a singer learns to sing in several languages without knowing or caring what the words mean. Actually he reads German, French, Latin, Spanish and Italian perfectly, and is eager for a chance to try speaking and writing them."

"How Tim would love to be with Jay!"

"Yes. We must think of some way to get Jay here. We need him, and I think we have much to offer him, too."

"If he would come, under the circumstances, I wouldn't want him," said Miss Page.

"That's the problem," said Dr. Welles.

"Hello, Stella."

"Hello, Dr. Welles. Miss Page said you wanted me."

"Come right in." Peter offered her a comfortable chair and set a dish of candies temptingly close while he talked. "I plan to have private talks with each one of our pupils fairly often, and help you with any problems you may have. Now that you have had a while to get settled here and get to know us all, we may as well begin our talks."

"Yes, sir."

"Is everything going all right? Are you happy?"

"Oh yes, Dr. Welles," replied Stella. "It's so interesting here. Miss Page is so good to me. And I can read all I want to."

"No troubles at all?"

"No, none at all."

"What have you been thinking about lately?"

"I've been thinking about what we were all saying about inspiration, and Tim gave me some books to read about dreams and their origins," Stella said, "and I think you must be right. We've been talking it all over. One thing I like best," she added in a burst of confidence, "is that even when they don't agree with me or understand me, they never act mean. I wrote a poem in which I compared myself to a timid bird, and my cousins or any other kids I ever knew would have chased me around for weeks yelling, 'Hey, timid bird!' and making all kinds of fun. But Elsie knew what I meant, even if she didn't care for the poem. She's quite blunt, but she takes things the way they are meant. And Tim is awfully kind. Even when they call me crazy, they don't act as if they're glad of it."

"Then you have no problems to set before me right now?" said Peter, making no comment on this innocently revealing speech, and giving no sign how much it had moved him. "Let's talk, then. Suppose you tell me, what is your philosophy of life?"

Tim would instantly have demanded a definition of the phrase. Stella only looked thoughtful.

"I never formulated one, I guess," she said. "I'd have to think about it. I never heard that expression before."

"Would you say your philosophy is simple or complex?"

"Fairly complex, I think."

"But don't you think a simple philosophy would be easier to apply?"

"Well, yes, but one must begin with a complex philosophy, because life is so complex, and the philosophy must fit it," said Stella carefully. "Perhaps it will simplify after a while, when I understand things better."

Dr. Welles nodded slowly three or four times.

"Suppose you tell me how you account for your being so different from your cousins and from other children."

"Right now I'm not sure about that. Tim says it's the radiations. But I don't understand such things. I had a theory worked out, but—" Her voice trailed off into silence and she looked doubtfully at Peter.

"I'd like very much to hear it," said the psychiatrist.

"I'm not sure you would understand."

"I'll try." Humanly speaking, there was nothing Peter Welles loathed so much as a person's assuming that he or she was too wonderfully unique to be understood. Professionally he was used to it.

"Timothy said that if nobody else thinks the way you do, you must be wrong."

"Well, suppose you tell me what your theory was, and how you came to formulate it, and what reasoning and evidence support it, and what is against it," suggested Peter encouragingly. He scratched a match and gave his attention to his pipe for a moment. The child spent the moment in concentrated thought.

"Cutting out inspiration made things a little simpler," she said, "but there are still so many complications and alternatives; perhaps you can help. I'll try to tell you. Where to begin?" she murmured, and then plunged in. "I guess it began when I was first taken to a museum. Pete was taking ancient history in school and Pat had to visit local points of interest, and my aunt took Pokey and Polly and me along. They ran around saying, 'Isn't this funny?' and laughing like anything, or else they were bored stiff and wouldn't look at all. They chattered and squealed so—"

"I know," said Dr. Welles, when Stella paused and gave him a look that begged for understanding.

"Either they all ran off and left me, or I slipped away, and there I was alone, wandering around in the great dark rooms and able to look quietly at everything as long as I liked."

"Dark?"

Stella frowned and tried to recapture the scene.

"They seemed dark. There was light to see by, of course, but it was shadowy. There were mummies and vases and things, and I wandered around for what seemed like a long time. Then I found myself before a great piece of stone with writing on it that I recognized as Egyptian. It was high and wide and solid, and for a flash I could remember it all. I knew I had been there, in Egypt, and had seen it many times before."

The child had lived the moment again as she spoke. Then she looked up, defiantly yet fearfully at Peter, who pulled silently at his pipe, his face without expression.

"That was the beginning," said Stella, and she waited for comment.

"Go on."

"Then I went into other rooms and saw other things. It was the same with cuneiform, almost. I almost remembered how to read it, although I could not remember seeing those particular inscriptions. Then the others found me and we went home. Oh, how they always chattered. So silly. Anything even a little bit different they thought was funny and would scream over it. Pat used to take care of children and she would show them pictures and say, 'See the funny man. He's all black. Isn't he funny? Look at the man with feathers on his head. Isn't he funny?' and if they passed a Chinese on the street they'd nudge each other and say, 'Look, look, isn't he funny?' What's funny about that?"

"Nothing whatever," said Peter, with such unexpected warmth that Stella took heart and went on.

"Then I asked my uncle about books on ancient times and places and languages and he would try to get whatever I wanted. He asked for story books first and when he brought me Haggard I was sure I was right. He took me to the museum again, without the others. At the library we got books about the different languages and I began to learn them again."

She seemed to expect comment, but the psychiatrist's nod was noncommittal.

"I got books in Arabic, Chinese, Hebrew, Greek, Hindustani, Sanskrit, Anglo-Saxon and Sumerian."

"Sumerian!"

"Yes. C. J. Good's *A Sumerian Reading Book*." Stella's eyes were shining. "Some of it is in cuneiform script."

"I see. Go on."

"So I came to work out this theory. I couldn't see that things made sense any other way except that I must be reincarnated and have a sort of memory of these other lives, unless I was inspired, and now I'm pretty sure it's not inspiration. Other boys and girls had no interest in these things; why should I have? They didn't think about things like life and death and time and personality and other religions—or even their own religion. How could I be so interested and know so much, and learn so fast, if it wasn't partly remembering? And stories I read backed me up. Kipling and—"

"Is there no other possible explanation?"

"I can't think of any. The other children wouldn't agree with me, I know, but I think they are the same as me only they don't know they are remembering anything."

"Do you believe this theory implicitly?"

"No," said Stella. "Sometimes I thought I was positive. Once I

asked our minister if reincarnation could be true, and he said he
didn't know. He said he once saw a little whirlwind moving along,
and when it came to a haystack it took on a body of whirling hay,
and when it crossed the road it took on a body of dust, and if it had
come to a pond it would have been a waterspout."

"In other words, yes?"

"He meant 'maybe.' But the analogy didn't seem quite right to
me. It's good poetry, but after all, a philosophy of life isn't only poetry. Poetry is true, of course, but you never know quite how it is
true or where it is true. It doesn't have fixed limits like material
things. You can't build your whole life on a lyric idea. Besides, I told
my uncle and he was furious."

The psychiatrist began to like Stella's uncle.

"How much did you tell your uncle of all this?"

"Nothing. I just told him I liked ancient history and things. He
told my aunt it was an odd taste but harmless."

"You said that on your first visit you recognized Egyptian writing," said Peter, laying a little trap.

"Well, I had seen some in Pete's history book," Stella said candidly.

"Have you worked out a time schedule for the various incarna-
tions? Is this the first one in the Americas?"

"I don't know anything about all that. I don't really remember
much, if anything. It's that it all seems to come back to me as I see
it again. And there is my poetry. It's beyond my years certainly. The
critics all say it shows extraordinary insight. If it isn't inspired, then I
must remember from past lives, to be so much older than my years.
And you said we can't imagine anything we have not seen, so that
simplified things even more."

"Go on."

"That's all. What do you think? Am I all wrong about this?"

"Do you want my honest opinion, Stella?"

"Yes, I do."

"I think you have worked it all out very intelligently," he said
slowly, "and I quite understand how you came to do so. But I do not
think your theory is true at all. I think you wished to be away from
where you were—to live away from where you lived—didn't you? And
you were especially eager to get away from the others at the museum.
You worked yourself into a semi-hypnotic state wandering about
alone in the shadowy galleries—a half-dream state. Many people have
been very deeply moved, or greatly thrilled, at seeing things from

these ancient civilizations. Their antiquity appeals strongly to the imagination. Probably the history book was your first glimpse of a world beyond your everyday life. You mistook the thrill for a stirring memory. Did you ever remember anything you had not seen or read of in this life?"

"No. Not that I could prove, anyway."

"Nothing you were positive of, you mean? I thought so. The book you read and also those you wrote were an escape from what you were living every day, as far away as possible in space and time, and they were also an outlet for your creative energy and imagination, your impulse to write stories and the like. *The Star Child* shows at least the wish to believe that you did not actually belong to the family, that you came from some other source entirely."

"I knew better by the time I wrote it," Stella said defensively. "But it made a good story, I thought."

"Of course it did. And *Incarnation in Egypt* shows the wish to live somewhere else, in as different a world as possible. You must have enjoyed living in Egypt in your thoughts, reading and writing about it."

"Don't you think reincarnation can possibly be true?"

"It has a powerful appeal to the imagination," replied Dr. Welles. "It promises a sort of immortality to those who can think of no other; but I don't see much use in living many lives if one must forget them all—"

"One could grow in them without remembering."

"One could grow much better with the aid of memory, don't you think?"

"I have heard of a law of conservation of matter. There might be a law of conservation of souls."

"There might be almost anything. One does not multiply hypotheses without reason. Have you any evidence for reincarnation?"

"Many civilizations have believed in it."

"I know. By the way, what is your religion? Egyptian? Buddhist?"

"Of course not," cried Stella indignantly. "Do you think I pray to cows and cats and beetles?"

"Have you ever lived as an animal or bird of any sort?"

"That wouldn't have to be."

"It depends on which religion of reincarnation you follow. Why was your uncle so angry with the minister you spoke of?"

"He said it wasn't Christian."

"Well, is it? This belief is contrary to the whole Judeo-Christian revelation and to most of our philosophy. Plato believed in a form of it, and I believe Origen taught some such doctrine. If you want to take it seriously you should study the teachings in its various forms and find out which is to be accepted and why. I've always followed that hardheaded old realist Aristotle, myself. I must admit I have never considered metempsychosis seriously. I believe it can be disproved by philosophical and psychological methods. Do you think you can prove it to be true?"

"I don't want to have an imaginary idea of myself or the world," protested Stella. "I'd much rather have a sound and true one, as you and Tim and the others think you have. Until I came here I thought religion was just something you took on faith without any evidence or philosophical reasoning. But . . . but—"

"Let us try to build up a philosophy that you can depend on," suggested the psychiatrist. "One you can test and prove. I'll give you books to study, and you argue against them all you can." He selected a volume from the shelf. "A practical man, Aristotle; let's start with him. How is your Greek?"

"Oh, this is in both languages," cried Stella in delight.

"I believe Aquinas has some relevant material in *Contra Gentiles*," said Peter. "Stella, your knowledge of Egypt is really remarkable, and your books are extraordinarily interesting."

"They must reveal a great deal about me," said Stella. "Tim said you could analyze stories and poems as you do dreams. Could we do that?"

"Certainly, if you would like to," said Dr. Welles. "But don't let it discourage you from writing more about these things of which you have so much knowledge, which you have studied so thoroughly."

"If I have a sound philosophy I can write more wisely as well as live more wisely," said Stella gravely. "Thank you, Dr. Welles. I'll try to find out what can be proved."

Peter relaxed completely when she had left and sighed in relief. One problem was off his mind. He knew what had been in the little girl's mind, and she had agreed to study under his direction. It would take months, perhaps years, to weigh both sides of the questions she had raised, but it would be good for all the children. Now there remained—

"I've got it!"

Peter jumped to his feet and dialed a number. "I want a plane reservation," he said, "at once if possible." How slow he had been to see the obvious!

"Jay? This is Peter Welles. I'm here in town. I've come to talk to your guardians, but I want your permission."

"But—what do you want to say?"

"I want to tell them about you," said the psychiatrist. "You can't keep the secret much longer; the school will unavoidably get publicity, and they have the right to know directly from us, before that happens."

"I thought of all that. But you must promise—" he hesitated.

"They may overhear what you are saying?" guessed Peter. "Do you want me to promise I won't ask them to send you to the school?"

"Yes, that's it."

"I give you my word. I won't even mention the possibility."

"Then come."

The doctor was there within half an hour, and the formalities of his introduction were soon completed.

"I represent," said Dr. Welles, "a school for superior children which is being started on the West Coast."

"We could not think of sending Jay away," said Mrs. Curtis.

"I was not going to ask you to do so," said Dr. Welles. "I have another request to make. I have come to ask you to help us there in teaching the children."

"You must be aware that I have lost my sight," replied Mr. Curtis, "and have done no teaching for many years. I retired from that profession in order to devote full time to writing historical works, some years before my sight failed."

"I realize that, sir. But hear me out. The children I am gathering for the school are of extraordinary brilliance. Although scarcely in their teens, they have written many books and earned fame as inventors and the like, under aliases. I can prove every word I say. What we require of our teachers is a sympathy with the gifted child, and a wealth of knowledge and wisdom to share with the children. They are eager to learn; you would merely be expected to talk with them for an hour or two a day. Let me ask you, are you familiar with the name of James Vernon Worth?"

"Why, yes. His books have been read to me by my wife. But he is not a child, surely?"

"He is your son Jay."

And then Peter told them the whole story. Their incredulity was soon overcome, the situation made clear, and evidence presented—chief of all the evidence of Jay himself.

"But, you rascal," protested his guardian, "when I read the first book which you say is yours, I dictated a letter to you to be sent to the author!"

"Yes, Uncle," said Jay, "and it made me mighty proud, too."

"I'm not sure whether I ought to be proud of you, or whether you played me a shabby trick," said Mr. Curtis.

"You ought to be very proud," said Peter Welles. "It was not an unwillingness to confide in you, or that he meant to deprive you of the pleasure of knowing what he had done. These children do not wish or need adult assistance, any more than any adult author—if as much. We must never betray their pen names. Their achievements must be kept in hiding, under aliases. But they do need to learn history as you can teach it, and I have come here daring to hope that you will do for these other youngsters what you have done for Jay."

"I made him promise he wouldn't ask you to let me go," said Jay. "But please, if you do go, may I go with you?"

"The whole thing is immensely appealing," said Mr. Curtis, "but I hardly like to consider trying to teach again—"

"Of course you'll do it, John," said his wife firmly. "You can write books as well there as here. We haven't taken root in this town forever, have we? And Jay must be with those other youngsters, but he won't go without us. Salary doesn't matter—there needn't be any. I'll teach languages, too, if you like; I'm a good linguist. We want to have a big share in this wonderful thing, don't we, John?"

"Yes, we do," said Mr. Curtis. "And thank you very much for the invitation, Dr. Welles."

So that, thought Peter as the plane sped him homeward, was that. The expense of the special trip was well repaid. He had Jay, and he had two fine teachers besides. He could start out the next month to interview more prospects, without nagging worries about either Jay or Stella. More problems would arise, but they could be solved in their turn. Everything was under control. Peter could relax. He slept.

PROBLEMS

Peter Welles and Timothy Paul stood together looking at their school, and sighed contentedly.

"It's all ready," said Tim blissfully. "It's all ready, Peter, and the other children are on their way now."

"Your dream came true quickly," replied Welles, smiling down at the boy. "Three months ago it was only a faint hope in the back of our minds, and here we are, ready to launch the venture. But it is too bad we couldn't have the buildings you first planned."

"Prefabs are good enough," said Tim. "After all, we are already fourteen years old, and the group may not stay together more than five or six years. That seems like such a short time, Peter! I know you didn't have time to get more than four new boys and girls last month, but I do wish everyone could be here from the beginning. And yet the only way to do that would be to postpone the beginning."

"Perhaps it is best not to have too many to start with," answered Dr. Welles. "We may have problems."

"Elsie and Stella had problems," said Tim, "and you put them straight in no time at all."

Dr. Welles shook his head.

"Elsie and Stella were eager to be helped," he said. "Suppose we get a boy or girl who refuses to be helped?"

"You mean someone who doesn't just have a problem, but *is* a problem?" frowned Tim. "Well, you can take care of that, too, Peter. You know you can."

"Some doctors can bury their failures, as the old joke says," answered the psychiatrist, "but I can't do that, Tim. You must face the facts. We can't expect a hundred per cent success with the Wonder Children, any more than with any other group. Dr. Foxwell and I will do all we can to help them, but they may have more problems than you can realize, and some of them, by the law of averages, will be tougher problems than Elsie and Stella. For that matter, the girls seem to be on the right track now, but either of them may go off it again. Frankly, Tim, I am glad I do not have to cope with twenty or thirty completely unknown Wonder Children all dumped into my lap at once."

Tim stared at his friend, appalled.

"But surely," he cried, "they are all so intelligent! and under expert care and guidance like yours—"

Peter Welles grinned wryly.

"Don't fool yourself, Tim," he answered. "Intelligent people have at least as many problems as anyone else, and they are often worse at solving them. And when a child of superior intelligence is a problem child, Tim, we really can have problems!"

"But they'll have intelligence enough to see that something is wrong and must be set right, and to know that you can help them," protested Tim. "That's almost the whole point of bringing them here. Of course they'll be glad to be helped. But I can see your point, Peter," he added thoughtfully. "It will mean a lot of work for you, keeping track of all of us and getting the others here too. Do Max and Fred and Beth and Jay have bad problems, Peter?"

"I can't say yet," replied Dr. Welles. "I don't know enough about them. Undoubtedly they have probelms; don't we all? Beth seems extremely shy and withdrawn. Max has always been desperately poor; he has had to struggle against poverty and work very hard. Now that his game is earning a great deal of money for him, he scarcely dares to believe it! Fred, like Jay, seems to have been accepted as a bright boy, but he has lived at a series of foster homes, and is delighted to come here. Max will probably miss his grandmother; there was great family love in his home, and since his grandfather's death he has tried to support himself and his grandmother also. She cannot run the store without him, and he is frantically anxious to work out a new game, or find some other way to help her to live in comfort. But his grandmother insisted that he should come to us."

"His game must be coining money. Everybody is playing it," said Tim. "How about Beth? Did her folks mind having her leave them?"

"No, they did not. They talked a great deal about how necessary it is for her to be forced to get along with other children and to be reconditioned out of her extremely anti-social ways. They are quite sure they know all about her, and that they understand her case entirely; but they have to admit that they don't seem to be able to adjust her."

"They don't sound as if they like her very well."

"No; but I am sure we will," said Welles, smiling broadly.

"What does she do in hiding?"

"I'll let her tell you that when she is ready," replied Dr. Welles. "I am not supposed to know it myself."

Beth, as her train drew near its destination, was tense with an almost unbearable excitement. People, particularly children of her own age, had always thought that Beth Burke was stiff, unfriendly and uninterested in things. She was the silent observer at all youthful gatherings, so quiet in school and around the neighborhood that she was often forgotten. Some adults declared that she was not co-operative; others said she was of a retiring nature. Kindly or bossy women tried to push Beth into group games, but soon admitted defeat and condemned the child as hopelessly shy. Teachers obsessed with ideas about "school spirit" and "team play" shook their heads over Beth and declared that she was anti-social. She did not romp and gambol with the others, and seemed unable to work or play like the average child. And yet she was often to be seen watching other people, and had a brief, shy smile for those who did not try to coerce or coax her to join in the doings of other youngsters.

In reality, Beth longed passionately for friends and playmates her own age. But she could no more make friends among them than she could make friends with kittens or puppies; for friendship implies equality. She approached people of any age, but particularly people of her own age, with the same diffidence that timid people show toward strange dogs, the same awareness of her inability to communicate with them or to make herself understood by them.

Now she was going to meet and live with people of her own age who were on her level and could speak her language. She knew this for certain, for she had exchanged letters with Tim, Elsie and Stella, and had been interviewed by Dr. Welles. Arrangements had been made swiftly for Beth to live and work with them and with the other children who had been blessed or cursed with this frightfully high intelligence which set them apart from the rest of the world. It had all been so sudden that Beth could not, even yet, bring herself to believe it.

"Most there now, little lady," said the porter, and at Beth's little gasp and frightened glance of appeal, he smiled reassuringly. "I'll see you get off all right, bag and baggage. I'll take this suitcase now, and be back for you in five minutes. You just relax and take it easy."

Always grateful for kindness, Beth politely tried to smile at the porter, but her mouth was dry and she was trembling.

But when she stepped off the train, Beth saw Dr. Welles coming toward her with long strides, and his welcoming smile banished all her nervousness.

"You are the first to come," he said, looking down at her as they walked to his car. "You'll get a warm welcome—almost too warm, I'm afraid. Tim and Elsie and Stella are almost out of their minds with excitement."

"I am, too," confessed Beth.

"Naturally," agreed Dr. Welles. "We're all in this together now, and we are all pretty well keyed up over everything. But if we live through this day and this week and this month without dying of sheer excitement, we ought to be able to make out all right."

Beth laughed. This was a welcome change. People usually said, "Don't be scared! Nobody's going to hurt you. Push in and play like the others."

As soon as Dr. Welles had unlocked the car door, Beth hopped in, and they drove in a cozy silence through the city and up the hills to the acreage, just beyond the city limits, where a dream was coming true.

"This fencing isn't to keep you in," said Dr. Welles as the car passed through the open gate. "It's to keep outsiders out. That second house on the left is yours—on the girls' side of the street, as we say. You'll be with Miss Page and Elsie and Stella. The first building on that side is the dining hall." He stopped the car, and Beth could see faces peering out from behind the curtains of the house where she was to live. "The opposite side of the street," Dr. Welles went on, as he took her suitcase out of the car, "is for the boys, and that barn-like affair is the hall, where we'll meet for our lessons and lectures every morning at nine sharp, starting next Monday."

His hand behind her elbow propelled her up the steps; the door flew open, and Beth's shyness vanished. Miss Page's arm was about her, Tim was shaking her hand with both of his, Stella was embracing her, Elsie snatched up the suitcase, and then they were all clattering off upstairs to her room. Tim carried the suitcase, Elsie her hat, and Stella her coat. Pausing only long enough to drop these

things, the children dragged her out again and downstairs, through
the kitchen—snatching apples from a bowl as they passed, and forcing one into her hand—and out they all rushed through the back
door.

Dr. Welles and Miss Page exchanged glances of satisfaction and
let them go.

"These are my cats, and that one is Stella's," said Elsie proudly.
"We have a rule that pets must be kept caged when not in use."

Beth smiled at the mild joke.

"Do you have any pets?" asked Stella.

"No. I'd like to, though. Can we play with the cats, now?"

"Oh, we want to show you everything first," said Elsie, scratching
Silver King's head through the wires. "After, we can. Tim's cats are
back of his house, and his grandmother's cats, too."

"Then your grandparents *did* decide to travel. Good!" said Beth,
who had heard much about many things.

"Yes; they decided that it was very fortunate for them to be able
to let me live at this nice school, and set them free to travel," said
Tim, who had labored mightily to achieve this end. "Come and see
my cats. There's nothing to see at Jay's house yet."

The children cut through the side yard, where newly-planted
shrubs were deliberating whether to live or die, and stopped short at
sight of a stranger.

"Play dumb!" muttered Tim in stern warning. "Reporter!"

"Run," urged Elsie, and they all sped across the newly-laid strip of
road between the two rows of buildings, and into Tim's house, where
the others warned Beth in whispers that they had a rule which
strictly forbade letting anyone outside the group know anything
about their achievements or abilities.

"Pretend you're only about 150 I.Q.," Tim explained. "Don't tell
anyone you have ever done anything—"

"She won't," said Elsie. "She hasn't even told us, yet."

They looked expectantly at Beth, who said only, "I know. I won't
tell anybody's pen-names or anything."

"Let's sneak out back and hide," said Stella. "Dr. Welles will get
rid of that reporter fast. Nobody has come but you; he wants to see a
big crowd."

The cleared land around the houses offered scant cover, but the
children were soon out of sight among the tangle of eucalyptus, bay,

poison oak, and toyon that grew over most of the land that was their domain.

"Have you had anything else accepted, Elsie?" asked Beth, when they were safely away.

"That second novel hasn't sold yet," said Elsie, "but about half the short stuff I send out sells. Of course I don't send those I think won't sell."

"Did you send the Cataline play?" asked Stella.

"No. I like it too well; I couldn't stand having it rejected."

"We'll put it on here," suggested Tim. "Peter—Dr. Welles—says we've got to do some things as a group, not only personal projects."

"Did he mean that kind of group work?" asked Elsie. "I thought he meant something creative, that we all created."

"We have to do something we can let the public in on," said Tim, reasonably. "If we try to keep everything a dead secret we'll have reporters hiding in the clothes closets and roosting in the chimneys. As it is planned, we let them think they can walk in any time, attend classes and all. But when they come we all play dumb."

"If we present a play that Elsie wrote," said Beth, "then won't everybody know?"

"Who's to know I wrote it, stupid?" asked Elsie. "Haven't you ever heard of pen names?"

"If it has never been printed, stupid yourself," retorted Beth—and she paused to marvel at herself, for never had she been called names and called them back, as equal to equal, in all her life before—"won't somebody think it's funny we have it to present?"

"Gosh, I didn't think of that," said Tim, taken aback. "Somebody with that much sense might come."

Beth thought of a solution.

"Have it printed in the East somewhere, and advertised," she advised. "You might even sell some copies that way. It won't cost much, and you can have it copyrighted and all. And then the school can see the ad and buy copies, and it'll all be on the up and up."

"Good," cried Elsie. "I'll do that."

"But real authors never have things printed at their own expense," protested the scandalized Tim.

"I can try to sell it first, then," Elsie said, "and if it doesn't sell within a year we can print it. Meanwhile we can be getting ready to present it here, any time we want to, after it is printed."

(And thus it came about that a small experimental school on the West Coast, with a cast of fourteen-year-old amateurs, presented

Cataline two weeks before the play's record run started on Broadway with Donald Garrick as Cicero and Sidney Siddons in the title role.)

"That bell means lunch in half an hour," said Elsie. "My aunt is the cook, and my uncle does work around the grounds. Come on, Beth, and wash up."

"Do we have bells and everything?" asked Beth, uncurling her legs and getting to her feet. "All kinds of rules, just like any school?"

"Sure, we have rules," said Tim. "The doctors posted a list in each bedroom. Got to be on time for meals, can't leave the grounds after supper without special permission, or at any time without writing in the book where you are going and when you expect to be back. Things like that."

"And the unwritten rules, too, like about playing dumb, and not asking each other snoopy questions," said Stella. "Of course it's nice if people tell what they do—just among ourselves, of course."

Beth did not respond to this broad hint, and they walked three or four paces in silence before Tim said cheerfully, "We have to take care of our rooms and the houses and the yard, too. Mr. and Mrs. Waters can't do everything, and we don't want other people around, so we have to do the work ourselves, don't we? And Peter says it's good for us."

"I don't mind work like that," said Beth.

"Beth, you have to unpack after lunch, I suppose," said Tim a little jealously. "The girls will help you. Jay isn't going to be in my house, he's going to be with his guardians, the Curtises."

"Max and Fred will be along soon," said Stella sympathetically.

"Well, Tim, here's soap in your eyes!" said Elsie as they neared the house.

"Don't spare the towels!" answered Tim. "That's what we make up to say when we have to wash, Beth. Is Elsie's aunt strict about scrubbing! Wow!"

Jay arrived in mid-afternoon, and Dr. Foxwell met his train. The boy was visibly conscious of his responsibility, for he had been sent on ahead to see that the house was ready for his blind guardian, and the kennels for the dogs. Tall for his age, lanky, awkward, talkative and self-assured, Jay was in complete contrast to Beth. He talked eagerly all the way from the train to the school, and as soon as they reached it, asked to see the house.

"The others are in the hall, I think," said Dr. Foxwell. "Come and meet them all."

"I'd like to, but I'd rather see that the house and the kennels are all right, and wire my aunt that everything is ready," said Jay. "It won't take long."

"Well, there it is—the third building on this side," Dr. Foxwell said, and Jay was off on his tour of inspection.

"I see why you had Beth come first," the big doctor remarked to his colleague, who came out and joined him, "and now I see why you had Jay come second."

"Jay has not had to restrain himself very strictly," answered Dr. Welles. "Everyone thought it was the Curtises' training and example that made him so bright. Even the Curtises thought so, I suspect. When they went to adopt a child they did ask for an intelligent one, but Jay was less than a year old, and nobody could have had the least idea how bright he actually was. Yes, Jay?"

The boy, running back from the kennels, passed by the men and greeted Tim, who had come slowly out toward the men.

"I'm sorry I didn't take time to see you first of all, Tim," said Jay. "You are Tim, of course? But I had to see that things were right for Uncle. He's not at all fussy, and Aunt and I have to see to things for him. Everything is fine, and it's grand to be here. Do I sleep here tonight?"

"This is your place," said Tim, a little stiffly. He was busy trying to convince himself that there was no real reason why he should have been called the minute Jay entered the gate. He was only a boy. The school was not actually his school, either. It was only his whole life—at the moment.

"Yes, and of course I don't want to take the new off some other fellow's room," answered Jay. "But can't we share a room for a night or two, Tim? There's so much to say to each other! Shall I come in with you, or will you come in with me?"

His eagerness made Tim pause. Who was Jay, to come rushing in, first ignoring Tim and then giving orders and making plans? And Jay was almost a head taller than Tim, too. But that didn't make it Jay's school. While he hesitated, some of the eagerness evaporated from Jay's countenance.

Dr. Foxwell rushed into the little silence with, "If you'd rather not be alone in the house, Jay—"

"It isn't that," the boy stumbled. "It's only that I never had a boy for a real friend before. I thought that—that Timothy would feel the same way."

It was the "Timothy" that did the trick. Jay's letters had been brief and formal, but they had been addressed to "Tim." Now, clearly, he felt that he had overestimated his welcome, and he was so hurt and bewildered that he made formal use of Tim's full first name. The smaller boy jumped forward.

"I'll come here, of course," cried Tim. "Then Dr. Welles can't bang on the walls for us to shut up and go to sleep. Right after supper I'll move in. Come now and meet the girls."

It was strictly against the printed rules for children to visit one another's rooms after bedtime, but neither doctor said a word.

The girls were in the hall.

"They've probably not switched on the recording wire," remarked Tim, "but don't say you weren't warned. They might think this was a historical occasion."

"You can keep a record of what goes on here?" Jay was delighted. "Can we all play it back and listen whenever we like?"

"Yes, and that way we can miss lectures if we want to," answered Tim. "It will come in handy. It's only this room that is wired—and the doctors' offices; but their records are private, of course."

"Have you read all the rules?" Stella asked when Jay had been introduced.

"Yes, and I know the unwritten rules too," Jay replied. "But I think it is silly that we're not to ask one another about our work. I should think we would be glad we have somebody to tell. And we ought to discuss plans for future work, too."

"That's fine if you want to do it," Tim said, "but we did not think we ought to make people tell, or to expect them to if they would rather not. So it's the rule that nobody has to tell unless he wants to. And we don't tell about each other, unless we know it's all right. Maybe something isn't ripe to tell, even."

"Well, I don't care if all the gang knows I am James Vernon Worth," Jay said, "and I have brought all my books along for the school library. Oh, that's where the books go, along the walls in here. I'll bring mine over as soon as I unpack. If it is against the rules, I won't ask questions, but I would very much like to see what all of you have done."

"We have a code," said Tim. "If you don't care who in the group —that includes the grownups too—knows you have written something, you put a star in the margin and write your real initials beside it. And if you find such a mark you can call it to the attention of any of the group. My stuff, and Stella's and Elsie's, is scattered all through here."

"And Beth's?"

"Don't you say a word unless you want to, Beth," said Elsie quickly.

Beth stood up and walked quietly across the room. She took a newspaper from the table and turned to the comics; and there beside all America's favorite comic strip, she drew a small, neat star and wrote her initials.

"Beth! You're the Scatterlees!" shrieked Elsie.

"Yes," said Beth. "I didn't tell Dr. Welles, but I think he knows. My family told him I could draw—everybody knows that—and a little later someone mentioned that it was funny how often the Scatterlees strip had something in it that had happened around our neighborhood. That's always the way in comic strips of the true-to-life type, you know. But I smiled to myself and Dr. Welles looked at me, you know the way he does—"

"I know," said Stella.

"I thought then that he guessed. But nobody ever used to look at me, and that is why I was careless about smiling."

"You meant for him to see it," said Tim.

Beth looked startled for a moment, then reflective, and then began to laugh.

"Why—yes, I think I did!" she said.

"How did you start doing the strip?" asked Jay, intensely interested.

"I was so lonely," answered Beth, simply. "All I had was grandparents, and the only way I could have brothers and sisters and young parents and aunts and uncles and cousins was to dream them up. By the time I found out I could draw, I had been living with the whole family for years in my mind. It was easy enough to work out a strip. I had the seven children to take turns with, and some ideas were good for a day and others for a week or two, and some could keep recurring with variations. And then I began to work in the neighbors and the boarder, Mimi O'Graph, and all—I don't think I'll ever run out of material. I listened and watched all the time for things to use, and I have several notebooks full, all indexed. There is always someone to pin things on. When I was standing on the sidelines and watching other people, I was really living with the Scatterlees. I have hardly scratched the surface of the material I have on hand."

"What are you worrying about, then?" asked Tim.

"Worrying?"

"You know you must be, or you wouldn't keep telling us how much you have on hand to work with."

Beth took a swift step toward him.

"Oh, you do understand!" she cried, and, looking about her, she saw the same understanding reflected in the other faces. "I'm afraid I'll be so happy here that I won't need the Scatterlees. And I hate to think of having them die."

Dr. Welles, who had just entered, had heard.

"You will always need to be creating, Beth," he said. "And we hope that the process of creating the Scatterlees will never stop. The reality you have breathed into them, because of your need for them to be alive to you, has almost brought them to have an independent existence."

"If you stop you'll be a murderer, and you ought to be executed!" Elsie said vehemently.

"I'd feel like one, too," said Beth.

"I feel rather like some sort of villain myself," Dr. Welles said. "But Jay and Beth haven't unpacked, and the rest of you have chores to do, Fred and Max will be here tomorrow. This will mean extra effort on all our parts until they grow used to us. So suppose you see how much you can get done today that has to be done."

Fred and Max arrived almost simultaneously the next day, one from the east and the other from the north. The first demand Fred made was to see the laboratory.

"I want to try to synthesize chitin," said Fred.

"What on earth is that?" asked Stella.

"Beetles," ventured Elsie. "I'm sure it is something about beetles."

"That's it; the hard case or outer shell of a beetle. It's the strongest stuff for its weight and thickness, and can stand so much vibration, that if it could be made synthetically for airplanes and rocket ships—"

"Just a minute, Fred!" said Dr. Foxwell, somewhat taken aback. "Listen, kids. One of the rules, one of the strictest of all the rules, is that nobody is to do any experimenting without the approval of Mr. Gerrold. No rocket ships—no space ships—no blowing up the whole place and everybody with it!"

"When is Mr. Gerrold coming, then? And what is he like?" asked Fred.

"He is a young man in his early twenties," answered Dr. Welles, "and something of a bright boy himself. He wanted to teach, but he doesn't like what Elsie used to call 'stupid people' and he wanted some time and money for research. I've known him for ten years, so I asked him to join us. His orders, with which he is in hearty agreement, are to let you do almost anything you like, but to see that you remain alive and intact. It is his responsibility to oversee everything that could possibly be dangerous, and he—not you—is to be the judge of that."

"It might be rather hard for the surviving stockholders to explain why your goings-on were allowed to become goings-up," explained Dr. Foxwell.

"He's sort of young, isn't he?" said Jay doubtfully.

Dr. Foxwell coughed so violently that Tim looked suspicous. The big doctor took a box of coughdrops out of his pocket and popped one into his mouth. Elsie caught his eye and grinned.

"Mr. Gerrold has done four years of graduate work in the physical sciences," Dr. Welles was saying, "and I am quite sure that he is far ahead of all my Wonder Children in laboratory work and experimentation. We gave up Tim's idea of separate laboratories and chose to have one large laboratory in common, so that Mr. Gerrold can more easily keep track of all that goes on. No one is to interfere with the work of anyone else, or even to examine it without permission. Please keep these rules and explain them to newcomers."

"Does he have to approve before I can start work? When is he coming?" asked Fred. His brow carried wrinkles of annoyance.

"He will be here on Monday. Yes, you must wait for his approval," Dr. Welles said.

"Well, does he have to approve before I start what I want to do?" Elsie asked. "It can't possibly be dangerous."

"What is it?"

"Auntie is keeping hens, and there are double-yolked eggs almost every day. I'm going to build an incubator, and hatch them, as soon as I can. That's all right, isn't it? Tim and I thought Dr. Foxwell would help us take the X-ray photos."

"But why?" asked Stella.

"Don't you think teratology is awfully interesting?" Elsie seemed to think that settled the matter. The doctors exchanged glances, and Dr. Foxwell offered Dr. Welles a coughdrop.

"This is the first I have heard of the matter," said the big doctor, "but I'll make myself responsible for the X-ray work, Dr. Welles."

"What do you think of Fred?" Dr. Foxwell asked Peter Welles later.

"I don't know," Welles admitted. "I must confess he worries me a little—that aggressiveness and self-assurance he displays outwardly may indicate deep basic insecurity. On the other hand, they may merely be disguised bashfulness in a new situation, and may disappear in a few days, as he becomes accustomed to the other children. Unfortunately, there is no way of knowing except by waiting to see."

"He was raised in a series of homes, wasn't he?" Dr. Foxwell said.

"Yes. When his parents died the usual lingering death of radiation sickness, two years after the Helium City blast, the state paid for his care with various private families. He picked up a fine knowledge of the sciences along the way, but apparently they are his only interest. I am afraid that he may regard the school as simply some sort of benevolent institution set up to operate for his benefit, with no effort on his part required in return. Certainly, having lived under these conditions, he may feel that the only reason people felt any interest in him was because of the money the state paid them."

Within a fortnight, things at the school had fallen into a routine. Officially, the children studied first year algebra, literature, English grammar and composition, and elementary social science. They were allowed to start a language also, and, since they were known to be superior children, their program was enriched by allowing them to learn any musical instrument of their choice, and to read more widely than children of fourteen usually do. They wrote frequent reports on this work, and these were kept in a notebook for the benefit of reporters and casual visitors.

Actually, the children gathered in the school hall every morning at nine, and spent three hours listening to the televised University Extension courses. In this year, 1973, the courses were in their third year. For three days a week, half-hour courses were given in astronomy, physics, psychology, biology, and inorganic and organic chemistry. On the other three days of the week, the lectures were on Renaissance art, economics, economic geography, European history, United States history, and philosophy.

The theory was that a student could choose from four to six of these courses, study at home, and by attending the yearly examinations at the University could obtain credit for the subjects. Later, more courses would be broadcast. Eventually a student could complete the entire undergraduate curriculum without ever entering a classroom. Mathematics, however, involved so much written work that it was still taught by correspondence courses only. Languages were taught by a combination of phonograph records and correspondence courses.

The Wonder Children studied such subjects as they chose. Elsie, for example, was struggling with analytical geometry.

After lunch, the children were free to work on their private projects. The laboratory was the chief attraction for some. Others retired to their rooms and wrote. The care of pets and the daily chores took considerable time, and games were not by any means omitted.

"At any rate we'll never have to worry about keeping them busy," remarked Miss Page. "They have more to do than they have time for. Being together is a great stimulus for them, too. Do they actually listen to all those courses?"

"No, of course not," answered Mr. Gerrold. "Most of them know the work already, and listen only for review, if and when they choose to do so."

Mr. Curtis, the blind historian, gathered the children together at some hour convenient to all, and talked to them about history, recommending books for them to read. They all liked the blind man who, being unable to see that they were mere children, constantly forgot their tender years and talked to them as if they were completely mature adults. It was his hope that each one of them would write some work based on history—a historical novel, a biography, perhaps a drama or a textbook—and several had already chosen a subject and started to gather notes for it.

That midnight, there was a great commotion in the yard.

"Hey!" shouted Max from his window. "What's up?"

"The dogs are all out," Jay shouted back. "I must have left the pens unhooked. Come help!"

Max and the other boys hastily pulled on pants, sweaters, and shoes, and hurried outside.

The darkness was a nightmare of yelping, scurrying shapes. Grigio, Mr. Curtis's guide dog, was the only one not at large. Guarda and her six pups, and Companion and her seven pups were all enjoying themselves hugely in a figure-eight race which began, as far as it had a beginning, at the cat-cages behind Tim's house, past the north side of the boys' house, across the road, past the south side of the girls' house, around the cat-cages where Elsie's and Stella's pets were housed, back past the north side of the girls' house, across the road, past the south side of the boys' house, and around Tim's cat-cages again. The cats were voicing their disapproval of this visitation in no uncertain terms.

The more the boys tried to catch the galloping half-grown puppies, the wilder became the scene. Jay and his aunt could not make themselves heard as they shouted commands to the dogs. The pups were still untrained, and although Mrs. Curtis and Jay tried to concentrate on catching the mother dogs, Guarda and Companion had caught the spirit of the occasion and were not willing to obey.

Elsie's uncle came hurrying out with a box in his arms.

"Bones!" he called. "I got bones. Maybe if you boys quit yelling and running around, we can get the dogs in."

"Good," said Mrs. Curtis. "Stand still, everybody—the more we chase them the worse they get. Stand here under the floodlight. Don't let go of the bones; try to lure the dogs back to their yards."

It was far from simple, but at last it was accomplished.

"You really must be more careful about hooking the doors of the pens, Jay," said Mrs. Curtis when the door was at last fastened on the pups.

"Aunty, I did fasten it," said Jay. "I remember shaking the door to make sure, because it was open one day last week, and two of Guarda's pups got out. That time I didn't see how I could have been so careless."

"Funny things happen," said Tim, yawning. "I was so sure I always lock my cats up, but my big Persian tom got out yesterday."

"Let's go to bed," said Mrs. Curtis wearily. "Thank you for the bones, Mr. Waters."

During the evenings, Dr. Welles and Dr. Foxwell sometimes listened to the wire recordings which had been made of the children's conversations in the school hall before lectures.

"Look, this doesn't make sense," said Elsie's voice.

"What doesn't?" asked Tim.

"This math. It says four over zero equals infinity."

"That's right." This sounded like Max.

"How can it be? Four over zero means four divided by zero. If you divide by nothing you don't divide at all. The answer ought to be four."

Several voices tried to answer her, but the doctors could not understand. Nor could Elsie, apparently, for her voice cut through the hubbub.

"Hey! One at a time. What did you say, Tim?"

"I said that's the right answer. It's a convention."

"You mean they just made up the answer and said it had to be right? How can you do things like that?"

"It is right. Like saying any number to the zero power is one."

"Holy cow! How can you use stuff like that in equations and have them come out right?"

"It works out right. That's how we know it is right."

"You mean people build bridges and fly airplanes with information like that? I don't get it."

"You've got the wrong idea, Elsie." This was Max again. "It isn't four divided by nothing. Zero isn't nothing. Zero is zero."

"Well, if it isn't nothing, I'd like to know what it is."

"It's zero, that's what it is. You want to read it this way: the ratio of four to zero."

"Oh! And what does that mean—if anything? You mean four is infinitely bigger than zero? There's no sense to that either."

"Yes, there is," Max said hotly.

"No. There isn't. Four isn't infinitely more than nothing. It's only four more. If I had no money, and then got four dollars, would I be infinitely wealthy?"

"I said the ratio, Elsie."

"Well, the ratio, then. Compared to nothing, four is still four. It isn't infinity."

"Listen, you," said another voice. "Save your breath. You'll never explain it so she can get it."

"If it made sense, Fred, they could," Elsie interjected.

"There must be some way to explain it," said Tim stubbornly. "The ratio—"

"I guess I know what ratio means," said Elsie tartly. "Ratio means relationship. It means one divided by the other. Tell me, what's zero divided by four?"

"Zero," chorused the boys.

"Well, that's all right. Nothing is still nothing, whatever you divide it by. But four not divided at all—"

"Say, Elsie, can't you shut up?" broke in a girl's voice. "I've got this page to finish writing before the program starts."

For a few moments the tape recorded only the usual small sounds of a room in which several people were gathered. Then the first words of the University lecturer in organic chemistry were heard.

"Today we are going to study esters," said the professor slowly.

"An ester is very easy to understand. You recall from your inorganic chemistry courses that when a base and an acid interact, a salt is formed. Now, when an organic acid and an organic base interact, the result is an ester. An ester is an organic salt. I repeat, an ester is an organic salt."

"Oh, I see!" shouted Elsie. "Just like Lot's wife!"

Tumult, and amid it the voice of Stella crying out, "Was that really her name?" Then, pandemonium.

The next morning, Elsie came late to breakfast. She went straight to Tim and Max, who were sitting together.

"I'm sorry I was so stupid yesterday," said Elsie. "I've got it all straight now. Max was right; I wasn't reading it the right way, or I would have understood immediately. It isn't four divided by zero, or the ratio of four to zero, it's four *over* zero. Then of course anyone can see the answer is infinity, because—" she looked around to make sure everyone was listening—"because if there's nothing under the four to exert a gravitational attraction on it, of course it goes into a free fall forever, all the way to infinity."

Peter Welles was sorry he could not watch all the faces at once. Some of the listeners caught on immediately and became helpless with mirth. Stella, who was not mathematical, looked bewildered; Max, who took his math seriously, looked with alarm at Elsie until he saw that she was teasing him, and Fred snorted, "She thinks she's smart," and went on with his breakfast.

Dr. Welles felt obliged to read Elsie a little lecture, later on in private, about showing off. But his heart was not in it.

"I really didn't understand about that old math," pleaded Elsie. "And then when I thought of that other way to put it, it was so funny. Besides, now none of us will ever forget the right answer."

"You ought to make an effort to understand it, not to remember the right answer mechanically by a jest."

"Oh, I do understand it," replied Elsie. "I thought that out afterwards. Six over two is three, because it takes three twos to make a six. But how many zeros make a four? An infinite number, of course."

"And Lot's wife?"

Elsie giggled.

"That just popped out," she said. "I don't think anything else can ever be so apt again—do you?"

"Suppose you wait for something equally good before you ruin the whole lecture again," said Peter, laughing in spite of himself.

During the third week of the school's existence, a newspaper was proposed.

"We can't have one," was Tim's opinion. "We have to play dumb. What's the use of a newspaper we can't show?"

"We have to show something," said Max. "Print one we can show. We have to send things home, and all."

"It won't be much fun to write a stupid paper," grumbled Elsie.

"In a way, it might," mused Fred, and some of the children looked brighter as they considered this idea.

"We can put in what people know about us," Beth agreed.

"Tim's cats and Jay's dogs—after all, Tim has a good breeding experiment to write up and Jay trains seeing-eye dogs—and some of the book reviews and some news items about the trips we take and things like that."

"We could use some of the stuff we wrote long ago that nobody would print," said Tim.

"And some of Stella's poems," Fred said maliciously. "They would be just the thing to confuse outsiders."

Beth came quickly to the rescue with, "I'll draw a cartoon for each issue. Everybody knows I can draw."

"Once in a while we could put in something good," said Elsie. "Is it to be a literary paper or a newspaper?"

After considerable discussion it was voted that the paper was to contain news primarily. Max was to be Editor-in-Chief, and the children were to take turns mimeographing it. They would allow a maximum of one page per pupil, including at least one full page of news notes.

"What shall we call it?" asked Elsie.

"Call it 'Not-A-New,'" proposed Tim. "That is a hint to all of us not to put anything really new in it."

"This school hasn't any name yet, has it?" asked Stella. "We ought to have one. Tim?"

"I haven't been able to think of a good one," confessed Tim. "Maybe some of you can think of one. I did think we might call it the A.A.A. school for Aristotle, Albert and Aquinas, but I don't like that very much."

"It's a horrid name," said Stella candidly.

"Yes, but it is fitting. Three such great thinkers, you know."

"Oh, if it is fitting," said Fred, "by all means use it. If the shoe fits, put it on. But I always thought triple A was as narrow as they come."

The children all roared with laughter.

"Fred is clever," said Tim, a little unwillingly, to Elsie.

"It was a terrible name, you must admit," said Elsie. "You'd better just choose one of the men and name the school for him."

"Oh, we may think of a good name," said Max. "Let it ride for a while. Who is going to hand in something for this newspaper? We want it out this Saturday, don't we?"

Among the things which did not appear in "Not-A-New" was Max's earnest effort to instruct Elsie further in mathematics. Max was a brilliant mathematician, and he greatly admired Elsie, in whom he had quickly discerned a different type of brilliance. At lunch time a few days after he and Tim had so notably failed to make Elsie understand about zero, Max, not knowing that Elsie had arrived at the explanation, brought up the matter again.

"See here, Elsie. Zero is infinitesimal."

"No, it isn't. It's nothing."

"That's the joker. If you put four over zero, the zero becomes something infinitesimal in comparison."

"That doesn't make sense!" cried Elsie.

"It does," said Max, while everyone listened hopefully. "Man is infinitesimal; in comparison with God, man is nothing."

"No, he isn't," shouted Elsie. "God didn't make nothing! He left that for the Arabs!"

"Got you there, Max," cried Tim in delight, and Dr. Foxwell was obliged to pound to table and call for quiet, while the unfortunate Beth, who had been drinking her milk as Elsie spoke, mopped herself as dry as she could with several proffered napkins, but refused to leave the room for fear she might miss something.

Elsie's vehement whisperings were drowned out by a heated conversation at the other end of the table where Fred and a new boy, Giles Bradley, were discussing absolute zero, without getting anywhere. It soon developed that Fred had been talking about mathematical absolute zero, while Giles, not unnaturally, had taken him to refer to temperature. Stella and Beth caught at the word and began a discussion of the Absolute in philosophy, in which Tim and Jay promptly took part, opposed by Fred who maintained that there were no absolutes at all.

Dr. Foxwell pounded in vain as the discussion grew heated, and then marched into the hallway and rang the dinnerbell.

"Quiet, please," he begged. "Conversation during meals should be non-controversial. The next child to say more than 'Please pass the salt' will leave the room."

The children saw the point and subsided.

"Suppose each of you prepares and submits to me an essay on some aspect of the Absolute or some correct use of the word," said Peter Welles. "We'll file the papers and, later, have a debate on the subject. That way the discussion will be kept orderly. Be sure to define all your terms clearly."

The adults in charge had set aside one evening a week for a meeting. This was sometimes postponed when Dr. Welles was out of town interviewing one of the Wonder Children. Upon his return from such a trip he always called a meeting and was told what had happened during his absence.

"I wonder whether there are any generalizations about these children that we can make as yet," suggested Mrs. Curtis on one such occasion. "We have had six weeks with them. Are they alike in any ways?"

"Except for their extremely high intelligence, I would say no," said Dr. Foxwell. "Those we have so far are by no means of the same psychological type, and those we expect to get, by the time we have all of them, will probably represent all the types there are."

"Some of them have one-sided development," commented Mr. Gerrold. "All of them need much more laboratory work. This is their most serious lack. Some of them have a good reading knowledge of the sciences, but others have wasted far too much time on literature, languages, history and the like."

Mr. Curtis said, "All scientific knowledge is of no importance whatever in comparison to the history of what human beings have done with their scientific knowledge, young man. History contains all knowledge, for it shows us what men do with their knowledge. Human nature in action, that is the chief thing."

"Pardon me, sir," said the young man stiffly, "I do not agree with you. This is a scientific age. What was done in the past, under very different conditions, concerns us little today."

"Human nature does not change," said Mr. Curtis. "Had the scientists during the Second World War had the most elementary knowledge of history, they would have known better than to turn the bomb loose upon the world."

"You can say that? Remember what produced these Wonder Children!" said Mr. Gerrold.

"An accident produced them, or a miracle," said the historian. "Nothing else but evil has come of the bomb. Russia would have used it against the whole world had not Stalin's death come when it did. We cannot always depend upon Providence to save us from ourselves. It happened before—in the days when the whole of civilization was menaced by the Tartar hordes—that the death of one man saved the world from destruction. However, this is all idle argument. Dr. Welles is in charge of the school, Mr. Gerrold, and we must defer to his opinion."

"He might say we should teach nothing but psychology and psychiatry," said Dr. Foxwell. "I might think medicine is the most important of all. But as a physician I would recommend a well-balanced diet. There is something in what Mr. Gerrold says; the worst deficiencies should be remedied, and the children are weak in laboratory technique and applied science. They have been able to study the humanities on their own."

"Certainly they should know some history," said young Mr. Gerrold politely.

"Certainly they must know some science," replied the blind historian with equal courtesy.

"Actually, there seems to be little danger of over-specialization," said Dr. Welles. "All of the children have wide interests, and those who were ignorant about a special field, or had no great interest in it, catch this interest from the others, or are in some way challenged by the greater knowledge of the others. As their teachers, I think we should encourage this tendency as much as possible. We must make them into well-balanced people. We cannot control their ultimate destinies, but all their interests and functions should be developed."

"How well do they work together?" asked Mr. Curtis.

"They like being together," said Miss Page, "but they would resent being organized."

"They work together without tub-thumping and flag-waving," agreed Dr. Foxwell. "But what would happen if we tried to make them co-operative according to the usual school standards?"

" 'Co-operation,' " quoted Miss Page sarcastically, " 'means doing what I tell you to do, and doing it quick.' I wouldn't dare take that line with them. Even ordinary children won't stand for it."

"You always did play fair, Pagey," said Peter Welles.

"I do not understand," said Mr. Curtis. "Aren't the children required to keep the rules?"

"Certainly they are. We were referring to the type of school which insists that all children must drop all of their own interests and activities to take part in something that the school has decided they should do; the type that insists all pupils must attend all ball games or that everyone must be at all the dances. Miss Page's policy has always been that rules must be obeyed, otherwise the children were free; no rhetoric, tear-jerking or prestidigitation about a child's amusements in his spare time."

"What, no 'school spirit'?" grinned Mr. Gerrold.

Miss Page smiled upon him.

"I was the girl who sold two stories to real magazines during the summer before my senior year in high school," she said. "During my senior year I gave all my stories and most of my spare time to the school paper. I also did all the write-ups that nobody else wanted to do for the year book. But I graduated with high honors instead of highest honors, and I found out why. It seems I was anti-social and had no school spirit. I didn't go to any of the ball games and I wasn't at the Senior Prom."

"Why weren't you?" asked Mr. Gerrold.

"I'd rather play ball than watch it," said Miss Page. "As for the Prom—no boy asked me."

There was a brief silence, and then Dr. Foxwell cleared his throat and spoke.

"I must mention an important and rather alarming fact," he said. "We have had several mean tricks played lately. I think we must face this fact and find out which child is guilty of them."

There was a silence, and the adults looked uneasily at one another.

"What has been going on?" asked Dr. Welles and Mr. Curtis together.

"The dogs have been let out twice so far," said Dr. Foxwell, "and on another occasion a puppy was found in the chicken pen. Mr. Waters was furious."

"That sounds as if it might be Elsie," said Mr. Curtis. "She seems to have very little natural affection for her aunt and uncle."

"It was her own suggestion that they be asked to come here," said Dr. Foxwell.

"She has such a violent nature at times," said Mr. Gerrold.

"She is trying to repress that violence," said Mrs. Curtis thoughtfully. "She may be bursting out in these little ways. There is such a thing as trying too hard to be good."

"I should rather expect her to blow up like a volcano, so that windows would shatter in all directions," answered Miss Page. "I would say—it is only my opinion, of course—that Elsie has enough outlet for her surplus energy without practical joking of this sort. There were other tricks also. On two occasions, one of Tim's cats was let out. And—"

"It is unlikely to have been Beth," said Dr. Foxwell. "One of the tricks was turned against her. It seems she was late with her Scatterlees strip, and worked all evening on it, saying it must go off by air mail the next day to meet the deadline. She left the material in the mail bag that night, stamped and ready. One of the boys put the mail bag in my car the next morning and I put all the stuff down the chute in the main post office, as I always do, without noticing what was going out that day. Two days later, Mrs. Waters, in cleaning the room, found the material behind a bookcase in the girl's house. We sent it off special delivery, and the strip was omitted only one day. But we fear that the person who played that trick hoped that the loss would not be discovered. They all know we can't be reached by telegram, since nobody knows who Beth is."

"If tricks were also played against Tim and Jay, it is not likely they are guilty," said Mr. Gerrold, "unless it was a means of diverting suspicion."

"I trust Tim absolutely," said Dr. Welles.

"It is certainly not Jay," said Mr. Curtis.

"It might be Stella," said Dr. Foxwell, "if she resents the other children for some reason. Almost any child might be jealous of all the others for merely existing at all. Has Stella ever recovered from the shock of finding out that there are other children as bright as she?"

"I would have said she had," said Dr. Welles. "But she loves mystery and magic. She might be pretending she is a witch or a poltergeist, or something of that sort. She is deficient in humor, and might think this sort of thing is funny, or be trying to be funny without knowing how."

"What about Max? That game of his—"

"Please describe the game," said Mr. Curtis.

"Oh, you go around the board, as in the old Monopoly game," said Miss Page. "Each time around, you collect a salary. If you land on a blue space, you get a boy; if on a pink space, a girl. You get a pink or a blue card, to keep track of your family. Other squares direct you to buy a dress for each girl, a suit for each boy, shoes for the whole family, pay rent, pay the grocery bill—that is decided by throwing the dice again and reading the amount you are to pay for groceries—and things of that sort. There is a card which gets you a raise in pay. Another square tells you to draw a What Luck card; it may be good or bad—a legacy, a doctor bill, twins, the purchase of a new car or other expensive items. These can sometimes be done on time payments."

"A complicated game," murmured Dr. Foxwell.

"It's great fun," said Miss Page. "The first time I played it, I accumulated seventeen children, and then got 'shoes for each child' three rounds in succession."

"It sounds rather anti-social to me," observed Mr. Curtis. "One would think it teaches the lesson that a family is too great an expense."

"Max has always been poor, and conscious of his poverty."

"Yes," said Dr. Welles, "but perhaps since he has made so much money out of his game, he feels contented. I know he invented the game before he came here, so even if he had some such feeling then, he may not have it now. The tricks occurred here. What reason would he have to persecute the other children?"

"And Fred?" asked Mr. Curtis. "He seems to be entirely above such doings."

"Surely, he of all boys can see how petty and silly such tricks are," said Mr. Gerrold, who had found an avid disciple in Fred, and consequently liked the boy.

"All of them have sufficient intelligence to see that," said Dr. Foxwell. "Dr. Welles, what do you think?"

"I would say nothing to any of the children about these things, except possibly Tim; but we must all keep watch. I shall not go on any more trips, or bring other children here, until we clear this matter up or until the tricks have ceased. There might be something serious to follow," Welles said, his mind still digesting most of this disquieting information.

"You don't think it is dangerous, do you?" exclaimed Mrs. Curtis. "The tricks are not of any importance, are they? Not nice, of course, but not dangerous."

"I think it is too soon to say. However," said Dr. Welles, "let us get this problem settled before we admit any more students."

A day or two later, Miss Page, sitting by her window during the afternoon, heard a racket break out in the side yard.

"Did you hear what Elsie said?" Stella was squealing. "An elderly man who used to be a teacher at some junior college came wandering in today, and he got hold of Elsie and me and started preaching to us, and he was talking about that essay on 'Climates of Opinion,' you know the one—"

"Yes, I read that," said Fred and Max.

"And he asked if we had read it, and when we said we had, he asked if we could explain what it teaches. And Elsie looked up at him so sweetly and said, 'Yes, sir, it teaches that on a rainy day we should all be drips.' "

There was a howl of joy from the children.

"I wish I had been there," said Beth.

"He was an awful old bore," said Stella. "You were lucky. Elsie and I had to show him around and listen to him for almost an hour."

"Elsie shouldn't have said that," said Fred. "She broke the rule about playing dumb. And she's always showing off, anyhow."

"He was too dumb to get it," said Stella.

"I wouldn't call that breaking the rule," said Tim. "She didn't tell what we wrote, or give away pen names or anything. After all, we can make a bright remark once in a while, I should think. This isn't a school for feeble-minded."

"Oh, you think everything she does is perfect!" Fred exclaimed.

"I do not," said Tim.

"And I think she ought to be disciplined."

"You just try," warned Tim.

"Try and stop me, and I'll knock you base over apex," said Fred.

"I'll knock you through an epicycle and two trochids," retorted Tim.

Miss Page, behind the window-curtains, made no sound.

"I'll knock you into a cocked hat!" Fred shouted triumphantly.

"That's a cliché," Stella observed scornfully.

"It is not," Fred contradicted. "It's a mathematical curve."

"What shape is it?" asked Elsie.

"I'll show you," Fred said, eager to illustrate his wit. And in no time at all the squabble was forgotten as all the children were drawing all manner of paths in the dust, and disputing amiably about the best locus to knock a fellow through or into, and also as to the origin of the cliché that Fred had been accused of using. They all streamed off in search of *Familiar Quotations* after a time, and Miss Page was free to jot down all that she could remember.

When she reported this to the other grownups, Mr. Gerrold had a suggestion to make.

"I have often thought we ought to have the recording tape in more places," he said.

"We can't listen in on all outdoors," said Mrs. Curtis.

."No, but we could wire the houses and—oh, I suppose it would cost a fortune." Then Mr. Gerrold's face brightened. "We could rig the tape in the hall so that it would go on whenever anyone went in."

"Is it fair to spy on them?" asked Miss Page coldly.

"Why not?" asked Dr. Foxwell. "They turn the tape on themselves the first thing every morning, and they know we listen to it sometimes. They know we hover around and listen behind curtains whenever we get a chance, too. As a group, they are not supposed to have any secrets from us."

"I agree with Dr. Foxwell," said Dr. Welles. "To set up wires all over the place, in houses and bedrooms, to spy on private conversations between two of the children, would be intolerable. But when they gather for recreation in the hall, which is open to all of us at all times, what is the harm in listening? We'd hear some wonderful things. Take the conversation just reported. There was nothing in it for them to hide, and yet none of them would have bothered to repeat any of it to us."

"Suppose I rig it in connection with the light switch," said Mr. Gerrold. "When the light is on, the tape will record. When the light goes off, the recording will stop."

The others agreed to this, and Mr. Gerrold made the required adjustment that same night.

Tim switched on the lights as he led the way into the hall.

"—like hitting yourself on the head with a hammer," Fred was saying. "The minute you say 'that's obvious' you stop thinking."

"That's all right if you have done the thinking first," said Jay. "Who wants to go on thinking about the same one thing forever? I like to get a few things settled, myself. Platitudes are true, of course. They are the concentrated, agreed-upon truths of all the ages."

"Not all of them," Stella disagreed.

"By definition," said Max loftily, "a platitude is a *truth* we have all heard about a million times. Sometimes people misunderstand or misapply one, of course."

"Isn't it surprising how often we work something all out and find, when we come to distill the essence, that we have a platitude for the end-product?" said Tim.

Fred snorted.

"I see what you mean, though," said Elsie. "You, Tim, and Fred, too. We feel sort of cheated to discover what everybody knows and has always been telling us. But it's something to have waked up to it, to know what it means and how true it is. And all the best thinking begins after you have come to realize that some trite truths especially are true."

The others made interrogative noises.

"You just have to take two statements that are both true, but that don't seem to go together," explained Elsie, "and think about both of them. Then you really get somewhere."

"You mean like 'Light behaves like particles' and 'Light behaves like a wave'?" asked Max.

"That's the idea."

"Or like 'I have free will' and 'God is all-powerful'?" said Jay.

"Who says those things are true, Jay?"

"I do, Fred, and if you give me time I'll prove them," said Jay. "Shall I begin now?"

"Oh, shut up," advised Max. "Don't go into all that now. It'll take more time than we've got before the meeting to get any sense into Fred's head."

"Somebody told him it was obvious that materialism is true, and he stopped thinking about it," said Giles.

"That isn't a platitude; that's all wrong, Fred. But cheer up; some day you'll know truth from its opposite," said Elsie with exaggerated sweetness.

"I can prove—"

"Nobody ever bothered to tell Fred how hard it is to prove a negative," said Beth. "Especially when it isn't true."

"Oh, quit baiting him!" pleaded Tim. "Some of us had a head start on Fred; we were taught right. Better get caught up on what we're behind on, ourselves. Aren't the others coming? We've got to get started. While the grownups are holding their meeting is the best time for us to have ours."

"Make a circle of chairs, so we can all see each other," suggested Giles, and by the time this was done, the others had arrived.

"I don't think we ought to wait any longer to track down all the rest of the group," said Tim, "before we begin to do what I hope we'll all want to do. There are a few more yet to come, and others to be located. But we are all here for a purpose and I think we ought to express that purpose and get to work on it. There are several purposes really. At first it was my idea that we should get together for companionship, which none of us could find, either with adults or with children. Then I found that some of us had to be set free, so we could do our best work, or so we could accomplish anything at all. The doctors could help us, and the teachers could help some, and I hoped we could all help each other. Some of us were locked up physically, others had no scope for their activities, and some of us were confused mentally or psychologically. Stella won't mind if I refer to her here. Stella, will you tell us all what you told me last week?"

"Yes, I want to. My idea of myself was all confused and wrong. I had worked out a sort of explanation, but when I met the rest of you I knew I might be wrong, so I had a talk with Dr. Welles and now I hope I am on the right track. But it was being here and knowing you that was the real help, because it got me to think I might be wrong. Dr. Welles said I had worked it out all very intelligently, but without sufficient knowledge of facts, so it all had to be scrapped. And to those of you who were all taking cracks at Fred a while ago, I'd like to say, give him time and treat him decently, because before I came here I had a great deal less sense than he has."

This direct hit at the boy who had been her chief tormentor raised a shout from all the others.

"Thanks," said Fred loudly. "May I answer that, Mr. Chairman?"

"Please, Fred, not right now," said Tim. "We can all dish it out and we can all take it. But we're here to get on with some business."

"Right," said Fred, subsiding.

"So I just wanted to bring out that we're all here to help and to be helped, and the grownups are ready to help us any way they can. The grown people are indispensable; they have the long experience, the training and practice and knowledge. But so many other things come up. For example, the question Beth and some of the rest of us were discussing with Dr. Welles last week: Why do so many bright children level out as they grow up? Does it have to happen to us? When we are grown shall we be hardly any brighter than other people? What can we do about that?"

There is a seriousness in children of which adults are seldom capable. These children, for all their intelligence, could still be completely serious when they were deeply interested. No cynicism, no self consciousness, no pose interrupted their earnestness as they considered this question.

"Max?"

"I think those others threw away their superiority for the sake of human companionship, out of mixture of despair and loneliness," said Max.

"Some of them specialized too much," said Giles. "Like Darwin; he threw away all music and poetry and all the arts, to concentrate on his work. When you once start to narrow your mind, it keeps on narrowing."

There was a burst of applause at this.

"We're starting a folder of papers about it," said Tim. "And there's a collection about the Absolutes, too. Well, that made me think of a plan for the group." Tim cleared his throat, squared his shoulders, and went on. "I think we've got to do something big. Not only our individual projects and our personal contributions, not only in developing each individual to his fullest, but also something as a group, too big for any one person, even for one of us. And I've been thinking about how we'll do it."

They were all quiet, straining to catch every syllable.

"The last man to know about almost everything that was known lived in the thirteenth century—Albertus Magnus. Since then, knowledge has advanced so rapidly that people have had to specialize. Even in his day it took a most extraordinary man to know everything that was known, and organize and correct it all, no matter how loosely we use the expression. But we, as a group, really can know the essentials of everything that is known, and something over. We have the intelligence, and the good will—I hope—and we have each other's help. We've got to understand and correlate everything as I see it. Each of us speaks two or three languages, you might say, the way Elsie understands both poetry and the sciences—though not mathematics as yet!—and she *is* beginning to understand philosophy. She translates science into poetry, philosophy into poetry, and poetry back into both facts and action. Truth is one, and we've got to look for and find the unity—that's the way I see it—and that one truth. I don't mean a philosophical truth, still less a religious one, and right now I don't even know what it is that we are after.

"When we have synthesized and harmonized all knowledge, and interpreted and shared everything, then we'll all understand. Each specialty, and we all have more than one, must be related to the whole, and each person to the group, for at last we have a group of people in this world of sufficient intelligence to understand the whole, even though its parts are so elaborate and complicated. We aim to simplify and integrate. I've talked this over separately with some of you, so I say 'we' because they all think the same way about this. It's not my idea only, but theirs, and I hope it will be the idea of us all." He paused a moment and then said, "Now I'd like you to discuss it, please."

Jay was the next to speak.

"Tim and I thought each one could choose a thing to specialize in, and work on that," he said, "but while we can't all know everything, we must try to understand everything. Take two truths that seem unrelated, and find out the relationship. We have to study all branches of knowledge enough to get the significance of everything. Thomas Aquinas said the thing he was most grateful for was that he understood every page he ever read in his life. That's the way we want to be."

"Didn't Korzybski do something like this?" asked Fred.

"He tried, I guess, but he left out an awful lot—whole branches of knowledge and experience, like religion," said Tim. "At any rate that's the impression I got. His writings are so confused sometimes— I haven't read them for years, but that's the impression I got, anyway. Anyway, we're going to do this. It'll take years and years, but it's what we want to keep in mind and work on."

"I'm going to take poetry and languages," said Stella. "Tim said languages are not important in this, but I think they are, once you get out of your own group of related tongues, and I'm going to prove it. Language is a factor in molding thought processes, and language has a relation to culture. Max is going to take mathematics as a language, and Giles is going to take music."

"I'm going to take psychology and philosophy," said Tim. "Do you know, there has been no synthesis of psychology. Each school has disregarded all the others. There have been all sorts of schools— behaviorism, Jung and Adler and Freud, and scholastic psychology, and functional, and parapsychology, and so many interesting sidelines too. Nobody has ever worked out Jung's animus stuff as well as the anima. I mean—" he was about to launch into an explanation, but Beth cut him short.

"You mean that Haggard's *She* and other books like that exist, but no woman wrote one about a man who was the animus."

Stella's mouth opened wide, and everyone looked at her.

"I believe Marie Corelli did," she gasped. "I never thought of that. I'm going to work on it. Why, some of my own—"

"Good!" exulted Tim. "You're exactly the one to do it, Stella!"

"I want to do something in psychology too," said Elsie. "Right now I plan to deal with abnormalities, physical and mental and psychological—any departure from the norm, favorable or otherwise. But Dr. Foxwell says I must wait until I grow up."

"And the philosophy of all these things must be expressed," cried Jay. "We must all work on it together."

"Sculpture and painting and architecture as they express and influence a culture," Giles reminded them.

They all talked together then, until Tim stood up again and thumped the table with the gavel.

"All right. So we all have got the idea. It means years of work and all the work must be respected, watched and discussed by all the group. We must all publish everything we can, so as to increase the general knowledge, but nothing relating to this work must be published prematurely."

"You said something about understanding everything we read," said Giles. "How could that be done? Some things are nonsense."

"We have to understand it anyway. We have to understand what the writer meant, what he was trying to do, by what psychological motives he was moved, and what was wrong and why," Tim explained. He ended happily, "Psychology is the most fascinating thing!"

"Relate poetry to music, and music to language," Elsie was chanting softly, "language to mathematics, and math to the physical sciences; physical processes to chemical—"

"—And chemical to biological," Max took up the chant. "Biological to psychological and psychological to metaphysical and philosophical—great gaps yet unbridged—things related yet not confused—"

Tim thumped the table again.

"And besides all this," he said, "we must carry on our separate work. Inventions and discoveries of all kinds must be sought after. And we must live here and now, so I want to say, time is up. They'll be in to chase us off to bed, and tomorrow anybody who is interested can come help work on the swimming pool. I staked out the place this afternoon, and if the good weather holds maybe we can get to work on it."

Two days later, as a matter of routine, Peter Welles played off the recording tapes which had been accumulating. He was not greatly interested in most of it, but when he heard the recording of the meeting, he went hastily in search of all his colleagues.

"What's up? Space ships being built? Or another trick?" asked Mr. Gerrold.

"More than that," said Peter.

They listened, and what they heard held them spellbound.

Finally Dr. Foxwell took a deep breath and said shakily, "I do believe they can do it."

"I'm sure they will," said Miss Page.

"They will change the whole course of history, and find a lever to move the world," said Mr. Curtis.

"Yes, and on the side they'll build a swimming pool and a space ship, no doubt," said Mr. Gerrold.

"No doubt," said Dr. Peter Welles.

There was a banging at the door. Rosy-cheeked and breathless from running, Beth and Stella pranced impatiently on the porch until the door was opened.

"Please, it's no use to start the pool yet, Max says," gasped Beth, "because the rains are coming so soon. Is it all right if we lay out a roller-skating rink and use the cement for that? We can skate all winter, and start the pool in the spring."

"We won't put it too near the buildings, because skating is so noisy," promised Stella.

"Great idea," said Welles. "Go ahead."

Two days later, they were again forcibly reminded that they had a more pressing problem than skating rinks or the improvement of the world.

Elsie came storming into the dining hall, late for breakfast.

"Who's been meddling with my incubator?" she raged. "Somebody turned the heat way, way up! The eggs are *cooked!*"

Most of the group looked shocked, but there were a few snickers.

"I thought those things had automatic regulators on them," said Giles. "How could it be turned up so far?"

"I didn't buy an expensive one," said Elsie fiercely. "Mine was home made and has to be taken care of. And I've been so careful—and some of the twin-yolk eggs were developing fine. And now—"

She jerked out her chair and threw herself into it, scowling.

"I don't want any breakfast," she said. "Especially," glaring at the plates, "not *eggs!*"

Dr. Welles signaled to the other children to be quiet. His face was grave. There were some sympathetic murmurs; everyone finished breakfast hastily and left the room. Peter Welles beckoned Tim into his office.

"Something is going on here," Tim said angrily. "That was no accident. And the other things weren't, either. Have you heard about them? What's going on?"

"That is what I wanted to ask you, Tim," said his friend. "Are you sure these things are not accidental?"

"I certainly didn't leave Beauty's cage unfastened while she was calling," said Tim. "When she got out I knew somebody was doing it."

"Have you any idea who it could be?"

"No," said Tim. "What sort of person would do things like that? All the dogs out—and the pup in the chicken pen—and stealing Beth's strip—and now the eggs! Who would be doing it?"

"Almost anyone might."

"But they are such stupid, mean things to do!" cried the boy. "You would never think anyone in his right mind would do things like that. It can't be one of the boys or girls, can it, Peter?"

"Almost certainly it is one of the boys or girls," said Dr. Welles. "Don't discuss it with them, Tim, but keep your eyes open and see whether you can find a clue."

"I hoped I'd given them something else to think about," said Tim. "And the skating rink, too. I tried—well, I guess we'll have to find out, that's all. I'd better not talk about it?"

"Just watch and listen. If you think you know, come to me," Welles said, but behind his calm features, he was deeply concerned.

But several days passed, and no more tricks were played.

It was late November and the evenings were cold. Most of the children gathered in the hall after supper every evening, where they played games. Max was working out a new and very complicated game requiring six players, three dice of different colors, and six separate boards, each representing a store owned by one player and patronized by the rest.

Some children preferred to spend much of their spare time making elaborate anachrostics or double-crostics for the others to solve— those which were easy enough were sold to magazines—and there was a perpetual chess tournament of which Giles kept accurate records illustrated by graphs and charts.

A favorite among the girls in particular was "Word and Question," which Beth had read of in a very old story-book, but had never been able to induce anybody to play. (Grown people all cried, "But that's too hard!") Each player wrote a word on a piece of paper, and the papers were tossed into a bowl. Each player then wrote a question on another slip of paper, and these were stirred in another bowl. The players then drew a word and a question, and wrote a rhyme in which the word was introduced and the question answered.

Stella commented that poetry did not need to rhyme, but both Beth and Elsie countered by appealing to the rules of the game, which did not specify poetry at all, but did specify rhyme.

"Practice in rhyming," Beth told Elsie in confidence, "will be good for Stella."

It was Saturday afternoon. Dr. Foxwell's phone began to ring.

"Hello? Hello?"

"Is this Dr. Welles' school?"

"Yes."

"One of your pupils has been killed in an automobile accident."

"What!"

"One of your pupils is dead. It happened in a car crash at For—"
There was a click, and the line went dead.

Mark Foxwell burst into Peter Welles' office a moment later.

"Come back to my office—we were cut off—he might call again."

But the phone had not rung again by the time he had finished repeating the message.

"We were cut off just as he was telling me where it happened," he said. " 'For—' —it could be Fortieth, or Fourteenth Street or Avenue. And Fourteenth Street goes clear to San Leandro. Besides, probably the child will be taken to a hospital or morgue or brought here—it all depends on who took charge on the spot. Pete—"

"Wait a minute," said Peter Welles. "Who is killed?"

"Didn't say."

"Boy or girl?"

"Didn't say."

"Who phoned?"

"Didn't say. Muffled, excited voice. Could have been a woman, for all I know. Who is out?"

"Saturday afternoon? Everybody, probably. Go ring the dinner bell and call everyone who is on the grounds. I'll check the book to see who signed out."

"You ring the bell," said Dr. Foxwell. "I'll start calling hospitals and the police, and get something definite on this."

The clanging summons brought the Curtises and Mrs. Waters, and Mrs. Waters was able to report, "They all signed out, Doctor, and so did Miss Page and Mr. Gerrold and my husband. And every one of the children signed up to stay out until half past five.

"If it's Elsie," she added, and began to sob.

"If it's Jay—" said Mrs. Curtis, and stopped short.

"I've called all the hospitals of the whole area, and the police," said Dr. Foxwell. "Nothing to report. Tied up the phone while I was doing it, so nobody could call us here. All the children carry identification, I suppose?"

"I'm sure they do. The first thing any child does with a new wallet is to fill out the identification card," said Miss Page. "Besides, some-one did call."

"Would it be any use to go cruise down the possible streets?" asked Mrs. Waters. "We ought to be doing something."

Dr. Foxwell shook his head.

"It would all be taken care of by the time we got there, and we'd go right past the place. No, the police or the hospital should be calling us back any minute now. Or someone will come. Can we be doing anything?"

"I'll sit by the phone," said Mr. Curtis heavily. "That much I can do."

"I'll go back to the gate, and watch there," said Mrs. Waters. "The other children may be coming back and I can be there to tell them."

"Why doesn't someone call?" Mrs. Curtis fretted. "Perhaps some others were there too and were injured badly. That may be why nobody's calling. I'll go straighten out the houses, just in case—They may be too busy to call, but they might bring the children here."

The two women left the room, and Mark Foxwell signed to Peter Welles to come outside, leaving Mr. Curtis by the phone.

"By this time," said Peter, "we should have heard. Almost half an hour has gone by." He stopped and looked at the big doctor.

"I'm beginning to think that myself," said Foxwell. "You mean, even if we were cut off—and that's a thing that doesn't happen very often—there's no reason why we weren't called again before this time."

"I don't dare to rouse false hopes," said Peter Welles. "But I am beginning to think it's another practical joke. You say the voice didn't say anything definite at all—not 'A boy was killed,' or 'a girl'; and if they knew the child was a pupil here, they knew the child's name. Either they knew the child by sight or they read the identification card. Usually people begin by using the name and trying to break the news gently. They'd say, 'Is—er—Timothy Paul a pupil of yours?' or something like that. It isn't really impossible that someone might say 'a pupil,' but it's unlikely. People almost invariably say, 'A *girl* has been hurt,' or 'A *boy* has been run over,' and—but I don't dare say so to the others."

"Best to wait," agreed Dr. Foxwell. "But I'm going to phone the police once more."

Two minutes later he hung up the receiver.

"No child has been killed in the whole Bay Area this afternoon, unless it happened within the last fifteen minutes," he said. "None that the police have a record of, at any rate. It could be someone was hurt, and the report exaggerated. But the children will be coming in soon."

"One of the girls is coming in the gate now," said Peter Welles, who was looking in that direction. "It's Elsie. I'll go ask whether she knows where any of the others are."

Mrs. Waters had already asked.

"Elsie says that she and Stella went to the main library together, and Stella wanted to read, so Elsie walked around the lake alone. She hasn't seen Stella since."

"I left my books, and then after I walked around the lake, I went in and got more books, but I didn't see Stella," said Elsie. "I didn't look very hard for her; I thought she'd have gone somewhere else by then. Why? It's early yet. What's the matter with you all?"

"It may be another of those jokes," said Dr. Foxwell, "but—surely we'd have heard by now! Somebody phoned in almost an hour ago, and said one of you children was hurt in an auto accident. But—here comes one of the boys! Fred, are you all right? Who was with you?"

By quarter past five, only Max and Beth were still out. The others awaited them with more anger than anxiety; and, just before the clock struck the half-hour, the two came hurrying up the hill, having caught the same bus from town.

No amount of questioning—and everybody questioned everyone else—got them anywhere. No two children had been together. Tim and Jay, exploring a large department store with a view to Christmas shopping, had left together and returned together, but had separated and met and parted again a dozen times in the course of the afternoon.

Tim privately insisted to Dr. Welles, as soon as he could get a chance to speak to him alone, that lie-detectors and word-association tests should be employed.

"I hate to think of that, Tim, but it may become necessary. Let's all take a few days to simmer down. After all, no actual harm was done," Welles said, though privately he had strong doubts.

"It was cruel! It isn't as if a specific name had been given. If the Curtises had been told Jay was killed, or Mrs. Waters that it was Elsie—No, you *all* had to be scared to death," said Tim bitterly.

"We were more bewildered than frightened, after the first few moments; and there was no grief, because we had no idea who to grieve for. When Dr. Foxwell's phone calls proved negative, we all began to suspect that it was only a joke," Welles said, trying to calm him.

"Do you mean you aren't going to do anything about it?"

"Tim, it could be Mr. Gerrold, or Miss Page, or Mr. Waters. So could all the other tricks."

"Miss Page!" snorted the boy.

"I have my choice here of treating all the children like criminals, or of being a little bit subtle," said Dr. Welles. "I promise you, I'll find out. But give me a little time. And don't take it all so seriously. There is no immediate danger, I give you my professional word. We are all on guard now, and are watching closely. Meanwhile, I positively forbid you to try any word-association tests or anything else of the sort. Absolutely no meddling, Timothy. Leave it to me. Promise?"

"One more trick, Peter, and all promises are off," said Tim grimly. "Until then, all right, I'll promise."

"One more trick, and I promise you I'll take any necessary steps up to and including thumbscrews."

"All right." Mollified, Tim stalked out.

A few evenings later, the children were gathered in the hall. Beth was putting the finishing touches on a cartoon for "Not-A-New." It pictured an elderly and dissolute-looking car driven by two old ladies who had just bought gasoline at a filling station. One old lady was asking the other, "Are you sure it's full?" to which the car replied, "Hic!"

"That is just about as bright as they expect us to be," said Max approvingly. "It's hard, isn't it, to keep down to it?"

"Well, we can be bright other ways," said Beth cheerfully. "How are you doing, Max?"

"Our big game is too hard, Mr. Gerrold says, but I have an idea for another. Sold anything more, Stella?"

"I'm concentrating on finishing the Petra novel," answered Stella. "What are you doing lately, Fred? Any more patents?"

"I haven't got anywhere with chitin yet," said Fred. "It's a tough proposition. But I have had a few ideas, and those two patents will probably be granted. And I have a good new idea to work on, if I can keep a few cows."

"Cows?" asked Giles. "I suppose we could use the milk. Have you asked permission?"

"No, not yet. I want to get the theoretical work lined up first," said Fred. "Then I'll need a few cows to test it."

"Want to tell us the idea?"

"This is the idea. You know how, if the cow has twin calves, and one is male and the other female, the female is sterile?"

"A freemartin," Elsie nodded.

"Yes. That's because the hormones of the young male get into the mother's blood and affect the young female, as I guess you all know. I thought it would be possible to develop a test—biological, if not chemical—so you could tell early whether the calf was male or female, if there was only one. It won't work on small animals that have large mixed litters. But it should be able to find out quite early, and then if you wanted a heifer and it was a bull calf, you could abort it, and not waste all that time," explained Fred. "It would work for human beings, too, I have no doubt; something like the rabbit test for early pregnancy. I mean to work that out, too; perhaps the doctors would find a place to test it, once I have it worked out."

The other children looked at one another.

"I suppose a mother might want to know whether to knit pink sweaters or blue," said Beth.

"Oh yes, I suppose it could be used to satisfy natural curiosity," said Fred. "But I was really thinking, since people seldom want more than one or two children, there's no use to have the kind they don't want. You could determine the sex of the fetus by the eighth week, and—"

"You!" Tim leaped to his feet so suddenly that he knocked over his chair.

"You're the one!" he cried. "You're the one who has done all these tricks!"

"But how—" cried Giles in amazement.

"How do I know? It's easy. He's the one who doesn't know anything except with his intelligence. He's completely undeveloped on the feeling-side," cried Tim. "He hasn't any right feeling at all. Only that sort of person could think of such a plan as he has just told us. He gave himself away!"

"That's right," said Elsie excitedly. "It has to be Fred. He doesn't know at all how people feel about their work, or about killing calves or babies or anything. How they feel about their pets. He doesn't want any pets. And the cartoons—how people feel about the Scatterlees, and how they'd miss them."

"Can't any of you take a joke?" Fred said hotly. "Those tricks were only jokes, whoever did them. I didn't—"

"Anybody who'd even think they were jokes," said Max grimly, "we know about. That's why Robin and Marie were put off coming, I suppose. Dr. Welles didn't say why, but we knew they were almost ready to start, and then they were put off. These tricks were spoiling the school for all of us."

"There's no reason why people should use my experiments for anything except to satisfy their curiosity," Fred said stubbornly. "I don't say anyone has to kill calves or babies, as you sentimentally put it."

"Jokes, he calls the things he did," marveled Giles. "Come on, Tim, give us a lecture on psychology."

"Well, you know how a person who lives on the feeling-level does the most incredibly tactless, stupid things if you put him into a situation where he has to think," Tim began. "Things without a grain of common sense in them? Well, just the same way, a person who lives only for his intellect and drives all the feeling-side down into the unconscious, does the weirdest things against feeling. If you drive a function completely down into the unconscious it takes revenge on you. It goes all primitive and sub-human—like Fred's tricks—and just the opposite to anything an intelligent person would do. It wants to compensate by over-emphasis on the other side, but can't do it any right way, and goes all archaic."

"You speak as if it were a separate person," said Giles.

"Well, that's a manner of speaking, but it expresses the way things seem to take place," answered Tim. "I never really understood it before this very hour. Fred couldn't love or even hate on a normal basis. He had to do something sub-human so it is below any sort of loving or hating we can understand, if we have developed our feeling-sides at all. That side of him exists, and it has to express itself, but it has had no chance to do so on a human level."

"What was all that stuff you were trying to talk about last week and the week before?" asked Fred sarcastically. "I thought you said that love was not an emotion, but an act of the will."

"Sure, that kind of love," answered Tim promptly. "But in a human being the affections go along with the will. A pure spirit might love with the will only—I suppose it would have to—but human beings have emotions too. What your will did was to repress all feelings as beneath contempt. But the will belongs on the feeling-side, because it chooses on a love-hate basis. You refused to do that at all; you tried not to love or hate but only to reason. You are the one who has no use for poetry or music or art or beauty or religion or anything of that sort."

"I thought you Thomists said religion was purely intellectual," said Fred.

"You never thought any such thing," cried Elsie. "You know that is nonsense. If you thought religion was supposed to be purely intellectual you wouldn't be so opposed to it."

"First, I thought it might be someone else," Tim said, righting his chair and sitting down again. "I thought about you, Max, until I watched you play your game."

Max gasped and stared. "Me?"

"I thought you might have invented that game because you didn't like children, and were trying to prove it costs more than it is worth to have a family," explained Tim, "until I saw you play it. Then I knew you loved to get more and more children, and the game was really a way of getting children or being one of a big family, and the expense part was a sort of compensation—you had to keep reminding yourself that they were expensive, because you wanted them so much, and your grandparents had all they could do to bring up one of you."

"Well, what do you know," marveled Max. "I never thought a thing about all that. Sure, Tim, you're right."

"And then I thought it might be Elsie, trying to be too good, because when you can't blow up openly in a big way you're likely to blow off sneakily. But I think Elsie is too honest to do sneaky things. She'd let pets out, maybe, if she wanted a row, but then she'd stand around and laugh at you. And I even thought of Stella, because some sides of her are still so undeveloped. She might have some undeveloped faculty that would result in odd behavior with no sense to it. I had to think about everybody. I even thought about Mr. Gerrold and Mr. Waters."

"I know what you mean about me," said Stella, "but it's on the sensation-side I am least developed, and I'm working on that with Dr. Welles, you know."

"But Fred has always exaggerated his intellect," Tim went on. "That was what folks liked about him—he was such a bright boy. The only other value they saw in him—or so he thought—was in the money the state paid them for taking him in. Maybe he was always so much better that way than any other, there wasn't much you could like about him. He's so cold-blooded about everything. Elsie might kill babies perhaps if she was mad at them, but there'd have to be a reason—like that they made a racket when she was trying to write a poem. Hate is the other side of love and pity and is akin to love, but Fred doesn't know anything about the feeling-side at all; he repressed all that. He thought the only good thing about him was the thinking-side, but we all have four faculties and we must develop them all somewhat. You can't just be one-sided, you have to be four-sided. Very intellectual people do the oddest things. Anybody who develops one faculty to the exclusion of the others is all out of balance."

"What are we going to do about him?" asked Max, looking critically at Fred. "Shall we kick him out of the school?"

"We ought to report him to Dr. Welles," said Giles.

"Well, I don't know," said Tim. "Why don't we handle this ourselves?"

"You mean, make him leave?"

"First, let's see what he has to say, now we know he did it all," suggested Tim.

"No real harm was done," Fred said vehemently. "I don't know what all this fuss is about." But his cheeks were red with mingled shame and anger.

"That's just what we're complaining about," exclaimed Elsie. "You *don't* know!"

"Look, do you want to stay here, and work with us, and do you want to be cured?" asked Tim.

"Cured!" Fred said angrily. "I've nothing to be cured of. You talk as if I'm sick or crazy."

"What would Dr. Welles do to him?" asked Giles.

"Cure him, that is, if Fred wants to be cured," answered Tim promptly. "He'd develop his other functions, so he'd have right feelings and good intuition and proper use of his senses. Fred knows a lot—perhaps more than any of us about some things—but he doesn't understand any of all this. No love-hate choice is permitted him by his all-powerful intellectual side. He would have to change his will so he could consent to develop that side."

"All this appeal to sentimentality," said Fred. "What do I care for that?" He stared coldly at the other children.

"Don't you care whether we like you or not?" asked Max. "Or even whether you can stay with us?"

"I can work at home," said Fred. "I don't care whether you like me; why should I? If that's what you think about me—"

"You're human," said Max. "I know you want us to like you, because you're human. Maybe your reasoning powers won't let you think why, but you do. I think, though, you were jealous when you found others were as smart as you, and wanted to get even by annoying us all. And I think you want to forget we exist, most of the time —if you go home you can try to do that, but you'll always know it was wrong. Look, don't you want to share life with us, Fred, and learn to develop all the sides of yourself?"

"I should say the real question is, do we want him to," said Elsie.

"Yes, we do," said Tim, "because we're human. He's one of us, and he could be so likable, and we admire him some ways, and we aren't afraid of him enough to have to kick him out. Of course, now we all know about him, he won't be up to any more mischief. But will he stay and learn? Will you, Fred?"

"How many say he can stay, if he will?" asked Jay, and Elsie's hand was the first to go up. "See, everybody would rather you stayed, Fred. You'll find it interesting, on the knowing-side, to learn about psychology, Fred. Let Dr. Welles teach you. You needn't say why."

"Psychology isn't a science," said Fred.

Tim grinned.

"I've heard you say so before. Neither was astronomy or biology or physiology in the days of Albert the Great," said Tim. "Suppose you get in on the ground floor and help us make a real science of it, then. Start with what Dr. Welles knows, and see what can be built up. The proper study of mankind is man, and if a science of psychology doesn't exist yet, we'd better get busy and build one up."

Fred, for the first time, looked interested.

"I haven't tried to study psychology—not the kind you are talking about," he said. "There may be something in it, if you found me out like that. I thought you'd find out by—oh, by Sherlock Holmes methods, to use an archaic example. But most of what you say sounds like awful nonsense."

"If Dr. Welles were here—or Carl Jung or somebody like that, it would all have been better put."

"Well, let's make a bargain, then," said Jay briskly. "We won't tell on Fred, and the tricks will stop, and everybody will forget about them. Fred will go to Dr. Welles and give the thing an honest try. Fred, you can tell him you heard Tim and me and the girls talking about all this stuff and you want to know about it, to investigate this science—or this so-called science if you want to put it that way; but you'd better be polite to Dr. Welles. It will take time, of course, and you want to understand what goes on."

"You can't deny your own human nature, you know, Fred," said Tim. "Give the whole thing a chance to prove itself."

"I'll try," said Fred. "But I warn you I don't expect to be able to make any sense out of this psychology."

"Give it a fair trial," said Tim. "That's all you are asked to do. Just say to yourself that there may be some sense in it and you're willing to see whether it has."

"If it has," Fred said, "I'll find it."

Tim and the other children kept their word, but the recording tape told Peter Welles and Dr. Foxwell the whole story.

The grown people were white-faced as they looked at one another while the tape reeled it all off to them.

"Oh, Tim, Tim," moaned Dr. Welles. "Why did you blurt it all out like that?"

"Is it all true—what Tim said?"

"The point is, should he have said it?" the doctor answered. "What boy can stand having such a shower of bricks cast at him? And Fred is terribly proud."

"I don't see what he has to be proud of," said Mrs. Curtis.

"He has intellectual pride to an extremely high degree. Theologians tell us that this is the sin by which the very angels fell—and if that is not true in a literal sense, Mr. Gerrold, it is certainly true in a psychological sense. All sorts of dreadful things have just been said to Fred, with a frankness of which only children are capable. He is proud of being very, very superior, and they called him sub-human. They said he knew nothing about feelings, was completely undeveloped in a very important side of his nature, that he knew nothing about the nature of man, and that people valued him for nothing but his intellect. And by telling him that he had almost everything to learn, they belittled his intellect and understanding."

"You don't think his pride can take all that," said Mr. Curtis. "It was a stiff dose. But toward the end they appealed to him and he appeared to respond."

"Yes; but did he mean that honestly?" asked Miss Page. "He may be only pretending. Of course he doesn't want to be sent away in disgrace. If he resents having to admit that others can be his intellectual equals, how much more he must resent being made to feel otherwise markedly inferior to them!"

"I wouldn't bet too much on his good will," admitted Dr. Welles. "For the moment, his intellectual curiosity may be aroused. He may consent to hear what I have to offer, even though he may fight it all the way. He may listen only to refute all that I try to teach him. We sometimes find that state of mind in an atheist who is undeveloped on the feeling-side and resists every reasonable appeal in regard to religion because, to him, all religion is a surrender to feeling."

"Many religious people are very much shocked at any suggestion that reason should ever be brought to bear on religion," commented Dr. Foxwell. "However, as to Fred—do you think you can straighten him out?"

"It will take careful work to keep him from falling back into his old blindness to all but the intellectual side of his psyche, once the effect of the shock he got today has worn off."

"I can do nothing if his will is actually set against me," said Dr. Welles. "If he worships his intellect to such an extent that the will is entirely a puppet of the intellect, and all feelings are rejected, it will be a hard struggle. 'A man convinced against his will is of the same opinion still.' There are two strikes against me: Tim gave me no chance to break anything gently; he told Fred all the things that Fred least wished to know, and openly before all the others. The only thing left to Fred's pride is that he believes we adults know nothing about it. Now we shall have to rebuild his pride. We should try to show that we value him for things other than his intellect."

"Yes, and we must value him as highly as we possibly can," said Dr. Foxwell. "After such a shattering attack, he needs all the encouragement we can possibly give him."

"I am afraid he is potentially dangerous," said Mr. Curtis. "I wonder whether we should not, after all, send him away."

"No," said Dr. Welles. "We must try to help him. He is a human being and a boy, in our care. He has the same value as any other child, and the additional value of being extremely gifted. And he needs us more than any of the others do. I would rather send the others away, and keep Fred."

"If he is dangerous, all the more reason why we should keep him and try to cure him," added Dr. Foxwell. "We can't turn him loose on the world and take no thought for our own responsibility as to the results."

"Yes. All the others are deficient in some degree in one function or another, but only Fred is badly deficient in every way but intellectually. As a psychologist I would say that to exalt any one function at the expense of the others to such a degree is dangerous—not only to the boy and to us, but to the whole world. People who valued only the intellect made the atom bomb and turned it loose upon the world, not knowing or caring what might be done with it. A better balanced inventor, long before, invented the submarine, and destroyed his plans because he feared mankind might make a bad use of such an invention. I don't know what Fred may invent; but I want to save him, if I can, from forgetting all about human nature and human feelings, and what the feelings can do. It is our nature to be developed in four functions, and the man who denies his own nature is in danger and is dangerous."

"Even partial success would be worth while," said Dr. Foxwell. "You can't fail completely, Peter. And you do have a chance; he promised to come to you, and the others will see to it that he keeps that promise."

"I must go hunt up some books and think what to offer him first," said Peter Welles, rising slowly to his feet. "Books are best, because they are impersonal when they attack. He can face the attack alone, and there is no one to witness defeat, no one to fight back against. I can only hope that Fred does come to me."

He should have had more faith in the Wonder Children, for Tim and Fred came to his study that very afternoon.

"Hey, Peter?"

"Yes, Tim?"

"We were telling Fred about the four functions of the psyche and all that, and he wants to learn about it," said Tim. "Do you think you could take some time to teach him the theory?"

"Yes, if he wants to learn about it," answered Dr. Welles, looking up calmly, betraying no sign of his tremendous relief. "I can recommend some books to you, Fred, and have a talk with you once or twice a week while I am in town."

"Are you free now?" asked Tim.

"I'll be free in about half an hour, if you want to come back then, Fred."

"All right, Dr. Welles."

Fred did come back, alone and of his own accord. And that, thought Peter Welles, was as much as could be expected for a beginning.

CHILDREN OF THE ATOM

The next few weeks passed peacefully. There were no more tricks, and as the grown people had good reason to believe there would be none, several more children entered the school—Robin Welch, Rose Jackson, Marie Heath, Alice Chase, and Gerard Chase. The last two proved to be second cousins, only vaguely aware of one another's existence, since they had been taken under guardianship by unrelated branches.

Robin's specialty was paleontology, but he also had a lively interest in snakes of all kinds, and spent his spare time in the woods, adding to his collection. He was overjoyed at permission to build a special house for them, and did not in the least resent the careful inspection the senior members of the school gave to his rattlers' cage.

"My family didn't like my snakes," he explained, one day not long after Christmas, when Elsie came to see his new snakes.

"This ring-necked snake is the prettiest," said Elsie. "Beautiful coral color! And I love that spiral it gets its tail into. What mathematical curve is that, I wonder?"

"We'll have to ask Max," said Robin, returning the small snake to its cage. "You ought to see a coral snake, Elsie; they're beautiful. But Dr. Welles doesn't want me to buy poisonous snakes."

"If no rattlers get out, maybe he'll let you have some other dangerous snakes," Elsie consoled him.

"When are more kids coming?" asked Robin. "Gerard wants to get up a ball team."

"Dr. Welles hasn't had time yet to interview everybody. There were thirty or more born, and only two are known to have died, but we haven't located everyone yet."

"Want to help me dig worms for the snakes?" asked Robin. "Hi, Fred—did you want to see my snakes?"

"No, thanks, I've seen them," said Fred. "I'll help dig worms, if you like."

"Why don't you have a pet, Fred?" asked Robin, taking up a spade and a garden fork, and handing Elsie a jar for the worms.

"I don't see why I should," said Fred, choosing the fork and motioning for Robin to lead the way.

"Dogs are sometimes useful, but I don't need a Seeing Eye dog, and I'm glad the pups are sold at last. Most people like dogs because dogs are so devotedly servile, living only to adore, like Ben Bolt's Sweet Alice. It makes the owners feel important," he said.

"Oh, is that so," said Elsie, sarcastically. "And cats?"

Fred forked up a clump of wild grass and extracted a worm from its roots. He dropped the worm carefully into the jar before he answered.

"Sensuous people like the feel of fur," he said, "on a warm, purring animal, especially. And cats are such merciless hunters, some people enjoy a vicarious cruelty in them. Hey!" for Elsie had incontinently flung the jar, worm and all, at his head, and he had ducked just in time.

"When I want to hurt something, I do it myself," said Elsie, quite unnecessarily.

"What did that poor worm ever do to you?" asked Robin, picking up the worm and the jar.

"Do you mean me or the Lumbricus?" asked Fred. "Listen, Elsie, I know you keep cats, but you don't have to throw glass jars at me. If you ever do any such thing again, I'll make you sorry! and you, Robin—"

"I wasn't calling you a worm," said Robin honestly. "I'm new here, and—say, Elsie, do you often do things like that?"

"I'm sorry," protested Elsie, scarlet-faced. "It was a—a sort of reflex. Fred, I didn't mean to throw it, really. It just happened. Shall we call it square now about the eggs?"

"Eggs?" said the mystified Robin.

"Oh, skip it," said Fred, reddening also. "I didn't mean you, anyway, Elsie. I meant why people buy Tim's cats. He gets good money for them, so I see why he raises cats. But I don't know why most people keep cats; I was just trying to think why, and now I see it didn't sound very complimentary. You keep cats because Tim does, I suppose. I mean," as Elsie showed signs of not liking that very well either, "he offered you some, so you took them. But they are such a nuisance—all pets are. So much work, when you could be doing other things. I don't mind digging worms—" he drove the fork into the ground, turned over a clod, and broke it up—"once in a while, but I'd hate to have to do it every day. That's one thing about snakes, they don't bark, or jump all over you—"

"They don't have to be fed every day, either," remarked Robin.

"Well, it wasn't because I have cats, or not even about the eggs entirely—but you make me so mad, Fred! You don't understand *anything!*"

"Why do people keep cats, then?"

"What eggs?" asked Robin.

"Oh, that was a while back, Robin," said Elsie impatiently, and returned to the real issue. "People keep cats because they like cats! Don't you even realize that people can like things you don't?"

"Lots of people say cats are sneaky and treacherous, but I don't think so, any more than snakes are," said Robin, manfully accepting the fact that the matter of the eggs was not to be explained to him. "They just act according to their natures. As Fred says, cats don't bark. Not being scavengers, they come quietly to catch their prey; and a cat has as much right to eat its dinner as any other creature."

"I like cats because they are independent," said Elsie, "and they are graceful, and so efficient—I think they are the most perfect of all animals, the way they move, the way they spring, the way they relax. And they are good company, when they want to be. But, Fred, you do assign the most perverted motives to people!"

"After all, a pet is, by definition, something to pet," said Robin. "I don't know if you could call a snake a pet at all. Most people like a pet to be a little responsive. I keep snakes because they are interesting."

"There are three worms in that clump!" cried Elsie, pouncing upon one. "Fred, I'm sorry I threw that jar at you. I always used to throw things when I was—"

"In the hospital," Fred supplied hastily.

"Oh, it's no secret—in the asylum. I'd go tell Dr. Foxwell on myself, but then I'd have to explain, and—"

"Oh, cancel it out—cancel it out," said Fred. "I'm sorry about the eggs, too. There's no sense making a mystery out of things. I played some fool tricks when I first came, Robin; turned up Elsie's incubator and cooked all the eggs, for one thing."

"No need to tell," said Elsie, "but since it came up, I suppose it's better. I'm sorry I mentioned it, I just didn't stop to think. Only you know, Robin, we can't go all the way back and explain everything, every time a new boy or girl comes."

"I'm out of sorts today anyway," admitted Fred. "That's why I came out. I was looking for Tim and the others, and thinking about asking them something. You too, Elsie—you're one of the old-timers. Do you know where Tim is? You know, Robin, Tim is sort of head boy around here."

"They're all in the hall, I think," said Robin. "This is enough worms. You go on; I'll stay and feed my snakes."

"No, I want you to come with us," said Fred. "There's no secret about it, just so we don't have to go into a long explanation of the whole background. I want your help too. Come on!"

Most of the boys and girls were in the hall, reading, listening to the radio, and eating apples, when the trio arrived; and Fred, after a glance around to assure himself that most of the "old-timers" were there, went up front and smacked the table with the gavel.

"If you aren't too busy, I want to ask you something," he said. "I was thinking about it, and then Elsie made me mad, so I'm going to."

Beth switched off the radio, and they all came nearer to listen.

"I've been talking to Dr. Welles for a whole month," Fred said, "and reading all he gave me, and I can't see that we're getting anywhere. You know how grownups are, they take forever to get anything done. We live at a different tempo. Now, some of you know quite a lot about this business of developing the neglected and repressed functions of the personality—and those who don't will please shut up; I'm talking to those who do—and you don't know as much as the doctor, maybe, but you wouldn't be so slow about it. Some of you have read more than I have, of course, and you must understand it better than I do, because I don't understand it at all. I can't find any practical suggestions, and that's what I want. I want something to work on, so I can see whether I get any results. Elsie just said I don't understand anything about anything. What's the sense of all this stalling around? It's nonsense to tell me I ought to develop this function and bring that function up and un-repress the other function, if nobody tells me how. You tell me how, then, and I'll try."

There was a stunned silence, in which everyone looked expectantly at Tim.

"I don't think I ever thought of it exactly that way," said Tim, and he took a large bite of apple and chewed reflectively.

"There must be some specific things you can do," agreed Max.

"If we could think of them," Elsie consented.

"Well, think, then," said Fred.

"We can't produce a whole program in five minutes," said Jay, "but I should think we could each make a couple of suggestions within a day or two. Will that do, Fred?"

"I'd appreciate that," said Fred. "But I'm right here, in case anybody thinks of anything now. I wouldn't expect a whole program; just what you might call a few simple exercises to try."

Tim nodded.

"I get it," he said. "Like, if a person's blood count is down, it's no use just to say he's anemic, and ought to be strengthened up, or dither around waiting to find out how he got that way, but it might be some use to tell him to eat an egg every day. That might not do a lot of good, but it would be some small specific help right away."

"Eggs again?" said Elsie, a little too loudly. Then she hastened to add, "It might do the rest of us some good, too. We could work on our own deficiencies the same way."

"And test the suggestions," said Jay, looking very much interested. "Can't anybody think of even one? Let's all stop chattering and think!"

"Well," said Tim, "I've remembered something. Will you do anything we say, Fred? And try it out honestly, and take time to do it right?"

"Sure," said Fred, "if you really mean it. Anything reasonable."

"Since it is your intellect that is over-developed, it isn't likely you need anything reasonable," Stella pointed out.

"Anything within reason—anything possible—anything I can do," said Fred impatiently. "You all know what I mean. Tim, what was your idea?"

"I read a story about Agassiz," said Tim slowly, "and a student of his. Agassiz gave the student a fish in a bowl and told him not to use any reference books or anything, but just to sit and look at that fish until he had learned everything he could from it, and he'd come back when he thought the student would be done. So the student worked on it for a couple of hours, and thought he was done, but Agassiz didn't come back, so he tore up his notes and started over, and really did look at that fish. He worked a week and then Agassiz came and when he had read the notes he said they wouldn't do. So the student spent another two weeks at it, and by then he had done a really good job." Tim paused, and bit into his apple again.

"I suppose that develops the use of the senses," said Max.

"It could," said Tim. "But in one of Gerald Vann's books he said that mystics of all faiths all over the world, in all times, have developed intuition in their disciples by having them take some little thing, like a leaf, or a flower, or a pebble, and hold it in their hands and stare at it by the hour until they had really learned to see it and to know its significance."

" 'Flower in the crannied wall,' " quoted Beth.

"That's right. So—" Tim carefully took a small bite and spat something into his hand—"For your first exercise, Fred, you take this apple-seed in your hand and look at it carefully and steadily until you understand how long before it will grow into a tree, bearing fruit."

There was a tremendous roar of laughter, and Fred jumped to his feet, his fists clenched.

"I mean it," said Tim. "Are you going to try it?"

"You promised," shouted all the others in chorus.

"You mean it? Just hold that seed, and stare at it, and think—?"

"Until you understand some things a little better. Yes," said Tim.

Fred walked over to Tim and stretched out his hand.

"Quiet, everybody, please," he said. "I could go away and get some quiet, but I want you all to see me doing this. I'm a man of my word."

While Fred sat grimly staring at the seed in the palm of his hand, the others exchanged glances. Some of them began to scribble on bits of paper, and occasionally passed these to someone else, or signed to have them circulated. Some of the group went on with what they had been doing, glancing at Fred from time to time. One or two tip-toed to the shelves and selected books for study. When Alice Chase entered, her cousin signed her to silence, and beckoned her outside, where he explained what was going on.

After what seemed like a long time, Fred's expression changed. He looked thoughtful; then he looked interested; and then he began to grin. Finally he got up and stretched.

"Do I report progress?" he asked. "I understand several things better. For one thing, I see the joke; not as a nasty slap or a smart crack, but as a very apt object lesson in patience and in waiting for things to grow. And I understand how the two things you read complement each other, Tim, and how they fit into all this. And I see what you mean by an egg a day; this is today's egg. My gosh, have I been staring at that seed for a solid hour? or—or was it *only* an hour?"

Nobody spoke for a minute. Then Tim cleared his throat and asked, "How do you feel, Fred?"

"I feel fine. A little stiff, that's all. But I feel more friendly toward all of you, and I know now that you all want to help me and that you are friendly toward me—now I know why you all laughed."

"Would you mind telling us how you did it?" asked Jay.

"You've all told me not to think so much, that I reason too much and am too intellectual, so I knew I had to do something else," said Fred. "First off, I was plenty mad, and all I did was seethe. But I remembered you said to think how a seed grew into a tree, and I supposed you didn't mean 'think' in the same way as when you talk about the 'thinking function,' so all I could do was to try to visualize it, as if I were watching a slow-motion picture of it. I did that over and over. And one time when I saw apple-blossoms dancing in the breeze, I saw beauty that was a promise of something—ah—riper. After a while, I saw fruition and fulfilment. A fish in a bowl can be seen only as a fish, I guess, but a seed must be seen in its potentiality. So that's about all I've done so far."

"It looks to me," said Elsie judicially in the awed hush that followed this speech, "as if you gave him the wrong thing, Tim. Instead of an apple seed you should have given him a radish seed. Or is there anything that grows faster?"

"Well, it all goes to show," said Max, "that you can do almost anything, Fred, if you try."

"All right," said Fred. "I'm ready for more exercises. We'll see whether the final crop is a radish or a barrel of apples."

"For some general principles first," said Jay, "I should suggest that you contemplate and act upon the general principle, 'There are no uninteresting things, only uninterested people,' as Chesterton puts it. You've always been saying that you can't think why people do this or that, or why they like something or other. If I were you, Fred, I'd try some of those things one by one until you begin to see what other people see in them. Things that almost everyone else likes, I mean."

"Yes, and he ought to take other objects and stare at them the way he did at the seed," said Stella. "And he ought to read poetry."

"He ought to read all our favorite books that he didn't like, and write a series of little essays explaining why we like them," suggested Elsie, "and to try to imagine how we feel about things, and—this is what helped me most—to think how it takes all kinds of people to make a world, and the other psychological types have their place, and a right to exist and to be themselves, just so they're good of their kind. Remember the essay Giles wrote on 'The Right to Be an Introvert'?"

A new game, a new fad had been born. It swept through the school and engulfed even the astonished teachers.

"Shouldn't we stop this amateur therapy?" Dr. Foxwell worried.

"How could we possibly stop it?" asked Peter Welles, "you might as well try to stop an avalanche. What can we do but stand aside and let it roar on? I can't pretend to foresee what it will accomplish for either good or harm, but they are keeping full notes of the experiments and their immediate results, and as a mere student I am grateful for the opportunity to observe all this."

"Most of it is good, I believe," said Dr. Foxwell, "but I am afraid they are rushing things too much, forcing things—still, it is all spontaneous and they are doing it willingly and gladly."

"They set their own speed now," Welles pointed out.

"Quite true," said Miss Page. "If I had not worked with children of this age for more than thirty years, I wouldn't have believed such a change could take place so rapidly in Fred."

"He tapped these buried functions and got a gusher," said Peter. "I only hope, to continue the metaphor, that all his resources won't be wasted, as happens in an oil gusher. But, after all, why should that happen? These things which were under pressure are now gushing forth, but by the time this fad has run its course, I think we'll have everything not only opened up and flowing freely, but under control."

"Would you risk this sort of thing with ordinary patients?" asked Mr. Gerrold.

"Ordinary patients resist. A co-operative youngster with great enthusiasm and zeal for self-development, combined with high intelligence, rarely becomes a patient of any psychiatrist. Fred's challenge was genuine, his curiosity was awakened, and he was willing to make a test of anything suggested. And apparently he meant what he said."

"He went about it intelligently, too," said Mr. Gerrold. "Do you know, I am surprised by these geniuses of ours."

"In what way, Mr. Gerrold?" asked Mr. Curtis.

"I am still waiting for a real problem child," explained the young teacher. "These children aren't problems at all."

"No?" murmured Dr. Foxwell.

"A serious case is bound to crop up at least once in this generation of children," continued Mr. Gerrold earnestly. "For example, there might be a child who, after his parents died, was transferred to an impoverished and unstable home, ran away from it and joined the underworld. With such an intelligence, he would actually succeed in taking care of himself, becoming an expert criminal, with a long history of escape from reform schools and a national record in juvenile delinquency. Probably such a child would lead a double life as a reputable authority on criminology, and in his spare time make hundreds of thousands of dollars mass-producing detective fiction. With a childish enthusiasm for melodrama and sensationalism he would get a thrill out of being the Invisible Detective."

"Something like the Spider in the Michael Innes book?" asked Miss Page.

"I haven't read that work," said Mr. Gerrold.

"There are several contradictory statements in the situation you have outlined," said Mr. Curtis.

"Well, it gives the general idea," said Mr. Gerrold. "And there might be, and probably is, at least one paranoid child. The paranoid is always dangerous, because he is convinced that people are against him, and all his logic is based on that false premise. His logic would be so good that no one could disprove it to him, and he would be out to dominate and hold in subjection the whole world in revenge. But at the very least I would have expected these children, or some of them—Fred perhaps, if he hadn't changed so abruptly—to see in himself the natural destined ruler of the whole world. He would be too intelligent to go about it as Hitler did by mass murder, but he might easily have become a world menace. He was only a mild nuisance, and now he goes about like Ferdinand the Bull, smelling the flowers!"

"Out of a maximum of thirty children, the chance of getting one who is really insane is slight," said Dr. Welles. "So far, all these children are sane. Though unable to establish rapport with the world, in some cases, they all had sufficient intelligence and sanity to realize that the intentions of other people toward them were not evil. They were bewildered and frustrated, but did not think they were menaced. We may meet something like your monsters of iniquity yet, Mr. Gerrold, but I have no real expectation of doing so."

"If I may say so without extreme discourtesy," said Mr. Curtis, "I would suggest that perhaps Mr. Gerrold retains something of a youthful appetite for sensationalism and melodrama himself. He would like something dreadfully—I use the word deliberately—dreadfully exciting to happen."

"By retreating safely into history and the past," Mr. Gerrold retorted, "it is easy to think that Alexander, Genghis Khan, Napoleon, and Hitler are all dead, and that, therefore, all is for the best in this best of all possible worlds."

"Nevertheless, are you not a trifle disappointed that Fred has metamorphosized into Ferdinand the Bull rather than into Attila the Hun?"

"I was about to suggest," interrupted Miss Page tactfully, "that we follow the example of the children, and try some of their exercises, and make reports as they are doing. Dr. Welles might consent to direct us."

"If it would lead to a better understanding between me and Mr. Curtis, I would be glad to do so," said Mr. Gerrold. "And if there is truth in his allegations—"

Mr. Curtis smiled suddenly.

"I did not mean to be offensive," he said. "I was recalling my own youth, which is not so distant as to be beyond memory, and attributing the same characteristics to others. Mr. Gerrold will excuse a man of my age seeing little difference between the late teens and the early twenties."

"If you will recommend some historical works which will tend to make me a better balanced individual," said Mr. Gerrold, with only the slightest sarcastic inflection, "I shall be glad to recommend and to read aloud some scientific works which might benefit you."

"I accept your generous offer," said the blind historian, "and agree that we might all benefit by entering into the exercises which the children are trying out. As for other exercises, since I am unable to stare at apple-seeds or to contemplate my navel, what do you suggest, Dr. Welles?"

"We might do what the children are doing with music," suggested Peter Welles. "They were having a hot debate over music not long before I left them this morning. Marie had been taught that no music 'means' anything, that it is all purely subjective, so that one person may take a certain opus as expressing light-hearted joy and another person may take it as expressing melancholy tragedy, and both be right. Most of the children violently maintained that the composer had, in all cases, some specific mood or emotion to express, but they were divided as to whether this should be laboriously expressed in words or whether the music should be allowed to speak for itself. They agreed, therefore, to listen to a series of musical records, and each one was to listen to what the music was saying and write down what it conveyed, but without discussion and without consulting any explanatory works. At the end of a fortnight or so they intend to compare notes and repeat certain selections, listening again. We might do that, using the same selections."

"Sometimes it depends on the musician's interpretation," Mrs. Curtis said. " 'Humoresque' has two—as a light, pretty piece, very happy; and as a heartbreakingly pathetic one."

While Dr. Welles was getting the first recording for this experiment, Mr. Gerrold whispered to Miss Page, "Don't you think anything exciting is ever going to happen here?" and she whispered back, "The happiest people, like the happiest countries, have no history. Fred's successful adventure with the apple-seed is as exciting and interesting to me as if he had gone to terrible extremes, and much more satisfactory." And when he did not look very much satisfied, Miss Page added softly, "Cheer up! Something dreadful may yet happen!"

The next three weeks were full of activity. Fred, at Stella's command, read *The Lady's Not for Burning* and complained that he could not understand what the author was driving at.

"That's because you're trying to think about it," Stella explained. "Don't think; just enjoy it."

Since most of the children were agreed that reading poetry developed the intuitive function, Fred was overwhelmed with collections of everybody's favorite lyrics, and was obliged to announce firmly that he would not read poetry for more than an hour in any one day. Max presented him with a beautifully bound copy of the Psalms, and added, "You wouldn't get much out of Job until you have known deep tragedy, but you ought to read it a few times anyway."

"We ought to find out why people go to church and what they get out of it," Robin said, "and what different churches have to offer."

"People go because they think they have to, don't they?" asked Rose.

"No," said Jay confidently. "Of course they don't. If they didn't get anything out of it, they wouldn't go."

"Let's go to as many as we can, then, and see what people can be getting out of them," suggested Giles.

"Do you mean out of church-going, to that particular building on that special day, or out of religion?"

"Church-going," said Robin emphatically. "Let's look each time for something of value there that day, and leave religion for full study later."

This led to a heated discussion which Alice Chase unwittingly cut short by coming in with two books for Fred to read—*Once in Cornwall* by S.M.C. and *Perelandra* by C. S. Lewis—and a question to ask her cousin.

"Could I ask, Gerard, what you are working on? Or is it a secret?"

"I meant to ask you all to a showing of it soon," said Gerard, "but we have all been so busy, I didn't get around to it. I want to, because I thought we might base a group project on it, for everyone who is interested."

"Tonight?" asked Alice hopefully.

"Tomorrow night, if that suits everybody. I want to ask the grown-ups, too," said Gerard.

Since Gerard's work was known to combine microscopes, moving picture cameras, modeling in clay, much tinkering with bits of metal, elaborate lighting effects, and large checks from a literary agency, excitement ran high when the suggestion of collaboration was included. Everyone promised to be on hand at the appointed hour.

"What I have to show you," said Gerard, "is a series of short movies, and some stills. What I have to propose is a full-length movie upon which we could all work, on a share-the-profits basis or for the benefit of the school."

There was a stir of interest.

"My father," said Gerard, "was a metallurgist specializing in photomicrography of metal specimens. My uncle wasn't so much interested in this field as in other kinds of photography, and he taught me photography and a good many tricks of the trade. I fooled around with it, indoors and out, and by the time I was twelve, he turned over all my father's equipment to me. I used to take pictures and then make up stories about them. This first still, I took when I was ten."

A color photo appeared on the screen.

"I wrote my first story about this. Defending force here—" Gerard used the pointer, "attacking force here, coming up this way, along this crest; sorties dividing off through here on the left and this passage through the cliffs on the right, and retreat this way. This whole formation looks large enough for armies to swarm over, but it was really only a piece of highly eroded red sandstone, or something of that sort, about three feet long and a foot and a half high. But I set myself to imagining what could happen on it, if it were full-scale or if people were very small. It looks more like a sort of rough Petra, and that's the way I dreamed the story up. I illustrated it with these photographs—" the pictures on the screen changed as he spoke, "and drawings. Here are the drawings, people in action at the right places on this blown-up bit of landscape."

Murmurs of polite appreciation came from the children.

"That was only an adventure story. I didn't do many of that kind, but when I got my father's stuff I really did begin work. I took short movies of microscopic things that moved, and stills of those that didn't, for backgrounds; and I watched things and dreamed about them, and combined the various backgrounds and actions—my uncle had taught me the tricks of the trade, I told you—and then I wrote the stories, with people in them, and illustrated them. Now, can you forget all this and watch the movies? Maybe I should have done this the other way around. The first reels show a tree on the planet Venus."

Sitting on the edges of their chairs, the children watched. A sort of leafless tree waved sinuous branches idly about, apparently under water. Into view swam a small creature with a segmented body. It had two antennas like hairy carrots, and behind them, two smaller ones; it had two stubby tails, from each of which trailed two appendages that looked rather like the backbones of fishes. Clinging to the sides of this creature were clusters of globules. It had only one eye.

This creature swam past the tree, touching one of its limbs in passing. Instantly the limbs went into action; the small creature was grasped firmly and, in spite of its struggles, was stuffed into an opening at the top of the trunk, which widened to receive it. Then, smug and bulging, the tree stood alone, waving its clustered limbs gently.

"This tree," commented Gerard as he put on the next reel, "can travel."

First the hero—or the villain—of the first reel was seen to glide along on its base. Then, bending over, it touched its limbs to the ground, released its base, and swung itself over in a somersault.

"Some of you may have read the story based on this creature," said Gerard. "My pen name is an anagram of my own name, with one letter changed."

"You're Roger Schaed," said two or three of the children at once.

"That's right. And these creatures in the films? Somebody can name them, no doubt?" asked Gerard, putting in another reel as he spoke.

"It's a hydra," said Dr. Foxwell. "A hydra eating a cyclops, in the first reel."

"That's right. The next reel shows the hydra's thread capsules and stinging capsules in action."

In rapid succession, reels showed an ameba ingesting a flagellate; euglenoid movement of a green flagellate, followed by the capture and eating of the euglena by a stentor; a nereis ("This is the Venusian dragon," explained Gerard), a fan-worm, and planaria orienting to lights going off and on and to water currents from a pipet. Elsie was delighted with "those cute cross-eyed worms" and wanted to see the film again.

"I got some good ideas from the life cycles of the obelia and the aurelia, too," said Gerard, "and, if you've read my stories, you know what I did with these lovely little horrors. In my imagination, I make myself small enough to live in this microscopic world, or make it large enough for me to live in. Now, as soon as this light bulb cools off a little, I'm going to show you some films in which I put this sort of action on to different backgrounds—magnified mineral surfaces, and clay models, and the like, sometimes on quite different scales of size. Now, what I want to do, if a few of you are interested, is to work out a full length movie combining human actors and—"

The enthusiastic uproar which greeted this proposal drowned out all speech for several minutes.

"Well, that ends tinkering with the psyches," said Mark Foxwell to Peter Welles, when the children had been packed off to bed.

"I was hoping for a distraction before they tired of it," Peter answered. "But they won't drop it entirely."

"They have been concentrating largely on developing intuition in Fred, haven't they? What about developing Fred's feeling?"

"Tim has something in mind," Dr. Welles answered, "but it'll have to wait until the edge is off this new craze. I hope this project won't prove to be beyond them; it provides a marvellous field for co-operative action."

"And a whale of a lot of fun," said Foxwell.

For two weeks, nothing was done or talked about but photography, microscopy, science-fiction plots and plans for the movie. As the magnitude of the task they had undertaken became apparent, the first excitement wore off and it was agreed that, to avoid lavish waste of expensive material, everything must be planned and rehearsed completely, and models built, before any actual shooting could begin. Responsibility for various parts of the work was dealt out, and Max and Fred were given intensive training in photography so that Gerard himself could appear in some of the scenes. Gerard set to work on the scenario, providing parts for everyone at the school and for others also, since they expected others to join the school before shooting began.

"I want to know what kind of costumes we are to wear for it," said Rose. "It's to be mostly underwater, isn't it?"

"It'll have to be," said Gerard. "Most of our non-human actors obviously live in the water. It will have to be filmed underwater—our parts—in the swimming pool, when we build it. That will give a good blank background."

"It looks as if swimming lessons will be a prerequisite."

"You bet they are, Giles. Anybody who is not a good swimmer will be cast for comic relief."

"But what about the costumes," Rose went on. "Diving suits are so hideous, and you can't tell one person from another in them."

"We'll use all plastic headpieces," said Gerard. "We're still arguing about the rest. In a warm place like Venus, a bathing-suit would be enough, but you girls don't want to look like imitations of pin-up girls, and, besides, can people swim in diving helmets? So we think we'll make some kind of plastic suit, like a diving suit, in different colors for each person, and use clear helmets. We can say they are cooled as the water on Venus is too warm, too. And they would be some protection against stinging things and all the other creatures. If anything is supposed to be in deep water, we can use diving suits, of course. Under the plastic diving suits we can wear bathing-suits, but they'll have to be designed some special way—a uniform, or something."

"I can swim," said Rose, a little doubtfully, "but not well enough. Should I take lessons at the Y, or can we have them here?"

"Both," advised Giles.

"Well, Fred, how are you doing?" Tim asked one day.

"You mean the functions and stuff? Pretty well, I guess. But I don't quite understand the differences between the types. Could you make it clearer, do you think? I suppose I am the thinking type, because I want to know things."

"But you can know things in all four ways," said Tim. "That's the whole point. Like viewing an object from all four cardinal points of the compass—if you look at only one face, or from only one viewpoint, you don't know it half so well. You ought to look at everything at least three ways. I think of the functions like four planes flying, together, or four ships in formation going somewhere together as a fleet. One usually leads, but two others come up on either side, and the fourth trails, but has to go along with the others. If they all start going in different directions you have trouble. See?"

"Peter said he had a patient once, a woman," said Stella, "and when he told her that she ought not to choose a husband by feeling or by intuition alone, she said, 'But if I used my reason it would only say, "If he isn't rich, don't take him," so I don't want to do that.' He had to explain that reason would have a lot more to say than that, and might not say that at all, except that a man who can't or won't support a wife and family isn't a good risk."

"Oh, I can see that. What do the functions do, exactly?"

"Well, a sensation-type just uses his five senses," said Tim, "and one who was born blind, deaf and dumb would have almost no senses left, so that would be the opposite. Thinking goes on a true-false basis, and feeling on a love-hate, but the irrational functions, sensation and intuition, just perceive. They see a thing as it is. Intuition is the best major function, I think, because it sees everything, right in place, and without casting out things because they are bad or untrue, but just accepting and recognizing them for what they are, the meaning of them and their place in things. And, of course, then you have the other two functions flanking it, to test truth and right feeling, and keep everything stable, and the senses tag along and can be used whenever they are needed. Now, you're a thinking type, Fred, by development if not by nature, so your two assisting functions would be sensation and intuition—"

"That's why you chose Agassiz' fish and Vann's seed," said Fred.

"Well, I just thought, since they were one for each, they ought to help one or the other. Feeling is opposed to thinking, so it'll be a little harder. If I give you an exercise on that, a hard one, will you give it a real try-out?"

"I want to know things," said Fred stubbornly, "and from all around."

Tim therefore came into the hall one afternoon a few days later, bringing a cardboard carton, which he placed before Fred.

"This is your new exercise," he said. "Stand back, everybody—this is all Fred's."

Fred looked at Tim, then at the box. A sound came from it, and Fred knelt down and cut the string with his pocketknife, and folded back the flaps.

Huddled in a corner of the carton was a small whimpering white puppy.

"Great day!" cried Fred.

"She's yours," explained Tim. "She's a mongrel, and nobody wanted her. She's cold and frightened, and most likely she's hungry. Dr. Welles says you can take care of her until you find out why people like dogs. Nobody else is to have a thing to do with her."

"But—I don't want—" Fred corrected himself hastily. "I don't know how to take care of a puppy."

"Jay and the Curtises can tell you."

Fred looked helplessly at Jay.

"You'd better take her out of the carton, first," said Jay. "Is she housebroken, Tim?"

"I wouldn't guarantee it," said Tim. "Take her outside, Fred."

Fred scooped the pup up awkwardly, put her on the floor, and then started for the door, calling the puppy, which only crouched shivering on the floor and whimpered. Fred returned, picked up the pup, and carried her outside; the others followed.

"What's it afraid of?" asked Fred.

"Probably this pup had good care until she was weaned, and then, being a female and a mongrel at that, she wasn't sold, so she was taken out and dumped somewhere. She probably got kicked around and chased around, and kids took her home and had to put her out again, until somebody had heart enough to take her to the pound. I got her there."

"Pat her, why don't you," cried Elsie indignantly. "Look how scared she is."

Fred crouched down and began to stroke the pup, which licked his hand timidly.

"What kind of dog is she, Jay?"

"Mostly fox-terrier, I should think," said Jay critically. "Those ears and eyes look sort of chihuahua, and I don't know about the tail. I don't know much about those small breeds. You'd better feed her, Fred."

"Bones?"

"Warm milk. Test it with your finger—it mustn't be much over blood heat. I'll get you some puppy biscuit; I think we had some left," said Jay, who had laid in a supply in anticipation of this event.

This time the puppy followed Fred, a little uncertainly, for a few steps; but when Fred walked on, the pup sat down and began to whimper. Fred stopped, went back and picked her up.

"I don't know what's so darned funny," he said, "just because I never had a dog before."

"If you take good care of her, you'll probably find out why people like dogs," said Jay.

"You mean that stuff about, if you work for somebody, you get to like them?" asked Fred scornfully. "There must be more to it than that."

"There is," said Jay.

Tim and Dr. Welles and Jay had already coached everyone. Though always ready with advice, nobody helped with the care of the pup, or fed or patted her. Gently but firmly, everyone else repulsed her and summoned Fred.

Fred dutifully fed the puppy, and prepared a bed for it in a box. When the pup whined and yipped piteously in the night, it was Fred who padded sleepily down and, when all else failed, in desperation took the puppy to bed with him. It was Fred who in grim silence cleaned up after the puppy—"She's housebroken," Jay explained, "but she's awfully young yet, and you've got to take her out often, especially in this rainy weather." It was Fred who said "No, no!" and "Hey!" when the puppy, gaining in confidence and friskiness, chewed everything chewable, leaped into chairs, tried to lick faces, and capered off with the evening paper. It was Fred who chastised her for these misdemeanors, according to Jay's instructions, with a folded newspaper—first trying it on his own hand, to make sure it did not hurt too much.

And it was Fred whom the puppy followed, into his lap she insisted on climbing, at his feet she always wished to sleep, with her head on his shoe, and Fred's slippers and socks that she preferred to chew. She watched him with bright brown eyes, and wept when he left her, until in exasperation Fred asked Jay whether this would go on forever.

"She's only a baby," said Jay soothingly. "You haven't had her long enough; she isn't sure of you yet."

"Hey!" shouted Fred angrily, and the pup dropped the pencil she had been chewing and fled to the other side of the room, looked back anxiously, and then bounded to him, leaping into his lap and licking his face. Fred pushed her down, but she leaped up again. He put her down, and patted her.

"Simmer down there, Pup-Dog," he said. "Sure, I still love you—when you're a good girl. Chew your rubber rat."

"Er—have you found out yet why people like dogs?" asked Jay, a little diffidently.

"I don't know why you like yours. But this little pest, this wriggling nuisance, I'm getting kind of fond of."

"Is it because she flatters your ego by liking you?"

"No," said Fred. "I'd rather be liked by something with more discrimination. But when I scold her for anything, she stops doing it right away and comes bounding to me like that, saying, 'You aren't really mad at me, are you? Did I do something you can't forgive? You still love me, don't you?' and if I sound really angry, or don't pat her, she looks so heartbroken. She tries so hard to please me and to be a good pup—she hasn't much sense of course, but she's learning as fast as she can. She so awfully needs somebody to love her, somebody she can trust. Isn't that so, Pup-Dog? Got nobody in the world but old Fred, such a mutt she is, and if Fred doesn't love her, who would?"

The puppy rolled on the floor in ecstasy at being addressed in affectionate tones, and Fred prodded her pink tummy with his finger.

"Going to keep her?"

"Guess I'll have to," said Fred.

"You could take her back to the pound."

"Then they'd kill her," said Fred. "I've got to keep her. What else can I do? I don't exactly want her—she takes more time than she's worth. But she needs me, and trusts me, and so I've got to keep her."

"Not because she loves you, but because she makes you love her?"

"That's it."

"Well, shall I tell Tim you've finished that exercise?"

Fred grinned.

"I'd forgotten that. I was trying so hard to be the perfect pup-tender, I forgot why I was doing it. Gee, I guess my psyche is getting along pretty well. Say, what happened to the rule that all pets must be kept caged?"

"We suspended it, because this pup was too young to be caged without a mama. You can begin to cage her any time now."

"Pup-Dog won't like a cage," said Fred. "If she's good, we won't put her in one, hardly at all. Put me in one, maybe, so she won't get at me and chew all my fingers off."

And when Jay reported all these things to his elders, Peter Welles commented, "You've got to hand it to Fred, what he undertakes to do, he does!"

The evening started out like any other evening. One group of children, challenged by Rose to name the eighteen orders of mammals, or representative animals from each order, fell down on it miserably, for in spite of their wide reading, which included much natural history, none had formally studied zoology.

"Do you mean to tell me that seals and walruses belong to the same order as dogs, cats and foxes?" cried Fred.

"I always thought coneys were rodents," wailed Alice.

"What floors me," admitted Tim, "is that spiny ant-eaters and scaly ant-eaters and great ant-eaters and Cape ant-eaters belong to four different orders. Four different orders, mind you!"

"Nobody got more than sixteen right," Rose said with satisfaction. "I'm so glad. All I got was fourteen, and I thought I must be too dumb to live."

Stella's aunt came into the hall just then, and, as she seldom did this, the children stopped their conversations to greet her.

"I came to see if I could watch Tommy Mundy on television, Dr. Welles," she said. "I could get him on the radio, but I'd like to see him, if you don't mind, for once."

"Certainly, Mrs. Waters," said Peter, offering her a chair. "He comes on at eight, doesn't he?"

"Yes—there was an announcement in the paper this morning. It said that he was going to give an especially important talk this evening, and since I've never heard him before, I thought this would be a good opportunity."

Peter Welles frowned as he turned the knobs of the television set. Tommy Mundy's increasing ability to draw publicity was an aspect of modern life that he found difficult to appreciate.

"Who is Tommy Mundy?" asked Stella, whose lofty indifference to the stars of radio, television, and the movies was so extreme that she actually had not heard the names of most of them.

"He's a sort of a lay preacher," Mrs. Waters explained. "I don't really know much about him, but he's very popular."

"He was studying to be a priest, I heard," Jay said. "He's not very young—he went to one of those seminaries for delayed vocations. But he left; some say he was expelled. Anyway, he left the seminary a few years ago, and since then he's been preaching on his own, spreading his unorthodox ideas. He's a sensation-monger. We were warned at Mass that he has no authority to preach."

"Has he been excommunicated?" Alice asked.

"No—that would have given him too much importance. Maybe he's managed to stay just within the limits. You can't really regard him as a Catholic, he's so obviously independent of the Church, and he has a large non-Catholic following. We haven't been forbidden to listen to him; I did, once, and it bored me, but I can see where he might excite some kinds of people who do all their living on a feeling level, and manage to ignore logic."

A great wave of organ music from the television set ushered in the program. Dr. Welles noted that the music, while vaguely reminiscent of several well-known pieces of sacred music, was actually a clumsily concocted hodge-podge.

The screen showed a pale curtain, which had been skillfully side-lighted to accent the vertical shadows of its folds. As the program began, the camera moved forward, focussing on the deepest recess of the largest fold. Dr. Welles smiled. If this program ran true to type, then he could expect a spotlight at any moment. . . .

It came, the beam directed from slightly above, so that shadows filled the eyesockets and gaunted the features of the small and intense man who stood motionless, drawn up to his full height, seemingly oblivious to his audience. A great wave of sound rolled over the audience in the auditorium, and, at the same time, the music faded away, and Tommy Mundy began to speak.

"Tonight," he said, speaking with careful restraint at first, "I am interrupting my regular series of talks to tell you something of the utmost importance to the world."

A new rustle ran through his audience. He moved forward, skillfully contrived shadows and lights following him as he stepped closer toward his audience. Welles could understand why he was able to impress so many of his listeners with this carefully directed performance.

Tommy Mundy suddenly seemed to grow two inches in height as he raised himself on his toes and flung his arms skyward.

"The world is in mortal danger!" he screamed suddenly. The impact on his audience of this sudden contrast to his former role was explosive. He began to pace up and down on the platform, pounding his fist into his palm, shouting and whispering alternately, gesticulating and stamping his foot.

"My people!" he shouted, "hear me! Listen, all you people around the nation, and especially you, my dear fellow citizens of Oakland, California." His voice fell to a whisper, gathering pitch and volume as he went on. "In the hills just outside our city limits, hidden from the watchful eye of the world, sunk in villainy, monstrous, blasphemous, foul, is a gathering of inhuman monsters! Spawned by the great explosion of Helium City's atomic plant sixteen years ago, these vipers, in appearance like ordinary, innocent, human children, are gathering from their hidden lairs throughout the country as they prepare to bring doom and destruction to mankind!" His shouts echoed through the great hall.

Mark Foxwell leaped from his seat with a roar, but Peter Welles thrust him back and sternly ordered "Quiet! We've got to hear this all."

"Hidden under the disguise of a school for gifted children, they have built laboratories behind a strong and high fence. There they make the secret and deadly weapons they will use against us, carrying out hideous experiments on helpless animals as they do so!" Mundy screamed.

"And is this the only plan they are brewing against us?" Mundy's voice regained a semblance of calmness once more, then rose again to its highest, most hysterical pitch.

"No, my people, no! Already these 'Children of the Atom' have penetrated into every walk of life through the crafty use of false names, making themselves heard everywhere, spreading their poisonous propaganda through the publications which you all take innocently into your homes!

"Their giant, inhuman intellects menace the whole world today! Let me tell you, my people, what they are!" With a flourish of his right arm, Tommy Mundy pointed a long finger heavenward, and his hysterical voice went on.

"They are a monstrous mutation born of the death and destruction of Helium City by the unleashed powers of the atom! Powers which God meant to remain under His control in the whirling universes of the atoms, powers which Satan for his own purposes has loosed upon the world! Under the appearance of flesh and blood, these Children of the Atom walk the world and plot your death and mine!"

Tommy Mundy drew breath, and the people in the great auditorium leaned forward to listen to his next words.

"They say they are more than men! They say they have greater knowledge and higher intelligence than any man who ever lived! But these Children of the Atom image no moral or spiritual good, because the only good they know is technological ability, skill at making money, and power over us whom they consider an inferior race! They judge and accept or reject people they meet on this basis alone. But behold the blasphemy! Can any mutation of man be true man, the man God created on the sixth day? Who has created these monsters? Blind force has created them! I think and know that man as God created him is the only true man! These Children of the Atom are entirely alien to God and to all of His creatures."

The open-mouthed children stared at the television screen, watching Tommy Mundy's grimaces and gesticulations with incredulous horror.

"They are outside the bounds of love and charity!" Mundy shouted. "What is loving or lovable about creatures who know themselves to be superior to and unlike every other member of mankind? And this superiority caused not by love but by blind destructive force? Satan himself, perverted as he is, is more lovable than these, for he was created by God to be an angel of light, even though he chose to refuse his high destiny. But how can we possibly love or even tolerate these Children of the Atom who claim that their nature, created by the physical force of a hideous explosion which brought only calamity to mankind, is superior to that of the men God created?"

Tommy Mundy held a pose, took a deep breath, and launched into the climax of his speech.

"Pray, my people, pray! This nest of vipers, this spawn of the atom, this fenced-in and secret gathering of monsters alien to all humanity and to all God's creation—" Skillfully, he drove his voice up to the breaking point, let it become incoherent with hysterical emotion, and buried his face in his straining hands. He gave a theatrical groan. "Oh, my people—my people—" He raised his face, and the spotlights threw it into sharp relief, so that the focal point of his audience's entire attention was his lips.

"Thou shalt not suffer a witch to live!"

The organ thundered again, and Tommy Mundy stepped backward; the velvet curtains parted to him, and he was gone. A gong clanged the program's end.

Jay switched it off, and turned stuttering to the petrified group, then bolted from the room.

Mrs. Waters was the first to regain the power of coherent speech.

"Well!" she said. "We certainly heard more than we bargained for, didn't we! I guess I'd better go lock the gates. I should hope that man doesn't represent *any* church, but he must have got his hearers pretty well worked up."

She hurried out, and some of the children burst into tears. Before they could be calmed, Jay dashed in again, followed by all the rest of the population of the school.

"Go bawl somewhere else," he ordered. "The rest have to hear the tape recording of that broadcast, right now!"

The two doctors shepherded the excited children out, and Jay bouncing with fury, followed them.

"Will there be trouble, do you think?" Dr. Foxwell asked Dr. Welles in an undertone.

"There may be. That—that rabble-rouser did not give our exact location, but it won't take people long to find out. News items and pictures about us have been in all the local papers. We've given out statements and let things be known, and this—this sensation-monger has put it all together in a witches' brew that—well, who knows how people may react?"

Elsie blew her nose and regained a semblance of calm.

"Shall we call the police, or what?" she asked. "If I didn't know us, after hearing that speech, I'd come and wipe us all right off the face of the earth!"

"But there's no sense to any of it," Jay cried. "It's pure blasphemy from start to finish. And he contradicted himself fifty times."

"I never heard such a mess of nonsense in my life," said Fred. "I'd like to analyze it semantically. In fact, I'm going to, as soon as I simmer down."

"What's wrong with that man, Dr. Welles?" asked Giles.

"He's a feeling type gone wild," explained Peter. "You can tell that by the way he despises and rejects the intellect, which, I might add, is a gift of God and not to be subdued or discarded. A man like this goes all out in love or hatred, without the least use of reason or stopping for an instant to think about true and false—either in his theology, or in the facts. A feeling type does find it hard to think logically, hard, or even impossible, but they can orient themselves to truth by perceiving, either with the senses or with the intuition, what the object of their love or hate actually *is*. Humph. I've lost track of my pronouns in the excitement—there is no excuse for that!"

"Yes, he could at least have come up and looked at us before blowing off to all the world like that," said Dr. Foxwell. "Come, now, children, go wash your faces—take an aspirin—get a grip on yourselves! Your little lecture did help quiet them, Pete," he added, as the children obediently left.

"Now if somebody would only quiet me," observed Peter, mopping his brow.

By the time the recording tape had played back the whole speech and the others had come out of the hall, bursting with indignation, an angry crowd had already begun to gather at the gate.

"I shall certainly enter a complaint," Mrs. Curtis was saying hotly. "To allow such a telecast to continue was inexcusable!"

"Please turn off the lights here," said Mr. Gerrold to Mr. Waters, as the first stone thudded near them. "Turn on the floodlights by the gate. Then we can see them but they can't see us."

"If the gate is locked, I don't see what harm they can do," said Mr. Curtis. "I'm sorry, Mr. Gerrold, but I am afraid you are going to be cheated out of an adventure."

"That speech was adventure enough," said Mr. Gerrold, fervently. "There!" as the lights went out by the houses, and went on over the gate. "They can't aim at us even if they have brought rifles. Now what? Shall I try to electrify the fence?"

"I wouldn't," advised Miss Page firmly. "If one of this crowd should get a slight shock, they'd all be convinced we were using ray-guns or secret weapons on them. Trust in the barbed wire. The boys tell me the fence can't be climbed."

"With ladders—" began Mr. Gerrold, but Peter hushed him.

"They are unlikely to have brought ladders," he said.

"They have cut the telephone wires," Mrs. Waters reported.

"We have an adequate and alert police force," said Dr. Welles. "They can't be unaware of what is going on."

"What do mobs usually do?" asked Alice.

"Oh, they throw stones," answered Dr. Foxwell, "and if they could get in they might smash things, or set fires, or try to hurt some of us. There hasn't been a lynching in this part of the world for a hundred years or more, and the makings for tar-and-feathering are hard to come by on short notice. If we can keep them out—there goes a window-pane!—I don't believe they'll do any great harm to-night."

"Yes, I think this gathering will be an anticlimax to the speech," said Dr. Welles. "The future, however, may be more troublesome. This poisonous speech has gone out everywhere, and it may be hard to discredit him entirely."

"I don't wonder he flunked out of the seminary," Jay's voice was shrill, "but he might sound right to some people—talking about God and love and all—"

"We have a number of powerful friends who know the truth about us," his uncle said. "The Archbishop will have something to say, no doubt. We can sue Mundy for libel and slander, he will be barred from television and from radio—"

"Why doesn't this crowd *do* something?" fretted Elsie.

"I'll slip around snake-hunting-like, and try to listen," proposed Robin.

Not long afterward, Robin returned, grinning.

"There seems to be some slight misunderstanding," he said. "Most of these people expected Tommy Mundy to come up here and lead them in an attack on us. But he didn't come. He just told them to pray, you remember. Right now, it's a mob without a leader."

"A mob without a leader," said Tim. "That's like a snake without a head."

He walked calmly into the lighted area and was standing with his weaponless hands outstretched.

"What do you want here?" he asked.

"We want to know what's going on up here," a man's voice shouted back, and the crowd cheered.

"Tommy Mundy told us about you," shouted another. "Now we know."

"You know more than he does, already," Tim answered clearly and quietly. "You're here looking at me. He has never set eyes on this place or on any one of us. He doesn't know the facts. We have just heard his talk, so we know what he said. He—"

"We want you to get off this land and our town!"

"This land belongs to Mr. and Mrs. Herbert Davis of Oakland," replied Tim. "They gave it to us. You know who they are, don't you? They've lived in this city long enough! They are respected citizens of Oakland. Why would they give their land to people who would harm you?"

"They don't know what you are," screeched a woman in the crowd.

"They do know what I am," Tim shouted back. "They've known me all my life. I've lived here all my life, went to the MacArthur School. If I come closer so you can see my face in the light, I think some of you may know me, too. If you do, speak up!"

Tilting his head slightly back so that his features showed plainly in the glare of the flood lights, Tim walked slowly forward.

A boy's voice rang out from the crowd.

"That's no atom spawn. I went to school with him for years. That's only Timothy Paull"

"Hi, Gregl" Tim answered easily, waving his hand. "Tell them who I am, then."

"I forgot he was here. The papers said so," said Greg. "He's the Davis's grandson. I know them, too—been at their house. Tim's no monster. He's in my Scout troop. Where are all the monsters, Tim?"

"I don't know any monsters," said Tim. "But you know me, Greg. If our phone wires hadn't been cut I could call plenty of people to prove who I am, people who have known my family for fifty years, people who have known me ever since I was born right down here at Merton Hospital, with Dr. Frank Roberts officiating."

"Who are all the rest of them, then?" yelled a man's voice.

"You may know some of them, too. How many of you have gone to the MacArthur School any time during the past thirty years? either as pupils or as parents visiting?"

There were several affirmative noises from the crowd.

Miss Page walked forward briskly and stood beside Tim, and several voices called her name.

"Some of you probably know our doctor, too," Tim went on. "He has been the psychologist for all the schools of the city for quite a while. You have heard him give lectures, you have seen his picture in the paper, maybe you have talked with him about your children's problems."

Peter Welles walked forward.

"Sure, I know him. He's a right guy, too," called a man. "Say, what's going on here, Doc?"

"What's going on is that a lot of you folks heard the same telecast we did, and came up to see what's going on," said Dr. Welles cheerfully. "After we had heard his talk, and heard you coming, we didn't know some of you were our old friends, so we closed the gates. We don't know Tommy Mundy and he doesn't know us. But you know some of us, and would you like to meet the rest? Mr. Curtis, will you come forward, please? Mr. Curtis uses a Seeing Eye dog, you will notice. This is John Curtis, folks, the historian. I think you know his name and his books. Mrs. Curtis, his wife. Jay, their son. These people train Seeing Eye dogs. Dr. Foxwell is our resident physician—come on, Markl—he and I are in charge here. Mr. Gerrold, our science teacher; those of you who studied at Cal during any part of the past eight years may have met him there. Oh, I see you do know him. And this is Mrs. Waters, Mr. Waters, their niece Elsie—" Rapidly he named the other children.

"Now, it's past bedtime for these children, and so I'd like to ask you all to come back some other time, during the daylight hours, and look things over, and meet and talk with us all as individuals. Mr. Mundy is welcome too, if he cares to come. But it is getting late, and we have had a strenuous evening; so, good-night, everybody!"

There were some murmurs at that, and a few voices were raised. But a uniformed deputy strode into the lighted area in front of the gate.

"The sheriff sent a few of us up to keep the peace, when he heard the broadcast," said the deputy. "As far as I can see now, the peace is being kept. But if anybody doesn't want to go along home quietly now, and let these kids get their sleep, we'll see what we can do about it."

"Does the sheriff know these people?" a woman asked.

"He sure does."

At the sight of the armed deputies, the crowd quieted.

"Aw—we just came up to find out what was going on," a man answered in a surly voice. "Nothing wrong as far as I can see. Mundy's a crackpot anyhow. I'm going home."

The crowd soon dispersed; the phone was quickly repaired; Mrs. Waters fed the children coconut cake and hot chocolate, and sent them all to bed. The sheriff had ordered a deputy to remain on guard all night, since the safety of children was involved. In answer to a phone call from the area's leading newspaper—for a reporter had mingled with the crowd and had hurried back with the story—Peter Welles issued a statement, and promised to prepare a complete refutation the next day.

"Too much has leaked out now," he announced to his colleagues. "Too much and not enough. Mundy's speech may circle the world forever, with our denials and statements never quite catching up. But now we must make a frank statement, as full as possible. We can't reveal all of the children's achievements and pen names, but we can and must tell the rest of it, and prepare for a real inspection."

"I'm going to deal with that Mundy rascal the first thing in the morning," vowed Dr. Foxwell. "The man's certifiable!"

"I think we should invite a complete investigation," said Miss Page, "and issue official statements from the guardians, teachers, friends, and neighbors of each child. The guardians should prepare these and gather sworn testimony from those who have known the children all their lives. I've written out a telegram and we can send a copy to each guardian."

"That was Stella's uncle on the long-distance right then," said Mrs. Waters, entering the room. "He wants to kill somebody. I told him we were going to take action, but he wants to talk to you, Dr. Welles."

"I'll get him off the phone and send those telegrams," said Peter.

The next few days were busy ones for everyone at the school. Reporters, photographers, lawyers and sightseers vied with friends and relatives in an attempt to monopolize the scene. Elsie complained that, to the best of her knowledge and belief, not one uninterrupted sentence was spoken on school property for three days. Every adult in any way connected with the school promptly used all his or her influence to deny the absurd charges and to support the denial with evidence of any kind available. There was a wealth of testimony on their behalf. Pastors—priests, ministers and rabbis—joined vigorously in the defense. Fred's semantic analysis of Mundy's speech, written the next day and released under his most respected pen name, was only one of many articles condemning the telecast; and the article by one of the auxiliary Bishops of the Archdiocese, a personal friend of Peter Welles's, completely discredited Mundy among his Catholic following.

Tommy Mundy, attacked on all sides, issued a statement also, in which he said, in effect, that he had been misinformed. If the children had been, as he was told, inhuman intelligences spontaneously produced by the atom-plant explosion, not born of human parents as he was now assured they were, his speech would, he claimed, have been justified. He was, he said, glad to have been instrumental in opening the way for them to clear themselves of the charges which had been brought before him. And, he added, he had not incited anybody to riot, but had merely asked his people to pray.

Not until the tumult had died down did Tim call an assembly of the children to consider the future.

"Dr. Welles has given orders to lock the gates during school hours and we're supposed to get back to our studies. Turn off those lessons, Robin; we've got to talk this all over. Max, will you switch on the lights? It's gloomy here."

"I should think we've talked about it enough," said Gerard. "I'm sick of Mundy's name. I'm sick of the whole fuss. Can't we forget it and get back to work?"

"In one way, we could," Tim answered. "The thing is, I want to tell you something. Tomorrow, I'm going back to the MacArthur School, and I want to ask all the rest of you to go either to that school or, still better, to scatter among the other big public and parochial schools of the city."

This bombshell was more shattering than Mundy's had been. Aghast, the children burst out in protests.

"You mean to close this school?" "Go back to the grades?" "Tim, you can't desert us like that!" "Dr. Welles will never let you do it!" "The grownups will be sick!" "To break up our group!"

"I know how you feel," said Tim. "I know what you think. But I've been facing it and that's the only way. That's how it has to be, for me at least. We did better when we stayed in hiding than when we locked ourselves up in this ivory tower. Let me speak, will you, Jay? I tell you I have thought it all out. You can talk when I've had my say."

"Give him a hearing," said Max.

"I don't want to talk about Mundy any more than you do. But there're two things to say about his talk. One is that people heard it and they'll never forget it. We all yelled him down—all those on our side—but it won't be forgotten. Bits of it will be coming up against us as long as we live. We can deny everything until we're blue in the face, but down in the minds of those who heard him, suspicion will remain, and fear, and hatred. Down on the irrational levels where no proof, evidence, logic, or reasoning can ever reach, some of it will be alive in spite of all that our friends and allies can do."

"He's right," said Stella.

"I'm afraid that's true," agreed Jay.

"And the other thing is," Tim continued, "that in all that jumble of lies and nonsense and false reasoning and jealousy and ignorance, warped and distorted as it was, there was some truth."

"If you mean those totally irrelevant misquotations about things being revealed to little ones—" began Marie angrily.

"Or that we hid behind pen names—"

"Or that God—"

"Be quiet a minute, can't you?" cried Tim. "This is hard enough to have to say. But I am going back to the grade school because intelligence is not enough. It isn't even the most important thing."

"If you're going to talk religion—" Fred began, but Tim shook his head.

"No," he said. "Psychology. None of this would have happened if we had not cut ourselves off from the world and from almost everybody in it. As long as we lived like other kids, nobody hated us, nobody feared us, nobody was against us. Some of you said, and the magazines and things said, that I saved us from real trouble by talking to the crowd. But it wasn't what I said or what I did, it was that somebody knew me. Some of them knew Miss Page and some knew Dr. Welles. But if you strangers to town, and the other strangers who will come, shut yourselves up here and live inside this fence, nobody will know you. And if I shut myself up here with you, nobody will know me. If they don't learn to know us all, and like and trust and have faith in us, all this stuff Mundy has put into their minds will blow up again some day against us. It must have been floating around in other minds for quite a while, more or less smouldering, and he heard these suspicions and fears. He made the most of what he heard, and then some, but he didn't invent it all. All he did was stew it together awhile and let it explode."

Murmurs of protest, murmurs of assent, came from the children but they waited for him to go on.

"So I figure it that we've got to go down to the regular schools, and mix every day with the rest of the kids. I don't want people who have known me all my life to forget me and believe lies against me, to see me as a stranger, a menace, a monster. If I had stayed in my own school and my Scout troop and gone to the other kids' houses after school and met their folks, nobody would have listened to any such stuff about me. So I'm going back and take up where I left off. And I think the rest of you ought to get yourselves known around town, not as a solid bloc at one school, but one or two in each school, to break up the solidarity we have here and to show everybody that we're human. Unless, of course, you don't want to be human, and want to be an alien race."

"You've got a point there," said Rose. "I tell you, I was scared. When he was telecasting, I kept thinking, I'm new here, nobody knows me outside this group. People could be afraid of us, especially as we grow older—the laboratory work and all."

"But to give up everything here—" wailed Elsie.

"Oh, have sense!" said Max roughly. "You meant for us to live here, didn't you, Tim? This is to be our home, together? Out of the whole calendar year there are only about forty weeks of school, aren't there? and school days are short."

"I checked on that." Tim was briskly businesslike again. "Of the five months of the fall term, last year, school was in session eighty-seven days; in the spring term, ninety-one days; a total of one hundred and seventy-eight days out of three hundred and sixty-five. On less than half the days of the year, to spend only about five hours a day to establish ourselves as real people—isn't it worth it?"

"Sure," said Fred, grinning. "Let's join the human race."

"We've always been human," Stella said swiftly.

"Yes; but some of us thought of seceding," Fred answered. "Let's get back in and stay."

"We have all summer for ourselves," Tim continued, "and by the time we get through high school and college, we'll all be known by hundreds of people, and we'll make them proud to know us. After all this publicity, the rest of the gang can come right in, as soon as they know it is safe—no secrets left. Now for the psychological part. It won't do any good just to sit through classes, you know."

"That's what I was thinking," said Beth. "Go on. We're with you."

"We've put in a lot of time lately helping Fred develop his psyche, and the rest of us did some work on ours, and had a lot of fun," Tim reminded them. "Now will somebody tell me what good that is? Our intellectual work we have been sharing, or planning to share, with the world, by publishing what we have done. But intellect is not enough. What's the use of developing right feeling if we don't go out to other people and let them see it in us and get the good of it, if we don't respond to what is likable in them? What's the use of intuition or sensation if we don't perceive other people and things? Mundy reached people on an emotional basis because any thinking person knew what he said was not true and was utterly unreasonable. But we can reach them on a solid basis of right feeling, value what is good in them, and respond to it, show them what is likable in us. That's the normal way of friendship. We've got to be friends with other people in this world, or they will take us for enemies. Most of them we can't contact by intellectual means. Fred can't make intellectual contact with the Pup-Dog, hardly at all anyhow, but he can and does form a rapport on the basis of affection, in response to the pup's need. People who are still a little fearful of us need reassurance; they need to know we have a right feeling toward them—and if we don't have it we'd better develop it as fast as we can. But we won't get anywhere sitting up here on the hilltop behind a high fence, playing the game of 'the Lowells speak only to Cabots, and the Cabots speak only to God.'"

"And what about our programs and plans?" asked Gerard, "as individuals and as a group?"

"This will slow them up a little, that's all," said Max. "It'll be worth it. I thought at first, Tim, this was the end of all we had begun, but I see you're right."

"That was a false start," Tim replied. "This is the real beginning."